Transforming

George Washington

The POTUS 1 Series

by

Gil Hudson

Copyright

Copyright ©2022 Transforming George Washington by Gil Hudson

All rights reserved.

No part of this publication may be reproduced, distributed, or transmitted in any form or by any means, including photocopying, recording, or other electronic or mechanical methods, without the prior written permission of the author except in the case of brief quotations embodied in critical articles and reviews. For information, address A Howard Activity, LLC, contact@ahowardactivity.com

This is a work of fiction. Names, characters, places, and incidents either are the products of the author's imagination or are used fictitiously. Any resemblance to actual persons, living or dead, businesses, companies, events, or locales is entirely coincidental.

Edited by Paula F. Howard, A Howard Activity, LLC

Interior design by Paula F. Howard

Cover design by Bob Hurley. Impressionsbookdesignservices.com

PRINTED IN THE UNITED STATES OF AMERICA

Aha! A Howard Activity Publication

ISBN: 979-8-9852263-5-5 Hardcover

ISBN: 979-8-9852263-4-8 Paperback

Available for purchase on Amazon.com and at TheWritersMall.com

Dedication

I dedicate this book to my sons, Curtis and Nathan Hudson who have made me so proud. No accolade or accomplishment I have ever achieved can possibly compare with the joy of seeing my sons succeed and develop into responsible contributing members of our society as well as become great fathers in their own right.

A Note From the Author

The POTUS 1 series chronicles the reemergence of George Washington into today's society and focuses on issues and problems he experiences while trying to adapt without giving up the values of his generation. It is envisioned that the most enjoyable reading experience would occur if the books were read in order, however, because each book has its own plot and can be read alone, it is not necessary to read each prior book in the series.

If you are new to the series, please read the Preface of each book in which one of the main characters of the series will introduce himself to you, and quickly bring you up to date so you can easily understand and enjoy the action contained in the novel you have chosen to read. Those who have read the books in order might enjoy each Preface update, even though they can just as easily start with Chapter 1.

Preface

Hello. My name is Dr. Palidore Hugh Montgomery VI, owner of Montgomery Cryogenic Services, LLC (MCS), located in Washington, D. C. In fact, the very building where MCS is located was once owned by my ancestor, Palidore Montgomery, Sr., who actually received it as a gift from George Washington, the first president of our country. My ancestor was given the building in exchange for his promise to treat and preserve the body of George Washington upon his death.

You see, my namesake's father spent many years in Egypt learning the mysteries of the pharaohs and their bodily preservation. He came into possession of a large quantity of the ancient chemicals before he migrated to the new world. Thereupon, his son, the first Dr. Palidore Montgomery, and his friend, Dr. Marshall Robinson, became adept at using these same chemicals to preserve the bodies of a few members of their church in the late 1700s. Somehow, our first president found out about their work and believed it might be a way for him to someday see how the country he helped create actually turned out.

Against my forefather's better judgment, he was pressured into accepting Washington as a prospective subject, and he provided Washington with a set of the precious chemicals along with instructions on how to self-administer them at the appropriate time. However, when Washington's favorite servant, Frank Khamisi, became terminally ill, he used his personal supply resulting in Frank becoming the fourth individual in my forefather's "inventory" of preserved bodies.

Washington was then given a second supply of the precious medicines to use upon his own impending death.

Even though he made a promise to Washington, my forbearer did not actually believe the president's body would ever be delivered to him. However, one night to his great surprise, Major Ronald Hudson did in fact show up with Washington's body, and our first president became the fifth person added to the ancient preserved human inventory.

Over time, the number of bodies preserved reached twelve and were faithfully kept in the MCS building throughout several generations of Montgomerys who cared for them throughout the centuries. A small amount of blood from each individual was also treated with the chemical compounds, kept beside each body, and regularly inspected. It was believed that when the samples began to liquefy, the same thing was happening inside each subject's body and that was the bellwether indicating it was time to try and revive the individual.

When the time was right, revival attempts were made on the first three subjects. Unfortunately, each one was lost and were unable to be saved. However, in 2025, we finally succeeded in reviving client Four, Frank Khamisi, then client Five, George Washington. The rest is history, so to speak.

Actually, no one knows about this remarkable achievement because I thought it best to let each ancient guest decide for himself whether to divulge the truth about their revival or proceed with new identities. We are currently waiting for Frank and George to make their own decisions.

The big task ahead for us now is to try and gradually bring them up to date on all events, historical and practical, that have occurred during the past 226 years while they have been in their preserved state. We are also trying to educate them on how to survive in today's society.

Fortunately, we have an excellent staff. Our psychologist, Dr. Lynn Radford, has prepared a series of educational modules that will allow our famous clients to select topics of interest and learn at their own speed. Her assistant, Susan Trott, is also most knowledgeable in the area of educating special-needs subjects. Together, they are being assisted by our company's communications director, Martha Vaughan.

One interesting note is that Martha's own husband, Stanley Vaughan, is currently in our human inventory, cryogenically preserved by MCS, and lies in state in one of our cryogenic preservation tubes.

We have no idea how any of this will turn out. . . or what will happen next.

Chapter 1

Washington DC, July 5, 2025

Palidore Montgomery and Lynn Radford sat at the end of the huge glass conference room table on the third floor of the Montgomery Cryogenic Services (MCS) building. Lynn glanced at the computer monitor displaying their sleeping patient in the next room, then looked at her boss.

"Okay Palidore, you said it was urgent, so let's hear it."

He looked at Lynn. "I know we had a plan to handle client Five and his careful re-introduction back into society, and I know we agreed you would be his sole contact early on concerning the new world he will be experiencing. I helped develop the plan and signed off on it."

"So now you're having second thoughts?" Lynn said raising one eyebrow.

"Oh, no, no . . . well, not really. I mean I'm basically totally happy with the plan, but it occurred to me that maybe we could tweak it just a bit."

"I'm listening"

"Well, I must confess I could be more helpful, at least initially." Noting the curious look on Lynn's face, he quickly added, "But I need you to hear me out, and perhaps you will agree with my reasoning." "You're the boss, Palidore, you don't need my permission to step in."

"I know, I know . . . but you know I don't operate that way," Palidore said, holding his left hand out as if trying to hold back her comment. "I really hope my involvement could be something we would both agree upon." Lynn gave him a "go ahead" look.

"I think our patient is going to expect to be seen by a physician. He certainly is going to assume he is receiving medical care and would wonder what's up if a doctor doesn't show up. I also believe he may feel a bit more comfortable if he also had a male figure to relate to. So, it seems logical that you could introduce me as his doctor, and we could proceed from there. I would, of course. follow the original plan and let you take the lead. What do you think?"

Lynn put her coffee down and let her professional, serious expression give way to a reassuring smile. "I'm not surprised at all that you want to be involved, and quite frankly, I would welcome your participation. At least if something goes wrong, all eyes won't be focused only on me. However, I do feel strongly that we should stick to the plan. It seems complex, but the short version is that our interactions must be focused on what the client wants and needs, and not on what we want to learn from him. We should just answer his questions and avoid asking him our questions. Are we clear on that?"

Palidore threw up both hands, surrendering the point. "Absolutely, I agree a hundred percent." Lynn glanced over again at the monitor and noticed her patient moving slightly.

"We'll soon find out about this; it looks like I need to get ready. Do you have a costume?"

"It's in my office."

Lynn smiled. "So, you anticipated my response?"

"I prefer to say that I chose to be prepared," Palidore said, grinning sheepishly.

"Ok then, get changed and meet me back here in five."

***

A short time later, Lynn said: "I'll go in first and you watch the monitor. When you hear me mention 'the doctor will be coming to see you soon,' that's your cue to come in."

"Got it," Palidore said.

Lynn entered the room and took her position in the chair next to the bed awaiting her patient's awakening. His color and complexion looked good; his breathing appeared normal, but somehow his face seemed to have a more mature, confident look today.

Maybe it's the white hair, she thought. Still, just looking at him gave her chills as she wrestled with what seemed to be the impossible: Just inches away from her lay the nation's first president alive after over 200 years in a preserved state. She knew each day her patient would be awake longer, and become more lucid, as effects of the coma drugs in his system began wearing off. She saw her patient begin to stir, then watched him drift back to sleep.

Thirty minutes later, George Washington opened his eyes and looked up at the ornate ceiling. Nothing looked different than the ceiling at home where he lived with Martha. The year, as he remembered, was 1799. His last memory was of being ill, but he felt much better now. Stretching his arms out, he was surprised to see a young woman seated next to his bed. She smiled at him.

"Good morning Mr. Washington." She had intentionally not addressed him as 'Mr. President,' since she did not want to let on that she knew.

"Good morning, Lynn," he responded. Her name had automatically come to him.

"I trust you slept well last night."

But Washington did not respond. He kept looking around the room. Something was different. Something had changed. "Where am I? I've been sick, haven't I?"

Lynn carefully weighed her words. "Well, you've been receiving medical care for quite some time, but I think you are doing very well now. In fact, your doctor, Palidore Montgomery, should be coming in soon." In the monitor room, Palidore recognized his cue and jumped to join them.

"Palidore . . . yes Palidore and I are friends, but I don't believe he is actually my *doctor*. I will, however, be pleased to see him,"

His comment caught Lynn by surprise. *How could he know Palidore?*

At that moment, Palidore entered the room and approached the bed. Washington sat up and studied his face.

"Good morning, Mr. Washington, I am Dr. Palidore Montgomery." He offered a hand to shake, but Washington did not take it. Instead, he looked directly into Palidore's eyes and tilted his head.

"*You* are not Doctor Palidore Montgomery. You favor him, but I know the *real* Palidore Montgomery, and you are certainly not him!"

Palidore suddenly realized that Washington was expecting to see his ancestor and quickly responded, "Of course, you are correct. I am not the *same* Palidore Montgomery whom you have known. I just have the same name as he did."

"'Palidore' is not a common name, so forgive me if I have trouble believing you," Washington responded.

Palidore held up one finger as if to say 'give me a moment,' then bent down, opened his bag, and produced the ancient photograph he had taken from his desk at the last moment while changing his clothes to 18th-century garb. Now, he showed it to the man who had just survived a 200-year leap into the future.

"Is this the 'Palidore' you were expecting to see?"

Washington took the photo, studied it and looked up. "Yes, that is Palidore and his wife, Anabel." He continued to point, "and that is Doctor Marshall Robinson with his wife, Sara; and, of course, that is my wife, Martha." He slowly lowered the engraving to his lap before turning to Lynn. "I'd like to see my wife. Can you please fetch Martha for me?"

Palidore was caught off guard by the request; he had not

anticipated this at all. Glancing over at Lynn, he saw her calm response. She was clearly prepared for this request.

"I am sorry, but Mrs. Washington is not here."

Washington handed the framed photograph back to Palidore who was anxious to change the subject.

"So, if you don't mind, sir, I would like to give you a quick checkup." Without waiting for an answer, he took Washington's wrist and began taking a pulse reading. Then he took out a stethoscope, held it in one hand to show the man. "This is a new instrument we use to listen to your lungs. I am going to place it on your chest and your back. If you don't mind, each time I move it, would you please take a deep breath?"

The ancient man, newly revived to life, said nothing but followed the routine as Palidore carefully placed the scope in different locations.

"I am going to place something on your forehead for a moment," Palidore continued. Without showing the item to his patient, he placed a tape thermometer on Washington's forehead and waited for a reading before removing it. He made a note on his clipboard. "One more small thing," he said, taking a small object from his pocket which had a small rubber tube attached to it. Placing it on his finger, he kept the battery-powered device in his pocket. He was expecting to be questioned about it, but Washington remained silent, his mind seemed to be elsewhere.

The whole purpose of what Palidore had done so far was more to establish a patient-doctor relationship than actually learn anything he did not already know.

"Well, it looks like you are doing fine."

Lynn was pleased with how things had gone until she heard Palidore ask something she didn't want to hear.

"So, how did you come to know my relative, the 'Palidore' in the picture?" the doctor asked.

Lynn shot him a look to kill, *That question is "off-script;" not part of the plan*, she thought. But Palidore was focused on Washington's response.

"I am not sure, but I needed to find something out. Wait a moment . . . I am sure I can remember, just give me a moment." He squinted, trying somehow to force the memory out. Then his eyes lit up.

"It had something to do with Richard . . . Richard Brockwell. Yes, it definitely had to do with him. Yes, his funeral - there was something wrong with his funeral - and he was Dr. Montgomery's patient or wait a minute - maybe he was Dr. Robinson's patient. I am not sure, but something was wrong with his funeral, and I needed information from both doctors."

Lynn noticed perspiration on Washington's face. It had changed color, and she was immediately concerned. She poured a glass of water and placed it into his hand.

"Please take a drink, and don't be too concerned if you experience some difficulty with your memory. That's why we are here - to help you." Washington took a drink and seemed to calm down. Lynn took the glass from him and placed both of his hands in hers. She positioned herself directly in front of him, cutting off his view of Palidore.

"You are doing really well today, but perhaps we should rest a while." The sound of her voice and the touch of her hands seemed to have a calming effect on him, and he laid back down as Lynn continued talking.

"Dr. Montgomery has to leave now, but I will remain here with you for a while longer. Can I get you anything? Are you hungry?"

There was no response. Washington was asleep.

Chapter 2

"Okay I know, I blew it!" Palidore said as Lynn walked into his office. "Big time!" she responded. "The plan was not to satisfy *our* curiosity, but to address his." Palidore waited before responding. "Well, I guess I wanted to get his mind off of wanting to see his wife, and the picture was right there, so it just popped out. I'm sorry, it won't happen again."

"That's right, it won't," Lynn said. "What on earth prompted you to put that photo into your medical bag in the first place?"

"Really, I don't know, I was getting dressed, excited about seeing the president and there was his photo sitting next to my bag. I just instinctively grabbed it and put it in. I don't know why or what I was thinking; it was just a spontaneous act. Then when he accused me of not being the Palidore he knew, I thought the photo would help explain."

Lynn accepted the explanation. "Ok then, but why ask him about how he came to know your ancestor? We agreed to answer *his* questions, not ask ours."

"As soon as I asked the question, I knew I screwed up. You are obviously better at maintaining protocol than I am, but I was just putting the photo away and the question popped out. I was making small talk. I can see we can't put pressure on him. I will try to do better going forward." There was a prolonged silence.

"He wasn't awake long, when do you think he'll be awake again?

Lynn knew Palidore could answer his own question. She audibly sighed. "If he gets excited, or becomes stressed, he'll tire fast. I thought you knew that. In any event, I expect he will sleep a couple of hours at most. He should remain awake longer this time, especially if we don't stress him out or put pressure on him. So, if you don't mind, I'll take the next session with him alone."

"I think that would be good. Yes, yes . . . just you this time." Palidore rose to leave.

"I am going to my office now. Please buzz me when he's awake so I can return to the monitor."

***

In less than an hour, he received a buzz on his watch and read the green and white message: "He's awake again, I'm going in." Palidore flew up the stairs to his seat in front of the monitor in time to hear Lynn say: "Well, I see you're awake again, can I get something for you?"

Washington ignored her question choosing instead to ask a question of his own.

"Where am I?"

Lynn calmly responded: "You are in Washington, D.C."

"Good, that's good. What is the date?"

"It's actually July 5th," Lynn replied

"Oh, did I miss the July 4th celebration?"

"I am afraid you did," Lynn said.

Washington went silent a few moments before saying: "You said it was July 5th, but you didn't mention the year and that seems to be an intentional omission." Lynn marveled at his intellect and ability to read between the lines.

"So, what year *is* it?" he persisted.

Lynn knew the moment had arrived. She had prepared for it and was hoping her response would not appear too rehearsed.

TRANSFORMING GEORGE WASHINGTON

"Mr. Washington, before I answer your question, I must tell you that you have been asleep for a very long time, and what I am going to tell you is going to be very difficult for you to believe, but we want to be truthful with you at all times. So, to answer your question . . . the year is 2025. That is 226 years since you went into a suspended trance."

Lynn offered nothing more but watched his face for clues as he processed the information. Washington seemed to be frozen in a moment of time. He moved only his eyes around the room. Then, he sat up and slowly got out of bed. He walked around the room, picking up various objects appearing to study them before putting each one back down. He then turned and walked back toward Lynn.

Palidore, watching on the monitor, didn't know what to think. He wanted to bust into the room but knew better, particularly after his last performance. His skin felt clammy although the humidity and air temperature were carefully regulated.

Washington returned to his bed and sat on the edge looking directly into Lynn's eyes.

"So, when you told me that Martha was not here, what you meant was that she is no longer alive, didn't you?"

Lynn felt like a witness being grilled by an attorney on a witness stand. Nevertheless, she was able to calmly reply.

"Yes sir, that is correct." She studied Washington's face, watching for any visible reaction to her answer. She found it interesting that Washington did not seem to display outward signs of grief. In fact, his face seemed to lack any discernable expression at all. The only thing Lynn could detect was a forlorn look of resignation. She was certain he had already deduced that it was not just his beloved wife, Martha, who was no longer here, but everyone he had once known . . .all were gone.

She wanted to tell him about his faithful servant, Frank, but thought it was too soon as Frank was not out of the woods yet. If something happened to him, she didn't want her patient to have to deal with that right now.

Lynn remained quiet, waiting for him to deal with the reality of all she had just told him. She didn't want to hurry the conversation or even change the subject just yet.

Finally, Washington spoke again. "But I clearly heard you say her name. Someone was with you, and you called her, 'Martha,' I remember. I couldn't see as I wasn't awake, but I clearly remember what I heard. You were near me and someone else was with you, and you called her 'Martha.' I tried so hard to speak, to wake up, to reach out. I tried so hard .... and ... my hand, I finally willed it to move . . . I touched her. I'm sure I did."

Lynn remembered the incident well. She and Martha Vaughan were in the room together and after his hand touched her leg, Martha had jumped from the surprise. She had bumped into Lynn causing them both to fall on the floor. Later they had even laughed about the incident. Lynn thought it had been just an involuntary movement. She had no idea he had tried to reach out, that it had been intentional.

"What you recall is correct. There was another woman in the room with me, and her name *is* Martha, but she is a different 'Martha.' Her name is Martha Vaughan, and she works here."

"Oh," he said, absorbing the information without changing his blank, expressionless stare.

Lynn wasn't sure what was next. At the outset of the conversation, she had thought he might try and question the veracity of the information she had given him. However, he appeared to accept it all. Now, wanting to reassure him, and move the conversation in a slightly different direction, she spoke again.

"Mr. Washington, we want to help you work through any emotions or doubts you may be experiencing."

Washington turned his head toward her and focused, once again, on her face.

"You cannot know the emotions I am experiencing right now, or how to deal with them. Of this I am certain, it is something only

TRANSFORMING GEORGE WASHINGTON

I can deal with. However, you can be assured that I no longer have any doubts . . . it is all starting to make sense to me now."

Lynn briefly allowed a questioning look on her normally placid face. Washington saw it.

"I have been telling you, while asleep or 'in a trace' as you say, I have been listening to you for quite some time. Nothing I've heard made sense to me then . . . but now . . . it's all coming into focus, so don't look at me that way." He appeared to be more energized and spoke in a somewhat demanding voice. "I want to see that Dr. Montgomery who was here earlier."

Lynn was surprised by the request, nevertheless, responded calmly. "Actually, he should be here any time now."

Palidore, glued to the monitor, heard his cue from Lynn. Now, he jumped up and bounded into the room to greet his patient, again. "Mr. Washington, pleased to see you up again."

"Pull up that chair, Doctor, we need to talk," Washington said, gaining composure.

Palidore did as instructed and when he was seated, Washington continued. "I feel I owe you an apology." Palidore gestured that none was necessary, but Washington continued without interruption. "I now realize the photograph you produced likely shows a distant relative of yours. I am beginning to remember things rather vividly now, and I want you to hear this. I think it will be most fascinating to you."

Both Palidore and Lynn were riveted in anticipation of what President George Washington was about to say.

Chapter 3

George Washington looked at Palidore and Lynn both standing before him wearing 18th century clothing. Nothing looked out of place to him.

"If you will recall, I mentioned the name of Richard Brockwell." Palidore nodded.

"Well, Richard was a good friend of mine who passed away, and I wanted to attend his internment. I was surprised to learn there would be none. The Brockwell family had a church plot so I could not understand what was to be done with his remains. It certainly wasn't for lack of a gravesite. I quietly inquired of the pastor and was informed the family had decided *not* to bury his remains. This was most irregular, to say the least. Later, I learned that two others had made the same decision and upon further investigation, it became apparent this was occurring only with patients of Dr. Palidore Montgomery and Dr. Marshall Robinson, so I invited them to meet with me, and there I confronted them with this information. What I learned was amazing!

"I was told that Dr. Montgomery's father had spent much time in Egypt and learned most of his medicine there. He migrated to this country and taught what he knew of these exotic measures to his son, the Palidore I met, and who is *your* ancestor shown in the photograph. This Paladore inherited a large supply of chemicals or "compounds' as he referred to them, from his father. These compounds, when applied properly, had the effect of perfectly preserving the remains of a person.

TRANSFORMING GEORGE WASHINGTON

Somehow the doctors were enticed into secretly treating people with their compounds and storing the bodies with the hope that at some point in a future time, these people would be revived and cured of whatever caused their demise. An exceptional idea.

"I became friends with both doctors, but particularly liked Palidore. I gained a keen interest in what they were doing and made a personal decision that when the time came, I wanted them to treat *my* body, too. It took a bit of arm-twisting, but ultimately, they reluctantly agreed, as long as I saw to having my remains delivered to them quietly, being a person of note. I think I was the only patient who made such a decision *before* becoming ill. In any event, I had no idea if it would work. But now, here I am, so I guess it *did* work."

The major details were not new to Palidore, however, hearing it from a person who had lived it was somewhat unnerving. At this moment, Palidore wasn't sure what to say. He looked at Lynn.

"Mind if I respond?" he asked.

"Please go on," she said.

"Mr. Washington, what you've just told us agrees with information we have gathered from documents left by your Dr. Montgomery's son, Hugh." Washington smiled at the mention of Hugh's name.

"You should also know that we have been in possession of several individuals who have been treated with the compounds before you, and some who have been prepared after your time." He let the information sink in, but Washington's face simply seemed eager for more information, so he continued.

"We were not able to adjust the time it took for the chemicals to wear off, therefore, we could not attempt to help any patient until the sign we watched for told us the compounds had pretty much released their effects on the bodies of the individuals. I'm afraid I don't have the time today to fully explain what we did once the compounds wore off, but suffice it to say that we were successful in reviving you."

Washington sat motionless a few moments, then abruptly

stood and blurted out: "I don't like this nightgown. I would like some real clothes."

Lynn was caught off guard by the abrupt change of conversation. "Well, we most certainly do have clothes available for you. Let me get them." She went to the wardrobe in the room and removed an entire outfit they had previously put together for just this occasion. The outfit was a replica of clothing shown in a drawing Lynn had seen of President Washington in his nonformal attire. They had been created to fit him exactly.

She brought the clothes over and laid them out on the bed. The trousers were light brown, had a button fly, and leather patches for back pockets. The shirt was white with long sleeves. There were ruffles on the front and at the cuffs. The shirt was crafted to host a large open collar. Both garments were made of fine cotton. She also laid out a belt, some underwear, a handkerchief, socks, and a pair of lace-up shoes. All items resembled clothing he would be comfortable wearing but were made with current-day materials and were likely to feel much more comfortable than his original clothing, especially the shoes.

"Why don't we leave you for a moment," Lynn said. "While you're getting dressed, we'll fetch some lunch." Washington was holding the clothes up for examination.

"Yes, yes, that will be fine."

"Okay, then, we'll return shortly." She and Palidore left the room closing the door quietly.

***

Washington quickly dressed, then stretching out his arms, took a deep breath and began walking around the room. He could not remember when he had last felt this good. He was also anxious for Lynn and Palidore to return with lunch as he had suddenly realized his hunger.

TRANSFORMING GEORGE WASHINGTON

There was a knock on the door but before he could answer it, Palidore entered, followed by Lynn who was carrying a large tray of food. Palidore cleared the table and pulled up three chairs as Lynn put the tray down. She couldn't help but notice how handsome Washington looked. His youthful face and short white hair picked up the color of the white open-collared shirt which suited his trim and fit physic. His entire persona commanded respect, and she felt a bit starstruck as if meeting her favorite actor. He looked strong, and completely in-charge. Somehow she felt he also knew it.

Almost forgetting what she was doing, she glanced down at the tray which held a clear soup, bread, slices of turkey, cheese, and diced fruit. Setting everything in its proper place, along with the pot of tea, she sat back and watched Palidore reached for some bread.

"Palidore, Since this is your house, I assume you will say grace," Washington said.

Palidore, was caught off guard by the request. He considered himself a Christian but had never verbalized it publicly, nor was he used to saying a blessing out loud. Lynn bowed her head to hide her amusement.

"Well, uh . . . certainly," he said. "Let's pray. Thank you, God, for this meal, amen."

Lynn grabbed a piece of bread, trying not to laugh, as they filled their plates. Palidore focused on what Washington was eating. The food itself was intentionally bland, but he did not want his famous patient to overeat for his first meal. He was pleased that Washington did not seem to consume much more than the soup with some bread. As they were finishing, Washington asked Lynn for a mirror.

"I have pretty much inventoried the room and have failed to find one. It is difficult to get properly ready without one." Lynn shot a quick look over to Palidore before responding.

"Well, again, you are correct. We've intentionally not put a mirror in the room because we wanted to first have a little discussion with you about your looks."

15

A concerned look appeared on Washington's face.

Lynn quickly continued. "We think you are going to *like* how you look. It's just that you are going to look much *younger* than you may recall. The process your body went through with the chemicals had the effect of stretching your skin and firming up your muscular tissues resulting in a more youthful appearance. So, except for your hair which is still white, you look more like a man in his mid-forties." She let her words sink in before continuing. "I'm also sure you may have noticed an improvement to your teeth."

Washington ran his tongue around and over his teeth. Then he smiled. "Yes, yes, I have noticed something different . . . my teeth no longer hurt. Did you fix them?"

"We did," Lynn responded

"I believe I am ready for the mirror."

Lynn got up, left the room for a moment, and returned with a small handheld mirror which she handed to him. Washington took it, held it in his lap a few seconds, as if trying to summon up the courage to use it. Finally, he raised it to his face.

They watched as George Washington took a look at his face for the first time in over two hundred years. He took his left hand and touched his short hair while moving his face a bit closer to the glass reflection. He opened his mouth wide and looked at his teeth, then held it further away from himself. As he stared at his image, a smile spread over his face, and he turned to Lynn.

"I'd like to keep this mirror."

"It's yours to keep," Lynn said with a smile of her own.

Chapter 4

That night, Washington slept well but awoke early to a slight pain on the edge of his right ear. He turned, and while fluffing his pillow, felt a small object inside that he thought might be the source of irritation. Feeling around for the object with his hand, he finally took the pillowcase off allowing him to see the object. It was a small, translucent round object, very lightweight, and made of a strange substance he had never seen before. Hollowed out on one side, it was only about a half-inch deep and on the inside, there were very fine lines. He squeezed it, but when the pressure was released, it returned to its previous shape. Twisting got the same result.

This is very unusual. Something this unique must be very valuable, he thought. Looking around for someplace to hide it, he decided to put it into a small vase that adorned one of the bookshelves.

***

Palidore heard the beep of his cell phone and knew why he had received a notification. Whenever Washington left his bed, a ping would be sent to him. Now he picked up his phone to see the monitor. It wasn't as good as actually being in his office in front of the large computer screen, but it was better than nothing. He watched as Washington was looking at something. The room was dimly lit by candlelight and Palidore couldn't see very clearly. But as he watched, Washington began walking around the room with a small object in his hand. Finally, when he held it close to a candle for a better look, Palidore could also see it. He immediately knew the object was the top of a plastic water bottle. Somehow it must have gotten mixed into the laundry and wound up in the pillowcase now on Washington's bed. Palidore was amazed at Washington's fascination with the object and watched as Washington hid it inside the small vase.

Why would he want to hide it? Palidore wondered. *Hmmm. How should I handle this? I can't possibly tell him what it is without revealing the fact that I watched him hide it. Then he'll know he's being monitored.* It also occurred to him that hiding something meant there was a distrust, some suspicion, some doubt. Obviously, Washington must not fully trust them.

I will have to find a way to win and keep his trust, Palidore calculated. *But then - aren't we keeping many things from him? Can he sense it? Is that the source of his mistrust?* Lynn had even admitted to him they had intentionally not put a mirror in the room. So why shouldn't he think they were keeping other things from him?

Palidore felt their initial relationship was good, but he could feel a small wall developing and he didn't like it. Even though it was early, he called Lynn and relayed what had just gone on. They agreed to meet first thing in the morning.

***

When Lynn arrived at his office, they discussed the bottle cap along with the implications concerning Washington's desire to hide it.

"The bottle top is not a problem," Lynn said. "We don't have to explain it to him. We'll just offer him a bottle of water at an appropriate time and when he takes the top off, he'll realize the purpose of his secret object. It's the mistrust issue that might be a bigger problem.

"I think we need to move the educational process along faster than we had anticipated," she said. "It's time to give him an overview of our proposed program to bring him up to speed. If we lay it all out for him, it should be reassuring, and help quash any trust issues."

"When do you propose we should have this conversation," Palidore asked.

"Right now," she said, and started toward the door.

Palidore grabbed her arm. "Wait a minute, have you forgotten that we're not in our costumes?"

"No, I haven't forgotten. The costumes were initially intended to make him feel comfortable when he awoke," she said, "but now that he knows what year it is - and if we are going to play straight with him - then he needs to see us exactly as we live now." She headed toward the door again. "Well, are you coming?"

Surprised by the invitation, Palidore caught up with her and they walked to Washington's room. Lynn knocked on the door and called out, waiting for him to answer.

"Mr. Washington, it's Lynn Radford and Dr. Montgomery. Is it okay if we come in to talk with you?" Washington was already dressed when he opened the door

"Certainly, please do. I am anxious to learn more."

They assembled around the small table in the center of the room. Palidore was surprised he had not seemed to question their clothing. Lynn was attired in a casual royal blue one-piece jumpsuit with a multicolored sash around her waist, white tennis shoes and simple silver jewelry. Palidore had on his usual attire consisting of a blue cotton shirt with a button-down collar, khaki pants and loafers that looked worn out.

Lynn didn't give Washington a chance to speak, but simply took charge of the meeting.

"Okay Mr. Washington, first we want you to know that we have been preparing for this moment for a very long time. A situation like this has never happened before. No one has ever been brought back, or revived, so we are not a hundred percent certain what we should do first.

"However, I will tell you that in all our planning, our primary concern has always been for *your* well-being. We have always been, and remain, concerned as to how the information we present to you might affect you. Though there is much we can learn from you, we strongly feel that, for now, it is more important *we* help *you* and answer all your questions. So. for starters we want share with you the plan we have developed for you." Washington was focused and appeared to be paying close attention to every word Lynn was saying.

"Initially, when you woke, we wanted you to feel comfortable, so we created an environment that would be familiar to you. This room, for example, resembles what you would have seen in your time even to the clothes we were wearing which resembled attire commonly worn in the 1790's.

"But now that you are aware of the year and what has happened to you, we feel you are ready to experience things as they *really* are. So, for example, even though there are many different styles of clothes worn today, what Palidore and I are presently wearing is clothing commonly worn by many Americans. You will no longer see us in the costumes we previously wore. There will be no more pretending on our part.

"However, for the time being, there will be a need to keep the knowledge of your existence and the progress you are making known to just a few people. We hope you can trust our judgement concerning this point, at least for now." Lynn paused to allow Washington time to take in what she had just said. Then returning to the theme of her earlier remarks, she continued.

"So, now for the rest of the plan. We have taken all the changes that have occurred since 1799, or at least all we could think of, and put them into categories which we refer to as Education Modules. Here is a list" She handed him a paper which he looked over.

"You can pick any one of these listed categories, in any order you want, and we can show you what has changed since 1799." Then pointing to one section on the paper she said "However we believe you should read this section first. It is a narrative describing how an average family lives today. It will take you through a typical day and year.

"Once in a while you will see a word displayed in red. That means there is an entire section devoted later on to that subject. Once you have read that section you can then pick any one of the modules or categories on the paper. They are listed in alphabetical order because we did not want to leave the false impression that there was any significance to the order." She pointed to a random category.

"For example, if you were to choose 'Transportation,' you would learn that today very few people use horses, wagons, or carriages, but rather they have automated carriages which we now refer to as 'cars' or 'automobiles.' They are powered by a motor or engine to go places. There are other forms of transportation used today, but all are covered in the Education Module called 'Transportation.'"

Lynn paused for breath and noticed Washington was now focused on the list of modules. She waited for him to react or finish reviewing the list before continuing. But he did not look up. He just kept looking over the list.

Perhaps, I have gone too fast, or covered too much too soon, she thought.

Finally, Washington put the list down and without looking up asked: "How long do I have to stay in this room?"

Where did that come from? she wondered. "Well, not too much longer in this room, but for now, it would not be safe for you to leave this building without proper knowledge of how we live in today's society. That's why we developed these Education Modules. Once we have covered a few of them, I think you'll understand why it might not be safe for you to go out just yet.

"There is another issue we need to deal with before that happens," Lynn continued. "You see, we believe that if people find out that you are alive again, they will not leave you alone. Huge crowds of people will follow you everywhere you go, twenty-four hours a day. Some will believe you are not who you say you are, and might even try to harm you."

Washington interrupted her. "Well, won't that happen whenever I leave?"

"Not necessarily, we can give you a new name, new identification papers, and place you somewhere you can live your life without anyone ever knowing who you actually are. You don't have to decide this right now, in fact, at the present time you probably shouldn't even try," Lynn said. "But we want you to know that when the time comes, it will ultimately be *your* decision to make, and yours alone. You can choose to let the world know who you are, or you can decide to keep that information a secret and set out on your own. We think you'll be in a better position to make that decision after you have had a chance to review some or all of the Education Modules."

Washington pickup up the paper again. "I would like to read about the presidents, I don't see that topic anywhere on the list."

"That would be covered under the module called 'American History' which is set out in a time ordered sequence by decades. It will certainly cover each president and much more."

"Well, I am sure I will want to cover that, but for now, I would like to read just a brief overview of each president. Is that possible?"

"If you want to read just a brief review of each president, yes, I can get that for you."

"Yes please, I would appreciate that."

"Of course; I'll get it for you now." Palidore rose and, once outside the room, quickly pulled up a list of presidents from Google on his cell phone. He began sending Wikipedia reports on each one to his printer. After sending the first few print commands he sprinted down to his office to pick up the papers. He then returned and handed the printouts to Lynn, who presented them to Washington. While he was reading the first batch, Palidore repeated the process until all presidents were covered. It turned out to be quite a pile as there were several pages on each person. When Lynn received the last batch, she looked over to Palidore. "Good job, thanks."

Washington was now sitting in a wingback chair engrossed in

reading the first batch.

"As you can see, there are a few pages per president, some more than others, but all together there is a considerable amount of reading here," Lynn said. "Anyway, this is the last of them. Is there anything else we can get you, or do right now? Washington looked up from the page he was reading.

"No, no, this is good. Thank you."

"Okay, we'll leave you to your reading, but should you want anything, just push this button." She took out a small device with a large red button and handed it to him. He just took it and put it on the table. What he was reading was holding his attention. Then he let out a laugh.

"Aha! I knew it! I knew Jefferson would get the job one day, but never thought it would take the House of Representatives thirty-six ballots for him to win!"

Chapter 5

Washington read quickly through the list of presidents who had followed after him. He stopped reading every now and then to reflect on something, then continued, letting some pages fall to the floor while carefully setting others aside in separate stacks, as he absorbed the information.

By the time he had read and pondered over every page, it was well past eight p.m. Lynn and Palidore had been watching on the office monitor the entire time, trying to analyze his expressions. They had ordered a tray of food for him but choose not to interrupt.

Finally, he put down the last few pages, stood up, stretched out, and picked up the remote control. Soon after he pushed the red button, Lynn entered the room carrying the tray of food.

"How did you know?" Washington asked as she entered.

"Well, you've been pretty focused, and it's getting late, so I just assumed you would like something to eat."

"Very perceptive of you," he said, obviously pleased. "Would you like to join me?"

"I'll be happy to stay with you, but I've already eaten supper," she said. They sat at the small table and Washington quickly consumed the noodle dish prepared for him, along with green beans and a side of pears.

When finished, he sat back with a cup of tea and looked over at his companion. "I've enjoyed reading about our presidents. There have been so many good men who have faced such tremendous adversities, but each rose to the occasion. What began as a social experiment has truly worked out well," he said in a pleased tone of voice. "Clearly, our country is now the most powerful in the world, and well-structured to continue. I could not have imagined all that has taken place in the past two hundred years. But it absolutely proves that our great experiment of good people governing themselves responsibly has worked out just as we had hoped it would. I am so very pleased. And how quickly you were able to provide me with the information! This world is truly a wonder."

"You're most welcome," Lynn said. "But going forward, you will not necessarily have to read everything. We now have the ability to present you with the same information in a more visual way. Tomorrow we can discuss it all."

"Uh, Lynn," Washington hesitated, "who was *your* favorite president?"

"I don't remember," she said without hesitation. "I've only known a few but, of course, over the past few days, I would have to say our first president has become my favorite."

Washington smiled. "We could have used your diplomacy in my time." He hesitated. "But I am truly curious. Other than myself, who would you select?"

Yes, there it is, at last. He just acknowledged that he knows he is our first president, George Washington, she thought. Then she refocused on his question. "Well, I didn't personally know him in his time, but I would have to say John F. Kennedy." She felt she was being tested, that somehow, he already knew what the best answer should be. Nor did he appear impressed by her answer. In fact, he sighed, and seemed to shake his head in disbelief.

"So, I guess that was not your choice?" she asked.

"No, not my choice. Certainly, there were many great leaders, but there is one who stands out above the rest, at least from what I have read so far."

Lynn did not want to ask, but her questioning look begged for his answer. Clearly, Washington was adept at reading faces. He continued as if the answer was obvious.

"In my opinion, Gerald Ford was the most significant and important president we have had."

Lynn was dumbfounded. She had *heard* of him, but could not, for the life of her, think of anything significant that he had done during his brief time in office. She truly had no idea why Washington would pick Gerald Ford out of all the presidents in history, no idea at all. She felt him waiting for her reaction, but all she could honestly say was,

"Well, *that's* an interesting choice."

Washington saw she did not understand his rationale.

"Would you like to know why I singled him out?"

"Sure, please enlighten me."

"Gerald Ford faced the greatest threat to the continued existence of our democracy. A sitting president was close to being removed from office, and the nation had witnessed an assault on the very fiber and trust so necessary for the continued success of our nation. Then almost out of nowhere came this decent, unassuming, but well-respected man who became the only person to serve as President *without first being elected.*

"As you know, or should know," Washington continued, "he was not on the ticket when, Richard Nixon was elected. Nixon's Vice President was, um .... I think the review said . . . yes, Spiro Agnew. Agnew was forced out, and Gerald Ford was selected by politicians of both parties to be the new Vice President. Then, when Richard Nixon was forced to resign, Ford became President, having never received a single vote. Had it not been for him and the confidence his peers, and the nation, had in him, our entire constitutional electoral system could have fallen into chaos. He handled it with a calm hand and guided us back while restoring confidence in our system of government.

"Then, he pardoned President Nixon knowing it would cost him any chance at being elected to a full term in his own right. He did that because he wanted to lift the country out of the mess it had been in for so long, and prevent it from having to endure seeing its own former president put on trial. It was an unselfish, brave, and correct decision. So clearly Ford, who was never elected, held this country together at a time of great turmoil and saved it from self-destructing. For all of that, he gets my vote as the best president to date."

"Well, I must marvel at your analysis and intellect, How quickly you have assessed the significant issues of our country over the last two hundred years and have come to some truly incredible conclusions," She felt conversationally inadequate, and wondered how she could possibly handle the rest of his re-education. Also, she knew it was her turn to speak. Should she change the subject, or stay on topic? Finally, she decided to be honest.

"Mr. Washington, I must confess, I feel a little intimidated here. It is my job to ensure that you receive the information you need to adjust and survive in our society as it exists today. However, despite all the time and effort we have invested in this, I must admit, I feel like my efforts may be inadequate."

"Well, why is it just up to you?"

"I don't know," she admitted. "I have experience dealing with people who have been separated from society for a long time, so I was brought in for this purpose. I've developed all the Education Modules for you to review, and I've developed the protocol, but in practice I just feel you are exceptionally bright and have so quickly grasped this future that it amazes me. I can see why you were an exceptional leader in your time. Still, I don't want to give up or let you down, and intend to do my best. But I need you to know that I am trying as hard as I can. I just may not have all the answers you need or desire."

Washington thought for a moment. "I don't know why it is all up to you. Perhaps someone else could help you. Maybe Martha, your communications person. So far, I have only spoken to you and Palidore. There must be others you could have me see."

"Well, perhaps you are right, but only Palidore and I are

familiar with the protocol."

"What is the protocol?"

"Well, in principal, it's really quite simple. We want to be available to answer all of *your* questions to assist you in acclimating back into society. We are trying to resist forcing you to answer questions that *we* may have for you. We need to first help you, before we can start seeking answers of our own." Washington thought for another moment as a small pleasing smile developed on his face. He reached over and patted Lynn's hand.

"Well, perhaps we should just talk, have a real conversation, without worrying so much about 'how to talk.' Think about it, and if you agree, then maybe you will not be so concerned about bringing Martha in, or someone else."

"Perhaps you're correct," Lynn said with relief. "But it's late now and perhaps we should both get some rest. Let's begin again tomorrow. What do you think?"

Washington smiled, "I think that will be fine. Oh, and Lynn, you should not worry. You are doing a fine job, and I look forward to working through this with you"

Chapter 6

Palidore sat alone at his desk; everyone had gone home, It was dark outside, and the only light inside emanated from a small lamp on his desk. He liked it that way. There was something calming about the subdued effect. He knew he had to call a meeting of the board but had been putting it off. Not because he feared it, but because he was unsure how much information he could or should share. Nor was he ready to answer all their questions.

I want to be truthful to the directors, but there is the obligation to my most famous patient, he reflected. *Sometimes it feels like a dream.* But the dream was really happening. *It's almost too much to comprehend,* he thought.

Palidore leaned back, put his feet up on the right side of his desk, and folded his arms behind his head, closing his eyes for a moment. *I need to focus, prepare for the meeting,* he thought. *Where do I start? Maybe I should talk this over with Lynn first . . . no, I know what she would say. She's heard the same thing . . . he wants more interaction. He's even mentioned Martha . . . by name, no less. Yes, Martha! If anyone would know how to approach, this it would be my communications director. I mean, why have her in that position if you're not going to use her?* His mind was racing now.

Yes, at the very least, she should be brought up to date. Just discussing it with her will be like a dry run for the board meeting. I need to call her. Palidore, looked at his watch, it was 10:30 p.m. *Too late to call?* Apparently, not.

"Siri, call Martha Vaughan."

Siri responded: "Calling Martha Vaughan's cell phone."

Martha answered on the third ring. "Hello?"

"Martha, this is Palidore, sorry to bother you so late, but I need to talk with you. Do you mind?"

"Okay . . ." she said uncertainly. "What's on your mind?"

"No, no, we can't discuss it over the phone."

"Alright, give me a few minutes; I'll be right there." As she hung up, she realized Palidore was not aware of her flat across the street. Lynn knew, however, so she figured she must have told Palidore about it. Quickly throwing on some jeans and a white V-neck, tee-shirt, Martha grabbed her purse and headed out. In less than ten minutes, she was at Palidore's office.

"Wow! How'd you get here so fast?" Palidore asked.

"Oh, I have a small flat across the street. I thought you knew."

"No, I guess I didn't, but nevertheless I'm glad you're here. Please, let's sit at the table."

They moved to his small conference table but had no more sat down when Palidore unloaded his burden of anxiety.

"A lot has happened since we last talked, and I need to bring you up to speed so you can help me plan for our next board meeting." For the next two hours, they talked non-stop with Palidore doing most of the talking. At half-past midnight, Martha returned to her flat. The day had been long, and she had consumed a couple glasses of wine earlier which added to her tiredness now, both emotionally and physically. However, sleep evaded her. So she poured herself another glass of Chardonnay and sat in her stressless chair, rocking back and looking up at her ornate ceiling trying to process all she had learned.

How wrong I've been about Palidore Montgomery, she thought. *He's actually quite decent and is truly concerned about his patients and obligations. I shouldn't have been so quick to judge him. But the good thing is that all my suspicions led me to this job and I'm really excited now. I need to destroy all the data and evidence I've been gathering.* Shortly after 1:00 a.m. she drifted off to sleep.

***

Lynn Radford also had trouble sleeping that night. Her mind keep going over her conversation with Washington and she started having an intense conversation with herself.

I should have anticipated his desire to know more about past presidents. I should have had a short module prepared. Thank God, Palidore came to the rescue.

Still, I can't believe how he stayed focused for so long and read all those Wikipedia excerpts, and then, of all things, he picks out Gerald Ford as the best president. Why? I mean, what was his criteria? What was the moral baseline against which he made his judgment? I know what he said, but could anyone be so morally good as to believe not looking for votes is actually the measure of a politician? No wonder he didn't want to be a king. Most people would have seized the power he had in his time with both hands. This man is truly unique!

She turned in bed; her mind continuing to race.

Funny, I've often wondered how future generations will view our history, but never about how past generations would judge us. Will future historians rate Gerald Ford as our greatest President? Somehow, I just don't think so. It's been a long time already, and so far, it seems only George Washington has put him on such a high pedestal. Clearly, Washington sees things differently. Why? He obviously has a different standard . . . different value system . . . on which to base his judgments.

Something clicked in her thinking, and she sat bolt upright.

That's it! We need to focus more on his moral baseline against which he weighs and makes his decisions. Once we understand that, we'll be better able to anticipate how he'll react to what we're trying to teach him. Ok, so now he wants to include Martha. Why Martha?

Maybe Martha is the only other name he knows, or maybe it's because she has the same name as his wife. Clearly, he wants more interaction. Perhaps he wants to avoid being hand feed information. In any case, we need to grant his wish, or he'll start feeling trapped. I need to talk with Martha right away.

It was 4:00 a.m. but she got up and called Martha.

I can't wait!

Chapter 7

Her ringing cell phone startled Martha out of a deep sleep. She sat up in her stressless lounge chair, her arm accidentally knocking over the empty wine glass. It shattered on the tile floor. Trying to focus, now, and locate her phone, she saw it ringing on the kitchen counter across the room.

"Alexa! Turn on the lights." She started across the room, trying not to step on broken glass, and reached the phone on its fourth ring, not wanting it to go to Voicemail. She grabbed it.

"Hello?"

"Martha, it's Lynn, I know it's late . . . or early, but could I please come over and talk with you? It's *really* important." Martha rubbed her eyes, looking around the room a second before answering.

"Sure, why not?" Geez, *I've become popular lately,* she thought as she hung up, before asking Alexa to turn the lights on brighter.

Martha cleaned up the broken glass and made a trip to the bathroom. She had just finished dressing and was coming into her living room when the doorbell rang. She buzzed Lynn in without speaking over the intercom. Within minutes, the elevator door slid open and the two women greeted each other.

"Come on in, can I get you anything?"

"No, thanks, I'm okay. And thank you so much for seeing me," Lynn said.

"Happy to help, but I must confess I was a little alarmed at the sense of urgency I heard in your voice."

"Well, it's more an urgent impulse inside me than an urgent *issue*, so I guess I need to apologize for bothering you at what . . . 5 a.m.? Sorry."

"No, I'm curious now, so spill it . . . I am all ears!"

Lynn slowly inhaled and held her breath searching for the right words but finally just blurted it out: "He wants to talk to you."

"Who? Who wants to talk to me?" Martha asked.

"Client Five, Washington . . . George Washington! He specifically asked for you to join us in doing his educational update," Lynn replied.

Martha was stunned, and her eyes showed it. Slowly she stood, put hands on her hips and began walking around even before turning her head back to look at Lynn.

"Are you sure he asked for *me*? I didn't know he even knew I existed." Lynn motioned for Martha to sit.

"I need to put this in context for you. You are not the first person he asked for. First, he asked for Martha, his wife. When I informed him that she was not available, he seemed to question my answer and told me that he *heard* me talking to someone named 'Martha.' I guessed he thought I'd been talking to his *wife,* but when I explained that I was probably talking to *you* and that your name is also 'Martha,' he seemed to accept it. The conversation went on for a while with me explaining your role with MCS. Toward the end of that conversation, he suggested perhaps someone additional besides me could assist with his re-education. That's when he specifically suggested *you*."

Martha's eyes opened wide, and she stood up again. "Oh, my god, the only time you and I were in his presence together was . . . when he touched me."

Lynn was nodding her head affirmatively. Martha, now looked at the ceiling while walking around thinking out loud. "So-o-o-o-o, he could *hear* what we were saying? Wow! I can't believe it! I'm trying to remember exactly what we said. Oh, this is not good, is it?"

"Calm down. I really think we're in a good place to move forward."

"Well then, what did you tell him?"

"About what?"

"About me working with you!"

"Oh that, Well, I told him that I would talk it over with you and Palidore," Lynn replied.

"What did Palidore say?"

"I haven't talked to him yet, I wanted to run it by you and get your reaction first."

Martha had a questioning look on her face. "Huh, that's funny."

"What's funny?"

"Well, Palidore called me over to his office late last night, around ten-thirty, and brought me totally up-to-date, but he never mentioned this."

Now Lynn was curious. "Hmm . . . that's interesting. I'm not sure what motivated him to do that, but he monitors all conversations, so, maybe he decided to jump-start the idea on his own. I don't know, but it looks like we're both thinking the same way. Anyway, are you up for expanding your role?"

"Absolutely! I'm . . . a little frightened, but excited to help."

"Well, let me give you a brief overview of how we have set up the Education Module system to work."

The talked for the next hour about what lay ahead.

***

Susan Trott entered Paladore's office. He was on the telephone but motioned her in and pointed to a chair. She took a seat in front of his desk and waited for him to finish his call. When he finally hung up, he smiled at her. "It's time," he said.

Susan knew exactly what he meant. Client Four had been revived, operated on, and placed in a medically-induced coma for healing. She had been faithfully monitoring him at his bedside while trying to keep up with Lynn's progress on client Five, hoping to learn from her experience. Now it was going to be her turn, and even though she felt she was properly prepared, the prospect still frightened her.

"I'm ready," she said, trying to feel confident. "When do you think he'll come around?"

"Well, you know, these things aren't as precise as we would like. You probably won't notice much for a few hours, but then you'll begin to see him stir. We've taken his feeding tube out this morning and administered drugs to help him wake." Susan sat in silence before speaking.

"Interesting, isn't it?" Palidore gave her a quizzical look.

"I mean, with client Five, we knew almost everything about him and his life, but with client Four, we know nothing, not even his last name. The two cases could not be more different. It just makes it more difficult to be prepared for anything that might happen."

"Well, we may not know for certain," Palidore said, trying to calm her nerves, "but we believe there *is* a connection between the two of them. History tells us that Washington befriended a slave known as 'Frank,' and enjoyed his company. We also know someone paid for Four's treatment. It just seems logical that it might have been Washington, himself, who did it. So, if that turns out to be true, it would be significant. Not just to us, but for both of them. Imagine, not only being revived hundreds of years into the future, but having a friend make the journey with you. How incredible is that?"

"Of course, you're right, and I guess we'll soon find out."

"I'll be at the monitor if you need me," Palidore said. "and if they're not too busy with Five, I'm sure Lynn and/or Martha will be at the monitor watching with me, too." Susan started to rise, but then sat back down.

"Martha? I didn't know she was going to be involved in this phase?"

"Neither did we, but Washington actually mentioned her recently and asked for her to be another one of his teachers. Incredible as that sounds, it just might be useful."

"Huh," was Susan's only answer as she stood up. "Well, I guess I'd better change into my costume and get ready to greet this gentleman."

"Yes, you should, but don't worry, you'll do fine."

With Palidore's words of reassurance, Susan left the office and headed down the hallway.
Palidore walked over to the monitor, but felt conflicted. He was anxious to get client Four to the same point where they had arrived with Five, but on the other hand, he felt things were moving too fast as if he was somehow losing control.

I'm not comfortable delegating important things to others, he thought, *it doesn't come naturally to me.* Yet, at the same time, everything happening was so exciting that he had trouble waiting for the natural sequence of events to occur more slowly. *I need to freshen up and wake up*, he thought and headed toward his private shower. *This is going to be another big day.*

Chapter 8

Susan moved to her post outside bedroom number two on the third floor of the MCS building. On her monitor, she watched as her patient moved a little. She drew her face closer to the monitor to double-check and after seeing another slight movement, headed into the room to take a seat on the chair near his bed.

Palidore found his chair in front of the monitor just as Susan was taking her seat in the bedroom. They both watched and waited for the sleeping man's next move.

An hour later, Susan was still focused on her patient when she noticed his eyes blink a couple of times before opening. No other part of his body moved; his eyes remained fixed on the ornate ceiling. Susan's heart started to pound as she watched. He remained so motionless, she wondered if he could actually see anything.

Maybe he can't see or he's having trouble focusing, she thought. Not wanting to startle him, she didn't say anything. *I want him to acclimate himself to his new environment without my intervention.*

After a while, however, she placed her hand on the mattress and applied just a little pressure causing an ever so slight movement to the covers. The patient's eyes seemed to squint slightly as if acknowledging that he had felt movement. Susan continued watching her patient intently. She noticed the covers over his feet give way to the movement of his right foot, then his left foot. Finally, his head moved a bit but instead of moving toward her, he moved away from her. His breathing quickened and she could see his lips part as his tongue slipped between them.

It's time, she thought and slowly rose from her chair, positioning herself in his line of sight. This time, his head turned toward her.

"Good morning," she said with a smile. Her patient didn't respond, so she continued. "My name is Susan, and I'm here to help you. Right now, I'm going to place a wet cloth over your lips. They look a little dry." What she actually used was a small damp green sponge on the end of a short plastic stick. She moved the sponge back and forth over his lips. He seemed to accept the gesture, then wet his own lips with his tongue.

Susan gently took his right hand and held it between both her hands. "If you would like a little water, please squeeze my hand." She felt his hand tighten. *We have found a way to communicate,* she thought, feeling pleased.

"Very well, then. I have this special bottle that will help you drink water while lying down. It has a long tube on it. I will place the tube between your lips, then you can suck on it." She gently placed one end of the straw in his mouth. He immediately began to suck on it rapidly.

"Not too fast now," she cautioned. "It will be better for you if we go a little slow at first."

Her patient stopped sucking and released his lips. Susan removed the straw and bottle, thrilled that he clearly understood her instructions. It verified that his cognitive abilities were intact.

"Are you feeling any pain?" she asked. He didn't answer, so she took his hand again, palm to palm as in a handshake.

"If you are in any pain, please squeeze my hand." Nothing happened.

"If you are feeling okay, please squeeze my hand." She felt his hand tighten around hers. "Good," she said, "very good. Now, I'm sure you have questions. Let me try to explain a few things. First of all, you are safe. You have been very sick and asleep for a long time. You are *not* in a hospital, but with people who are trained to care for you.

This will take some time. If you remain calm, we will be able to help you get stronger every day until you feel perfectly well again. If you understand what I have just said, please squeeze my hand." She felt his hand tighten once again, but this time, she noticed a small smile on his face. Slowly, Susan, herself, began to calm down. She was slowly gaining more confidence.

"Just a few more questions: If you think you can talk, please squeeze my hand." She felt his hand tighten. "Good. Now, if you would *like* to talk, please squeeze my hand." Nothing happened.   "Ok, would you like to continue using our hands to talk?" Again, nothing again. She looked at his face. Her patient had fallen back to sleep.

***

Lynn and Martha entered the room of client Five together. Washington was seated next to his bed reading the Bible. As they entered, he looked up at both women and rose from his seat.

"Mr. Washington, this is Martha Vaughan, our communication's director. At your request she's joining me today. Is that okay with you?"

"Most certainly. How do you do," he said, slightly bowing his head.

Lynn and Martha each had a bottle of water in their hands.

"Would you like some water?" Lynn asked handing a bottle to Washington. He took the clear, plastic bottle from her and looked at it curiously.

"Just twist the top off like this," Lynn said, as she took the top off the bottle Martha had handed to her. Washington followed suit and studied the small plastic top carefully. His eyebrows raised a bit as he seemed to recall the object he had found in his pillowcase.

Lynn was watching to make sure he made the connection.

Satisfied that he had, she continued talking. "Okay, then, have you reviewed your list of educational modules and selected a topic to learn?"

"Yes, I have, but before we begin, I want to go somewhere." The statement caught Lynn and Martha by surprise. They shot each other questioning looks.

"Where would you like to go?" Lynn asked in a calm tone. His response came instantly.

"Anywhere but here. I want to move to another room. I am tired of being confined."

"Of course. We can arrange that, but I'm not certain you've seen *all* of this room as yet."

Washington looked surprised and turned around with a questioning expression on his face. Finally, he stopped and focused on Lynn again.

"Let me show you," she said, and walked over to the large bookcase. Reaching for a small device, she held it in her hand and pushed a button. The bookcase began moving apart, one section going to the left, the other moving to the right. Behind the shelves, a small room was revealed. It measured some five feet deep and twelve feet long. Across the entire length of the back wall was an attached desk. It appeared to have three sections, with a chair in front of each section. Storage cabinets were positioned above the long desk along the entire length of the wall. Underneath were regularly spaced doors housing opaque glass that hid undercabinet lighting. The center section of the long desk held a large computer screen. In front of it was a keyboard and a computer mouse. The other two sections were equipped with notebook computers. Along with the notebook computers, there were, pencils, notepads, and pens at each station.

Lynn waited for Washington to take it all in. He walked over to the bookcases and started looking them over, up one side and down the other. He appeared to be more fascinated with how the bookcases worked than with the contents of the secret room.

Then he moved toward the desk and pulled out the middle chair which, like the others, was on wheels, and sat down. He noticed the chair swiveled and spun himself around, using his hand to stop when he faced the desk again. Lynn and Martha watched and waited. Finally, he got up and stood back, examining the entire area, before taking the remote from Lynn's hand.

"May I see this please?" he asked. Lynn released it to him. It was a simple device similar to a garage door opener. He studied it, then pushed the button. As he did, the bookshelf doors began to close, and he jumped back to observe. Once the doors closed, he pushed the button again and watched in fascination as they reopened.

Washington went to the right-side bookcase and put his head against the wall, trying to listen for a motor or however the movement worked. Once the doors were fully opened again, he stood there with his hands on his hips, still in possession of the remote. Holding it up, he looked at Martha. "I don't understand how this works."

"There is much we need to show you," Martha said, "and that device, which we call a 'remote,' is just one of them. The items on the desk will help us do that."

"Would you like to proceed with your first lesson?" Lynn asked. "We could do it here, or do you still want to go somewhere else?"

Washington looked over at the desk. "I think I am alright starting a lesson here. But I would like to keep this," he said and pointed the remote in her direction.

"You may keep it if you like, but now that you are aware of the special room we have for your studies, you may prefer to leave it open all the time."

Washington did not reply, but simply put the remote in his pocket and took a seat in the middle chair. Lynn took the chair to his left and Martha took the one on his right. Each of them pressed a finger on their touch pads and their screens came to life immediately displaying the words: "Montgomery Cryogenics Services, LLC" in blue letters on a white background. Washington seemed surprised to see the bright screens.

"Why does mine not turn on?" he questioned. Lynn had decided that it would be easier for him to use a computer mouse instead of having to learn all the commands of a touch pad or touch screen.

"Please place you right hand over this little black object and it will. We call this thing a 'mouse.'" She demonstrated how he should handle it by using a sample mouse in front of her. "Now, using your forefinger, push down on the left side of the mouse."

Washington did as he was instructed, and his screen lit up, showing the same phrase on it.

"Now move the mouse around to any blank space and push down on it again. We call that a 'click.'" Washington did as told and the screen changed, revealing the list of topics he had previously seen on paper. The same list appeared on Lynn and Martha's computers at the same time.

"Do you remember seeing this list before?" Lynn asked. Washington nodded.

"Okay, now just move the mouse around in circles and you will see a little arrow appear." While Washington was doing this, she continued. "As you can see, when the mouse moves, the little arrow on the screen in front of you moves also. Since our screens are connected, it also moves the little arrows on our screens. You are controlling that little arrow with the mouse under your hand."

Washington did not stop moving it until Lynn asked him to stop. When he was motionless, she swiveled her chair toward him, away from her computer. She then reached over and took his left hand causing him to swivel toward her. Once she had his full attention she said, "Before, when you saw this list on paper you were going to select one of the topics for us to start with today. You just did not know about this room yet. The topic which contains information about the devices we are using now is called 'Technology.' Is that the topic you were going to select for us to review today?"

"No"

"Ok, what topic did you select?"

"History."

"We can do 'History' first, if you prefer, or any other topic. There is entirely too much information on each topic to cover in any one session. Each session is designed to last about three hours. If that's not enough time to cover the entire topic, then it's broken down into sub-sections.

"At the beginning of each topic there will be a short introduction and, when appropriate, a brief description of how similar tasks or things were done in the early 1800's. So, for example, if under 'Technology' you picked the sub-section listed as 'Communications' you would first learn how people communicated in the early 1800's followed by a brief description of how, over the years, several other methods of communication were developed up to, and including, how we communicate today.

"Now for the first few sessions either Martha or I will be here to assist you, but as you become familiar with how to use the equipment, you will eventually be able to proceed without us, learning at your own pace. There is a lot of material here and if you went through every item non-stop without sleeping, it would take you approximately 57 days. Obviously, it will take much longer than that, probably several months.

"However, the more you do, the easier it will get, and there may be some subjects you have no interest in investigating at all right now. Which brings me to my disclaimer: Please understand that we did our best in putting this together. We tried to think of everything that would be important but, by no means, can we cover everything. Even after you have carefully completed this entire series, there will be much that we have probably, somehow, failed to cover.

"Our hope is that this series will bring you up-to-date enough for you to feel comfortable circulating in our society in this modern age . With that in mind, are you ready to begin?"

"Yes, please let's get started," he replied somewhat anxiously.

"Do you still want to start with 'History?'" Martha asked.

"No, let's do 'Technology,'" he replied.

Chapter 9

Lynn was a little disappointed that Washington had changed his mind. She felt she had indirectly influenced him to select this topic and that it wasn't really what he wanted to learn. Somehow, she had wanted him to stick with his first choice. But trying not to control the situation, she began instructing her famous student.

"Okay, now, let's move your mouse so the little arrow is over the words that spell 'Technology.' Now, push down on the left side of the mouse, or, as we say, 'click it.'" Washington did as told and a list of sub-topics appeared.

"As you can see, this topic is so large, it has many subsections so you will need to look at the new list and select the sub-topic you want to begin. Do you know which sub-topic you want to learn about?"

"The one that explains these devices we are using."

"Okay, then let's start with the sub-topic labeled 'Communications' by moving the arrow over that word." Again, Washington did as told and Martha instructed him to click on the word with his mouse. He was following her instructions when suddenly Lynn's image appeared on his screen and she was moving. He seemed shocked to see her and looked back and forth between the screen and the real Lynn. Martha used her pad to pause the program just as he turned to Lynn again.

"That's you! How is that possible?" Lynn turned her chair to look at them, but neither was looking at the screens, they were facing each other.

"Do you remember the photo that Palidore showed you?"

TRANSFORMING GEORGE WASHINGTON

"Yes, of course I do. I was present when it was taken."

"Well, now we have the ability to take a picture of people while they're moving and record what they're saying at the same time. We call that a 'video.' So, when that photo of you was taken, it captured how you looked at that one moment in time. In a video, the camera can take hundreds of pictures in rapid succession, so when they are played back, it looks like the people are moving. Later, we also learned how to capture sound and when we put the photos and sounds together we created a video. So, what is on your screen now is a video that I created some time ago when I was preparing this topic."

Washington looked back at the screen, then to her, then back at the screen.

"Well, it's not moving now."

"That's because I paused it," Martha said. "But we can resume it again, here let me show you." She rose from her seat and proceeded to the back of Washington's chair leaning over him to place her right hand over his hand and move the mouse.

The close proximity of their heads, and the warmth of his skin next to hers, stirred a feeling inside her that had laid dormant since Stanley's death. She froze for a second before she was able to refocus. Then she began moving the mouse under Washington's hand over the small triangle on the screen near the bottom.

"Now that we have the arrow over that little triangle, let's just press the mouse with our finger and see what happens." As she pressed down on Washington's finger, the screen came to life with Lynn speaking from the monitor.

"You have selected the 'Communications' topic," the monitor image said. 'Before we begin, let's take a look at how people communicated in the late 1700's and early 1800's."

Martha pressed on Washington's hand again causing the video to pause. She peered around so she could make eye contact with her student. Their faces were now only inches apart and Washington's eyes seems to sparkle as they locked onto hers. Martha's heart skipped a beat. *What is this,* she said to herself. *Why is this happening?*

She attempted to regain her composure. "So, um, as you can see it's easy to stop and start the video." Washington's body language, however, revealed that he wasn't as much interested in resuming the lesson as he was in exploring his newfound attraction for his teacher. His eyes glistened but never broke their gaze. Martha sensed his silent advance and fought to resist her own attraction, awkwardly continuing her explanation.

"As we go forward, umm, you can stop it at any time to ask a question or take a break." Standing up, she moved back to her own seat. "Think you understand how this works now?"

"I am not certain I understand *everything* I have experienced here today, but I must confess, I am eager to continue . . . learning."

Martha realized his carefully chosen words could be taken in more than one context and wondered if she had placed herself in an ethically-compromising position. Nevertheless, she felt certain that her new assignment was going to be very intriguing.

Lynn, whose attention had been momentarily interrupted by a message on her watch, failed to pick up on the non-verbal communication between the two of them.

"Are you ready to start this module?" There was a pregnant pause as Washington forced himself to break the gaze he had on Martha and turn his attention back to his monitor before he answered.

"Yes, of course. Please, let's proceed." He pushed the "play" button by himself. The screen came to life with Lynn's face saying into the camera: "You have selected the 'Communications' topic. Before we begin, let's take a look at how people communicated in the late 1700's and early 1800's. The primary means of nonverbal communication was the print media. Newspapers were common. The U.S. Postal Service Act of 1792 provided substantial subsidies allowing newspapers to be delivered up to 100 miles away for one penny. Mail was delivered based on the distance. Important mail was delivered by the use of personal couriers.

TRANSFORMING GEORGE WASHINGTON

The typewriter, a machine that allowed an individual to create a personal printed document, was not invented until 1878, so all personal mail was handwritten until then.

However, in 1840, the telegraph was invented which allowed for the transmission of messages using a series of sounds known as Morse Code to be sent over a special wire from one place to another. This allowed for almost instant communication at a distance, but it was not available everywhere."

Washington paused the video and asked Lynn if he could see the last part again. Martha, now back in her seat, pointed to the screen to show him how to rewind a portion. He followed her instructions and looked carefully at the video of people using the telegraph and listening to its beeps. He paused it at that point and asked what the person next to the machine was doing. Lynn explained that he was interpreting what the sounds meant by writing down the words they signified.

"Amazing!" exclaimed Washington as he hit the play button again. The video showed a series of telephones, starting with the old crank relics to the wall mounted larger antique versions. Washington and his two instructors watched as it went on to show telephone poles and lines being installed everywhere. Then it showed the huge cable that was dropped into the ocean which allowed telephone communication between Washington, DC, and Moscow in Europe. At this point, Washington paused the presentation again and pointed.

"Who is speaking on that telephone?"

"His name was President Dwight D. Eisenhower. After World War II, the United States and Russia emerged as the dominant powers in the world, both possessing powerful atomic weapons. Tensions between these two super power nations began to grow and it was felt that if the leaders were able to communicate immediately together, it might help prevent another world war."

"Brilliant idea. What an undertaking."

He hit the play button, again, and the module continued showing the advent of wireless communications from the first portable bag phone to the latest tiny cell phone. Lynn then used her own computer to stop the module.

"We weren't sure when you would reach this point, but we've been prepared from the outset that once you did, we would present you with a little gift."

Washington's eyes widened as he watched Lynn remove a small box from her purse. She opened it and turned it on before handing it over to Washington. He held it in his hand and looked at the small screen now displaying a picture of the MCS building.

"This is a cell phone for you to have and use. Right now, many of its features have been turned off so as not to confuse you too quickly, but it will allow you to call whoever you want." Washington held it up and turned it over. He even put it to his ear. Then he handed it back to Lynn.

"Thank you, but I don't think I have a need for this." Lynn and Martha both looked at him in complete surprise.

"But it's so useful; why wouldn't you want it?"

"I don't know of anyone I need to call."

Martha, looked a bit deflated and responded, "But . . . you could call *me*, or Lynn, or Palidore."

"Why would I call you? You're always here anyway."

"But, one day, you will be going out. You might need it then. Won't you at least try it for a little while?"

"Sure, I'll try it."

Martha showed him how to turn it on and where she had put in her number and the others. Then, she showed him how to access this contact list.

"See? Just touch the name of the person you want to call. Go ahead, give it a try." Washington pushed the contact icon for Martha and her phone began to ring. She reached into her purse and pulled out her cell phone, held it to her ear.

"Hello?" she said while smiling at him. Then she pointed at

him to put the cell phone to his ear. He did and repeated: 'Hello?'

"Hi, how are you?"

Upon hearing her voice through the phone, he gave her a curious look. Martha continued. "Go ahead and say something to me in your phone, so I can hear you."

"But you're right here," he said, somewhat confused. "Why would I want to use this to talk to you?"

"Well, we're just showing you how this works. Normally you would not call me if we were together. But, let's say I am not here. You could call me, or Lynn, or Palidore and have a conversation even though we may be miles apart."

"And you can call me?"

"Yes, of course."

"So, go into another room and call me."

Martha got up and went out into the hall before realizing she didn't have his cell phone number programmed into her phone. Then she remembered he had just called her, so looking at her recent calls, and touched his cell phone number. Palidore and Lynn watched as Washington held up his phone. Lynn showed him how to accept the call. He put it to his ear and said: "Hello?"

"Hello, George. This is Martha."

"I know it's you. You can come back in now." Then, without instruction, he ended the call. Martha re-entered the room and asked Washington if he had changed his mind about the cell phone.

"Okay, I'll keep it, so I can call you if I need to."

"Well, I think over time, you'll grow to enjoy having it, not just for making a call, but because there is so much more you can do with it. But let's resume our lesson.

Washington put the cell phone down, turned his chair back to the computer screen and started the video again. At one point, as it was covering the invention of television, Washington hit the pause button again, pointed at the computer screen, and asked: "Is this a television?" Lynn and Martha caught each other's eye, but Lynn fielded the question.

"What you are looking at now is a 'computer' screen. It can do everything a television can do and much more. Later, this module will explain in detail all about it under another tab."

Washington seemed satisfied with her answer and hit the resume button again. While Washington was engrossed in his studies, Lynn received another text message on her watch. This one came from Susan Trott.

"Can you join me? Client Four is awake."

"Give me five minutes," Lynn spoke into her watch to send her reply. As she stood, both Martha and George looked at her.

"I'm needed elsewhere for a while, but I think Martha and you can continue in my absence."

Washington didn't reply, but instead clicked the mouse to continue his program which he was enjoying. Martha, however, felt abandoned and shot Lynn a helpless 'are you kidding me?' look on her face.

"You're doing fine!" Lynn mouthed to her and gave a quick wave as she left the room, shutting the door behind her.

Chapter 10

Previously, Susan had briefed Lynn concerning Frank's initial awakening encounter and his preference in using hand signals to communicate. Now as Lynn entered the room of client Four, she saw Susan sitting in a chair next to the bed where Four lay; the head of the bed was slightly raised. She felt that Susan's approach had been perfect up to now, and that if at all possible, it was important for Frank to begin verbalizing his communications. She had promised to be there the next time he awoke.

Frank's medium brown complexion and facial features reminded her of a handsome young Sidney Poitier except for his white hair. His face seemed at peace and comfortable. Susan gratefully acknowledged Lynn with a nod of her head.

If it was necessary for client Five to have two people assist him, then it seems reasonable that client Four will also need two, Lynn thought. *Only I've run out of people. I guess I'll have to let Martha and Susan do the main work with each client and I will go back and forth between them as a support person for each of them.*

Lynn brought a chair over, careful to lift it off the floor and not make unwanted sounds. She quietly took a seat next to Susan. Frank did not seem to notice or acknowledge their presence but lay in his bed staring at the ceiling.

Then without warning, just as Lynn tried signaling something to Susan, Frank sat up, startling both girls. He swung his legs to the side of the bed as if getting up but stopped for a moment, suddenly realizing he had company. Susan and Lynn remained motionless. Then Frank stood up and uttered his first words.

"I need to go."

"Go where?" Susan asked as she stood in front of him.

"Home . . . Mount Vernon. I need to go now, or they will think I have run away. Where are my clothes?"

Lynn, now also standing, spoke in a calming voice. "No, they won't. They know you're here. There is no reason to worry. For now, you need to stay with us a little longer. Please sit down for a moment and let us help you understand what is going on." Frank, looking perplexed, began surveying the room as if looking for an escape route, or his clothes. But he remained standing for a moment longer before finally choosing to sit back down on the side of his bed.

"Would you prefer to sit in a chair?"

"Yes, I would," He replied.

Susan motioned with her arm to the wingback chair next to them. He stood without releasing his gaze on Susan and took the seat. As he did, the women repositioned their chairs to face him at more comfortable angles.

"Let's start with introductions," Susan began. "My name is Susan Trott, and this is Lynn Radford. We both work here, and right now our job is to help you understand what is going on. However, we only know your first name and were hoping you could share your last name with us." Frank did not immediately respond to the question and appeared to have trouble formulating an answer.

Finally, he said, "I do not use a last name. People just refer to me as 'Frank.'"

"Well, that may be true," Susan said, "but here, *everyone* has a last name."

"Many slaves don't have a last name, or don't know their last names." Hearing himself refer to his own self as a slave sent shivers through Susan's entire body. Lynn was also clearly taken aback by the comment.

TRANSFORMING GEORGE WASHINGTON

After an awkward pause, Lynn finally said, "Well, Frank . . . you are no longer a 'slave,' so you are entitled to have and use both a first and a last name. People can still refer to you by your first name, but for our records, we would appreciate knowing your full name."

Frank went silent again, his face taking on a more solemn look. A few moments passed with his eyes downcast. Then, looking as if he was studying the lines on his hands, he finally spoke in a voice so low, Susan and Lynn had to strain to hear him.

"The only other name I remember is . . . 'Khamisi' which is what my mother called me as a young child. I do not think it was my surname. I believe it may be my *original* first name. Later, I learned that it means 'born on Thursday.' So, if you like, you may refer to me as Frank Thursday." It was apparent to everyone that if Frank had a surname, he either did not know it or had long since forgotten it.

"Well, would it be alright if we called you Frank Khamisi?" Susan asked.

Frank raised and lowered his shoulders as if to indicate that he truly didn't care.

"Then that is what we will put down for you: 'Frank Khamisi,'" Susan continued. She wrote it down on her notepad. "Now, as we have just told you, we are here to help you understand what is going on. The best way is to simply answer your questions. That way you will receive information in the order you prefer. So, with that said, do you have any questions for us?"

Frank scratched his chin with his right hand. "You just said . . . I am no longer a slave. How do you know that, and what do you mean? Has something happened to my master?"

Instantly, Lynn knew it had been a mistake to have said he was 'no longer a slave.' Now she needed to answer his question. Her mind was racing. *I don't want to tell him yet that 'his 'master' is indeed alive. And I can't tell him that Washington set his slaves free in his last will, or he will assume Washington is dead. Then, he'll think we lied when he finally sees him.'* As she was still pondering an appropriate response, Susan spoke up.

"Slavery is no longer allowed; it has been abolished?"

Perfect! Lynn thought as Susan continued.

"We can discuss how that happened, but for now. let's just say that it happened while you were asleep, or as we prefer to say, 'in a prolonged trance'. However, perhaps you have some other questions for us right now."

Frank seemed to be cautiously considering what he had just heard. His eyes once again began scanning the room.

"Where am I?" he finally asked.

"You are in the City of Washington," Lynn answered. "This building *was* owned by George Washington but is now owned by Dr. Palidore Montgomery whom you have not met. yet"

"I think I may know him, that name sounds familiar."

"It does?' she asked, realizing his memories were starting to come back.

"Am I sick?"

"Not anymore, but you were. In fact, it was necessary for you to have an operation to help cure you of your stomach pain. You appear to have recovered very well. Although, we know you are still in need of a more rest and care."

"How did I get here?" Lynn jumped in before Susan could answer. "You were brought here by Mr. Washington."

Upon hearing the name of his master and friend, Frank's eyes took on a sparkle. No one said anything for a while. Then Frank opened his eyes wide and raised his head upward, as if he had suddenly remembered something.

"Yes . . . I was sick, I was *very* sick, I was hurting *real* bad. It hurt so much!" Abruptly, Frank stood and ripped apart the front of his gown causing a couple of buttons to pop off. Slowly he ran his hand over his stomach, feeling the scar his fingers found. After a moment he attempted to pull his gown back together and sat down in the chair.

"That scar is from the operation you had," Susan said.

TRANSFORMING GEORGE WASHINGTON

Frank said nothing but remained seated as if in a self-induced trance. They all sat quietly for a time. Then Susan broke the silence.

"Are you tired? Would you like to rest?"

Frank looked at her, then without another word, stood, got back into bed, and laid down. Susan brought his covers over him and smiled reassuringly. It took only a few moments before he was fast asleep.

Chapter 11

By 9:30 p.m., Palidore, Lynn, Martha, Renee, and Susan were sitting around the table in his office as he began the discussion. "Thanks for agreeing to this late-night meeting, I know you've all put in a long day, so I'm hopeful this meeting won't last long. After today, I believe it's imperative to bring our board up to date. A lot has happened."

Lynn and Susan had even taken to sleeping in their offices, or staying over at Martha's flat across the street, just to be available any time. They needed to always be sure their patients were sound asleep and without needs.

"So far, I've been fielding their questions," Palidore said. "But now it's decision time. I've been putting them off while I attempt to figure out how much information should be revealed at this time. I've already had brief discussions with each of you, one-on-one and I thought we should meet in the hopes of coming to a common consensus.

"Clearly we are way ahead of where we thought we'd be at this time. Indeed, sometimes I still have trouble believing it's all really happening - but it is!" Looking around the table he saw everyone's rapt attention.

"So, any thoughts?" Everyone remained silent, each glancing back and forth. When it became apparent that no one wanted to be the first with a suggestion, Palidore asked another question.

"Okay, let's try it this way: What should we *not* reveal to the board?"

Still, dead silence. Finally, Susan spoke up. "I don't think we need to update anyone about Frank at this time."

"Really? And why is that?" Palidore asked.

"Well, we really don't know much about him yet. The only thing we've confirmed is that he was Washington's favored slave. Washington has also been awake much longer than Frank, so couldn't we afford ourselves the same amount of time to get to know Frank, as we did Washington? Besides, we already knew a lot about Washington before he awoke, but we know nothing about Frank yet. I guess the real problem I have is that I don't feel like *I'm* ready to field questions that will surely follow such a disclosure. I mean, once they start asking, I don't want to be in a position requiring me to lie about anything."

"Okay, then does anyone disagree with Susan?" Palidore asked while looking around.

"I know how she feels," Martha said. "She doesn't need the added pressure. We're all feeling our way along this unknown pathway. Assuming we do not offer anything about Frank to the board, what should our response be if the board initiates a question concerning him?"

"Well, shouldn't we at least confirm that he's alive and doing well?" Lynn asked.

Everyone was silent again. Palidore finally offered a response. "Maybe we should just be truthful, then. We could say he is alive and well, but we don't feel comfortable about discussing his progress yet, and we're looking forward to updating them at the next meeting." All the women seemed to nod in agreement, getting used to the idea.

"Okay then," Palidore said, "that's how we'll handle questions about Frank. Now for the more difficult one: What do we tell them about Washington?"

Again, he was faced with silence and blank expressions. Slowly, he stood and walked over to his credenza. He opened the crystal decanter containing his special Edradour single malt scotch whiskey and proceeded to pour himself a handsome glassful. Then, he held up the decanter in an invitation for the others to join him.

"Maybe we need a little help in loosening up our tongues." They waved him off clearly indicating they had no interest.

"I don't know what you see in that stuff anyway," Lynn said, making a face at him.

"It's an acquired taste," Palidore answered. "As far back as I can remember, my family preferred it to other drinks, but it's getting harder to obtain. I actually purchased this bottle when I visited Scotland last year." He returned to his seat with his glass.

"Now then, where are we?"

"When do you anticipate holding this board meeting?" Martha asked, sipping her drink.

Palidore tilted his head up and out a little, pondering a response. "Not sure. Normally, we look for a commonly available date which is typically almost impossible to find. Usually, we ask board members to try and keep the last Wednesday of each month free from appointments not easily canceled or moved. That's when we try to book a date."

Martha looking at her cell phone's calendar. "Well, that would be the 24th, about ten days from now."

"I suppose so," Palidore replied. "What are you getting at?"

"Well, I have an idea that may be slightly off the wall . . . yes, I guess it is . . . anyway, never mind. Forget I said anything."

"You can't do that!" Palidore protested. "Don't leave us hanging like that. Let's hear it!"

"Okay but, promise you won't laugh or throw me out?"

Everyone encouraged her to just spit it out. She took a deep breath and said:

"Why don't we simply introduce Washington to the board

at the meeting?"

Everyone gasped at the thought, then went silent with their mouths open.

"I told you it was off the wall, but now that I've said it, hear me out, please."

Palidore made a motion with his arm. "By all means - the floor is yours."

"Well, Washington is growing tired of his room and has expressed a desire to get out, go somewhere, do something. He's also indicated he wants more interaction with people, indeed, as you will recall, that's exactly how I got involved. So, after we give the board a very brief update, I thought we could invite Washington to come into the meeting and introduce him to everyone. We certainly wouldn't allow anyone to question him. But I think we have time to prepare him for the meeting. I believe he would look forward to it. As for the board, I think they will be awestruck. And you know: Seeing is believing."

Lynn started shaking her head, 'no' but Palidore said, "I like it! You could not be more transparent than that! Lynn, you have some reservations?"

"I just don't know," she said. "Instinctively, I want to protect him. I'm not saying it *can't* be done, and maybe it's the right thing to do, but . . . I'm just not sure. Perhaps the idea will grow on me. In any event, at the very least, I don't think we should sign off on the idea just yet."

Palidore leaning back in his chair, hands behind his head, now came forward and looked directly at Lynn.

"I understand your hesitancy, but we have ten days to plan for this, so for now, I think we should assume this will be the course of action we will likely take. Therefore, I am going to proceed with trying to set the time and date for the meeting."

"Okay," Lynn said, "but let's not reveal any of this to Washington just yet. As you've said, we have ten days. We could use the first few to consider how to do this. Then we'll have the last few days to prepare him if we still want to proceed at that time."

Palidore rose and drained the remains of his Scotch. "I declare this meeting 'adjourned.'

Wonder what he'll think in the morning, Lynn thought, *without the scotch.*

Chapter 12

Martha knocked on the door to Washington's room and cautiously opened it a crack. "Mr. Washington? It's Martha Vaughan. May I come in?"

"Yes, of course," his voice responded quickly from the depths of the room. She entered and found her famous student seated in the room at the computer. He was dressed in a blue cotton button-down shirt and khaki pants looking very contemporary. He had no shoes on, just a pair of red socks, was clean-shaven and looked as if he had showered. He rose to greet her, his face beaming with pleasure.

"I'm pleased you have come to see me."

"You're already hard at work. I'm proud of you! Looks like you are mastering the process. How long have you been up?"

"I haven't kept track . . . a couple of hours, I suppose."

"I like what you're wearing. Decided to go a little more contemporary today, did you?"

"Well, Martha . . . I mean, *my* Martha, was always concerned with my clothes and the way I looked. She knew by the calendar, who I would be seeing, and what events were planned. She was always concerned about the proper selection of my clothes. It was something I never had to worry about but, now I see those decisions have been left up to me. Therefore, not knowing who I am going to see, or what events have been planned for me, I've decided that perhaps looking more like how Dr. Montgomery looks, or dresses, might be a safe choice. However, I couldn't find any shoes that looked quite like his, so I've just opted to stay in these colorful socks."

Washington's full statement caught Martha a bit off guard. *Clearly, he feels out of the loop. He doesn't have a calendar, or schedule of events, and hasn't been given any advance notice of what is being planned or when. I'm happy that he's aware and cares about it. We have been so absorbed with trying to answer his questions and letting him lead the way, that we've failed to provide any structure or guidance. Of course, anyone would want to know what to expect. This was a big flaw in our planning. I need to discuss this with Lynn as soon as possible.* Martha broke away from her thoughts long enough to respond to him.

"Well, we'll try harder to let you know what's happening next. But I must say, you do look nice; very handsome, right down to those bright red socks." Washington glanced down at his feet and wiggled his toes in an effort to show off his socks while smiling a little shyly.

Hmmm, was his selection of socks a bit of a social protest? Martha wondered. In an effort to change the subject she started drifting toward the computer desk.

"What have you been looking at today?"

"The U.S. Wars."

"Wow! That's really good. To get there you had to go to 'History', then to 'United States,' and then to 'Wars.' So, you're moving along pretty well," Martha said. "Lynn told me that when we first showed you these education modules that you had wanted to select 'History,' and she was afraid that she had indirectly influenced you to select 'Communications' instead, so I'm not surprised you've migrated back to your first choice. Find anything interesting?"

"It's what I didn't find that is so disappointing."

Martha's questioning look caused Washington to continue.

"Peace. I see no prolonged periods of peace. I was so hopeful that this country would avoid the trap that all great powers seem to experience. But I suppose some lessons are never learned.

"When we won our independence, we did not do it by beating

the world's most powerful army. We simply outlasted them. You see, when a country is fighting at home, the citizens help feed the army, house them, and care for the wounded," George said. "In our war for Independence, England had to bring its own food, supplies, ammunition, medicines, caskets, everything! I knew they couldn't do that forever, and I was right. So, that was the lesson we needed to learn. But did we? No. I see that we started sending our forces all over the world, just like the British did. Then our country had to provide everything just as the British did. It is a process that is just unsustainable. How many years did we fight and how many men died in Korea, Viet Nam, Afghanistan, and other places? What did it gain us really?

"I suppose I understand our involvement in the great World Wars I and II because we were attacked and needed to respond. If a war is global, then you are necessarily in it. But just because we are a superpower now, does not mean we have a duty to police the world. We can't just keep sending our brave young boys all over the world to fight and die. And that is what they are, 'boys,' just teenage kids in a uniform. It's their blood being spilled, and if it must be so, then undeniably it should be connected to the security and preservation of this nation."

Martha sat mesmerized as she listened to the wisdom of this great general seated before her. She didn't know exactly what to say, so she glanced over at his monitor. On the screen was a picture of Mount Vernon.

"So how did looking at the 'Wars' module lead you to what I see on your screen now?"

"Oh that," George said. "I'm not exactly sure how that happened. While reading about the various wars, I recalled how President Adams put me back in charge of the military at one time because he feared a war with France was coming. I preferred to handle most of those duties from my home where I felt a sense of peace. So, I just started the history module over again and this picture of my beloved Mount

Vernon eventually showed up, about the same time that you arrived.

"Ahh, very good. So, what if I showed you a shortcut that will allow you to find anything much faster?"

"Absolutely, that would help a lot."

"Okay, then, put your hand on the mouse and I'll show you." Washington did as she asked, and Martha, once again, positioned her hand on top of his. She moved closer so her face was next to his, and both were looking at the screen. She moved his hand and stopped the curser in a small black box near the top of the screen.

"See that little magnifying glass? Well, in this box, you can type any word. So, let's type in 'Mount Vernon.'" Once they did, she continued. "Now see this word on the keyboard called 'enter'? Well, just hit that, and we'll see what happens." Washington did as instructed, and a list appeared on the screen.

"See? Mount Vernon is mentioned forty-six times. These numbers show the page where that reference is located. So now move the mouse until the arrow is over one of those numbers, then click it twice very fast." Washington followed instructions again and the screen changed.

"See?" Martha continued. "Now it took us to a list of historical sites." Washington was amazed.

"But where did the list go? Do I have to do the magnifying glass again?"

"No, you don't. See that little arrow pointing to the left in the upper left corner? Just put your cursor over that and click on it. It will take you back to the last thing you were looking at."

Washington handled the task with ease and when the list reappeared his face lit up. "That is amazing! This is wonderful! It will save me a *lot* of time. Thank you so much. How far the world has come with information. I could have used this back during the war."

Martha smiled at his comment. "Okay, now click on the back arrow again." She watched him do it by himself. "Good, so you are now back to where you were when I came in. You can also go forward. Can you figure out how to do that without my help?" Washington studied the screen, found an arrow pointing to the right and repeated the process. When the screen returned to his search list, he actually clapped his hands together once in joy.

"I did it!"

Martha was excited for him and gave him a big squeeze. Washington turned toward her, all smiles, and for an instant, they froze while looking at each other. He quickly returned his focus to the screen and clicked the back arrow again. Martha stood up from her crouched position as he leaned back in his chair.

"By the way," he said, "I have noted they are charging admission for visitors to take a tour of my home. Imagine that!"

"Yes, they do. Mount Vernon is considered a national treasure and also costs a great deal to maintain daily upkeep. So, the entrance fee helps pay for that cost.'

"So, anyone who wants to go visit can do so by paying an admission fee?"

"That's correct."

"Could *I* go see it, if I pay an admission?"

Martha had not seen this question coming and it made her feel a little uncomfortable, but she kept her composure and calmly responded.

"Yes, I think that would be correct."

"Okay, then, I'd like to go."

Martha's mind went into overdrive searching for the right response. *I sure wish Lynn was here. How can I put him off? I'm supposed to be truthful.* Then because she sensed her pause was turning into a noticeably pregnant moment she spoke again.

"Well, perhaps, we can arrange that. I will have to check this out with Dr. Montgomery."

"Great, tell him I have nothing planned for tomorrow."

Martha was taken back. *I think he's serious. Shit! What should I do? I'm in over my head on this.*

"I'm just not sure *when* this can be accomplished," she backpedaled. "You have not been around other people yet, and there is so much more to do with your education." Washington started to say something, but Martha kept talking.

"But I will certainly pursue this for you."

Washington grew silent and turned back toward the monitor to look at the picture of Mount Vernon before swiveling his chair toward Martha again. She took her seat next to him at the computer. They both sat silently for a while before Washington reached over and took Martha's hand in his.

"I have become fond of you, Martha. I *enjoy* spending time with you."

Martha's heart began to race, not knowing where the conversation was going, but acknowledging that she was attracted to this man. Again, she felt him gaining control over her. The scary part of this situation was that she *liked* it, she liked *him – and there seemed to be a familiar feel to their budding relationship.* She even liked his control. She was speechless, yet somehow, enjoyed the comfort of his touch. A tear formed in the corner of her eye. She wiped it away with the back of her free hand, without ever breaking away from Washington's gaze.

"You should know that I am really not a very patient man," he said. "In fact, patience has never been one of my virtues. Once I set my mind to something, I will *always* do whatever is necessary to accomplish my objective. With that in mind, you need to understand that it is my intent to visit Mount Vernon as soon as possible. I believe I can count on you to help me accomplish that goal."

Without realizing it, Martha committed herself, while still engaged in a mutual trance with her student. "Yes, of course, you can count on me."

With that, Washington took his forefinger and raised Martha's chin a bit before cautiously leaning over and giving her a light kiss on the lips. She felt like a schoolgirl being kissed for the first time. She sat motionless without resisting. After the kiss, he drew back only a couple of inches before pausing again to re-engage her eyes.

"There, your promise has been properly sealed with a kiss."

Martha did not want the moment to end and fought back her own desire to re-engage the kiss. But she knew this blissful moment had to end, so she slowly pulled back and said in a playful tone

"Was that a *Presidential* Seal?"

"No," he said. "Presidential Seals are intended for governmental business only. This was a *personal* seal. I hope you are not too disappointed."

"Not at all," she said. *How fortunate for me,* she thought, *that right now Lynn and Palidore are monitoring Frank and not us.*

Chapter 13

Susan was in her costume sitting next to Frank's bed. It had been decided to continue with the 18th-century look until they had the chance to bring Frank up to date. There was a low level of light in the room emanating from two oil lamps. Palidore and Lynn, both in costumes, were at the monitor. The goal today was to introduce them to Frank at the right time. They were simply waiting for Susan's cue to enter the room.

Finally, Frank began to stir, and Susan sat up a little straighter in her chair. Then he turned his head toward Susan and blinked his eyes a couple of times, trying to focus in the low light of the room.

"Good morning, Frank," Susan said softly. She thought a slight smile developed on his face, but he made no response.

"Are you thirsty? I have a little water here." She held up a glass with ice and a straw in it. Still no response, but after a pause, he slowly sat up and reached for the glass. Susan handed it to him. He took the straw out, placed it on the table and took a healthy drink, then handed the glass back to her. Susan accepted the glass and placed it on the table. Frank looked down at his gown which was still missing a few buttons and spoke.

"Do I have any other clothes here?"

"Yes, of course. Let me show you." Susan rose, crossed the room, opened the large wooden wardrobe. She took out an outfit carefully selected for him. She brought the clothes over to the bed and laid them out. It was a simple outfit. A white button-up shirt, gray cotton paints, a black belt, and black socks. She returned to the wardrobe and fetched a pair of black shoes that resembled shoes of his day but had been made to feel more comfortable, complete with memory foam inserts.

"I'll leave, and let you get dressed," she said. But Frank wasn't listening, he was closely examining the shirt. When she returned a few minutes later, she was shocked to see the clothes she had left on the bed were still there. Frank was now dressed in blue jeans, a white t-shirt, and white tennis shoes.

"I guess you didn't like the outfit I selected for you."

"Not that. I just wanted to see what else there was and while looking, I found these. I have never seen clothes like these before. Where did you get them?"

Palidore and Lynn were now glued to the monitor to see how Susan would answer the question.

"Well, you have been asleep, or in a trance, for a *long* time, and during that time, many things have changed, including the clothes people wear. What you're wearing is what a lot of people wear every day now."

Lynn whispered something into Palidore's ear. They both got up and headed back to their offices to change out of their costumes and into their own clothes again.

"So, the men wear clothes like this . . . but the ladies still wear clothes like *you* have on?"

"Well, not really," she said. "I'm wearing a costume that we thought would look familiar to you. It was our goal to have you wake up in a familiar atmosphere." She waved her arm around at the contents of the bedroom.

"We wanted to move slowly before introducing you to the environment of today." Frank didn't answer. He walked over to his bed and began gathering up the outfit that Susan had initially put out for him, returning the clothes to the wardrobe. Then, he took a seat in the wingback chair near his table. Susan took one of the remaining chairs in the room and sat waiting for him to ask a question. There was an uneasy calm. Susan clearly did not know how to move on. She really wanted Frank to say something first.

Frank was trying to comprehend what he had just heard. Next, Frank picked up the bible on the table and fanned through it but read nothing. Finally, while holding the bible, he asked her an important question.

"How *long* was I in . . . 'a trance'. . . as you say?"

Susan was ready for this question because she always knew it would be asked. In a matter-of-fact tone of voice, she answered. "You were placed in 'a trance' in the year 1799, and our time now is the year 2025, so it's been 226 years since you went into your trance."

Frank remained motionless for a long moment, then looked down at his tennis shoes and wiggled his feet. Slowly, he rose and glanced at the bible still in his hand and began aimlessly walking around the room. Susan stood and watched. Eventually, Frank turned back to her and looked directly at her.

"You told me that master Washington brought me here. If that happened so long ago, *how* would you know *that*?"

Time to bring in reinforcements, Susan thought before answering. "There were some notes attached to you. But there are other people who will be able to answer your questions better than I can. In fact, I had planned to introduce you to them today. Would you be willing to meet them now?"

"I think so. Who are they?"

"One is Dr. Palidore Montgomery. He is a distant relative of the Dr. Montgomery you knew, and the other is a woman named Lynn Radford who is helping us with your care. So, if it is all right with you, I will step out and ask them to join us."

Frank returned to his wingback chair and sat, placing the bible back on the table.

"That will be fine."

"OK, I will be right back." She headed to the door to let Paldore and Lynn into the room knowing they had heard her conversation. When they entered. Frank rose from his seat to look at them.

"Hello, Mr. Khamisi," Palidore said. "Please remain seated, and we will join you at the table." They each took one of the chairs around the table and Susan made the formal introductions.

"Why did you called me 'Mr. Khamisi,'" Frank asked Palidore.

"I believe you have adopted that as your surname and using a surname when initially meeting someone is considered appropriate manners even in our time."

"I suppose you are right, but it is unusual for me to hear it. My name is Frank."

"Would you prefer us to use your first name?"

"I think so."

"Good, then you may use our first names also."

When it became clear that everyone was waiting for someone to take charge of the meeting, Palidore said, "It is understandable that you would have many questions for us. We are here to answer them for you to the best of our abilities, but perhaps it might be helpful if we give you a brief overview of what we know about you, how you got here, and what our plan is for helping you to adjust to the way people live now. Does that seem like a reasonable approach?"

"Yes, it does. Please do that."

Palidore asked Lynn to proceed with the narrative. "What I am about to say will seem almost unbelievable to you," Lynn said, "but it is the absolute truth. Before I begin would you like something to eat or drink?"

"No, please just proceed."

"Very well, Frank. We believe that you worked for President and Martha Washington at their home which is called Mount Vernon."

Frank nodded his head in agreement as Lynn continued. "At some point in 1799, you became very ill, and President Washington brought you to Dr. Palidore Montgomery, or his partner, Dr. Marshall Robinson, we are not sure which one, but they worked together. In any event, you were treated with some very special, unique medicine that placed you in what we call 'a suspended trance.' During that time, your body was perfectly preserved for a very long time.

"At the time you were treated, it was not known how long the chemicals would last, but a fairly ingenious test was put in place to reveal when the treatment was about to wear off. A small amount of your blood, also treated with the same special chemicals, was kept in a bottle by your side. When that sample began to return to its natural, liquid state, we knew the same thing was happening to you. At that time, we, as the final caretakers of your body, knew how to revive you because medicine had changed so much during the time you were in the trance.

"So, that's when Dr. Montgomery, or should I say 'Palidore,' since we are using first names, went into action. He and his assistants were able to revive you, but as they did, they were forced to operate on you to repair a hernia near your stomach. That is how you got the scar and why you are no longer in pain. You were also placed in a coma, which is to say, you were put back to sleep for a short period, to give your body time to heal.

"Only recently have you woken up, and now we are here to help you in any way we can. That is a quick overview of what has occurred. Do you have any questions about that?"

"I remember hurting really bad, and President Washington came to help me. He gave me some medicine, and I went to sleep. That is the last thing I remember."

Palidore looked surprised at what Frank just related. "Well, that is very interesting. We thought it was the doctors who gave you the medicine. Perhaps, he gave you something that made you go to sleep, and the doctors treated your body at a later date with the special chemicals. The point is that it worked, and you are now well again."

"You said you had a plan for me."

"Yes, we do," Lynn said. "The truth is that so much has changed, we think it will take some time for you to be brought 'up to date,' so to speak. Therefore, we've developed an education plan designed to allow you to learn about things in the order you want. For example, if you're interested in something like medicine, we can do *that* first, or, if you want to learn about new inventions, we could do *that* first. It's completely flexible and up to you. We will simply guide you through the process.

"Our hope is that once you've completed the course you will be able to go out into society and live a new life without our help. You will decide whether or not to tell anyone about where you came from. However, we do not think you can make a proper choice concerning that until you have been brought up to date with all the modern lifestyles of today. Are you willing to do that?"

"Yes, ma'm."

"Good, that's good." Lynn continued. "Now, Susan will be the person primarily responsible for helping you with this learning. I must say, however, that you appear well-educated. Your language skills seem quite advanced, given your previous occupation."

"I would not call what I did an 'occupation.' But you are correct. As a young girl, my mother worked for years at a large church before she was brought to this country. The priests and nuns at that church took an interest in her and taught her how to read. So, as a boy, my mother taught *me* how to read and properly speak the language. My readings enriched my education, and once I was brought to Mount Vernon, Mr. Washington took a liking to me. He gave me books to read, and we frequently spent time together talking in the cellar. I would tell him about my mother and what I had seen and done, and he would share many things with me.

"At times, he even inquired about what I thought of certain things he was doing, especially about improvements he was making to his home. He also sought my opinion on how the help was doing, and what they might think about certain things. It was not uncommon for us to enjoy a drink of his special whisky together. He was an honorable man. I am going to miss him greatly."

At that point, it was everything Susan could do to hold back the news about Washington. She wanted so much to tell him that his master was alive and in the next room. But she was not authorized to do that, so she decided to get back on the subject at hand.

"Okay then, let me show you something that will help us with your new education." Susan headed toward a set of bookcases and took out a small remote. She pushed the button. And with that, Frank's education began.

Chapter 14

Washington was busy at the computer when Palidore knocked on the door and entered. "Sorry to bother you at this time, but everyone has left for the day, and I thought I might show you around if you're interested."

"Of course," Washington said. "I've been at this for weeks now and any break in my routine would be a welcome reprieve."

"Well, I'm not surprised; follow me. I'll give you a little tour." They headed for the door and Palidore began his narrative. "As you can see, we need to go through this door to enter a small hallway."

They proceeded down the hall and Palidore opened another door which led to a third door that he opened. There, he ushered Washington into the large conference room with oval glass table and an assortment of chairs, all different in color and design. It was early evening and there was sufficient light coming from the outside making it unnecessary to turn any lights on.

"This is our conference room. We have a board of directors consisting of twenty professionals. As you can see, each one has their own 'favorite' chair. I usually sit here." Palidore indicated a large, black executive-type chair with padded seat. "We try to meet at least quarterly to go over company business."

Washington stopped and slowly canvassed the room. Then he walked over to one of the windows and looked out before eventually turning around and crossing to the other side to look out the opposite window. Finally, he placed hands on his hips.

"This looks familiar. I think I 've been here before. In fact, I think I used to *own* this building."

"Yes, you did, until you conveyed ownership to my ancestor whose name I bear. It has remained in our family ever since. Why don't we have a seat over at the table."

They moved to the table where Washington sat in a chair near Palidore's seat. Palidore swiveled his chair a bit and leaned backwards eyeing Washington.

"We're going to have a meeting of the board here next Wednesday. If you feel up to it, I thought it might be appropriate to introduce you to the directors then. Please understand, they only know that you are alive and doing well. However, they are most interested in your progress. I have struggled with how best to satisfy their desire to know more about you. Actually, it was Martha who suggested that presenting you at the next meeting could be the best approach."

To Palidore's surprise, Washington did not immediately jump at the opportunity. Instead, he asked, "Did Martha discuss with you my desire to visit Mount Vernon?" Palidore had not anticipated the question but fielded it in the best way he could.

"Yes, in fact she did. We agreed that it should be a goal once we felt it safe for you to matriculate into public places. So, meeting with the board is our first effort to move toward that goal."

"So, if the meeting goes well, then we can plan the trip?"

My God, he's negotiating! Palidore thought. *Ever the politician.* But now Palidore felt trapped into relenting. "I think that would be the logical next step."

"Then, yes, I would like very much to meet your board." Washington held out his hand to shake on the deal they had just struck. Palidore reluctantly shook his hand.

"Shall we continue with our tour?" Washington said rising from his seat. " I am anxious to see what you have done with my old building."

Palidore had not planned on showing him much more but

decided to comply with his wishes. "Yes, certainly. Let's take the elevator, or 'lift,' as some call it. Have you studied or read about elevators yet?"

"No, not yet."

Palidore pushed a wall button and the elevator door silently slid open. With an outstretched arm, he signaled Washington to enter, then watched as he investigated all sides of the enclosure.

"Well, they're pretty simple. It's just a box, really," Palidore said. "People get in so they can be lifted or lowered with a motor using a set of pulleys." He hit the button for the first floor and watched Washington's face as they rode down. When they arrived on the first floor, the doors opened, and both men stepped out.

"This area is where our guests are greeted," he said indicating the large, curved reception desk. Washington stopped at the decorative water fountain and examined it.

"This is nice. I like it. How does it work? Where does the water come from?"

"Well, actually it's the same water rotating all the time. There is a small motor behind the wall that sucks water up here where it falls out and collects down here. Then it circulates back to the top again and repeats the action."

Washington was silent and hunkered down low to examine the object closer. Then stood up and put hands on his hips while continuing to marvel at the object. Palidore waited patiently before finally asking, "Shall we proceed?"

Washington started moving slowly while keeping his eyes on the waterfall before he replied, "Yes, yes ... that would be good."

What's he planning? Palidore wondered. He walked toward his business office. They entered and proceeded to Palidore's desk where he picked up the antique picture of his ancestor and handed it to Washington

"This is the photo that I previously showed you. It is my most cherished possession."

"Yes, of course, I remember it well," he said and handed it back to Palidore. Then Washington noticed the diploma within a glass case to the right. "Did this diploma belong to the Palidore I knew?"

"Yes, indeed. As you can see, it has a special home in my office. These other diplomas also belonged to my family members, all of whom looked after you throughout the years."

Washington slowly made a 360-degree turn examining all the walls of the room covered with diplomas.

"What an amazing commitment for one family to take on. This is just amazing."

"I feel the same," Palidore said. "Actually, they did not always adorn these walls. They were being held in one of the storage rooms until we needed the space. I found them, and not knowing what to do with them, thought I would display them here."

"A brilliant decision. They truly give this room a special meaning."

Trying to refocus now, Palidore said, "Well, obviously this is where I work and meet clients or employees. My door is always open." He no more got those words out when Martha entered the room.

"Palidore, I saw your light was on and . . . oh! Sorry, I didn't know you had someone with you."

Upon hearing her voice, Washington turned and smiled. Martha gasped.

"Oh, it's *you*."

"Yes. Palidore was just showing me around."

"Why, that's wonderful," she said, controlling her surprise. "I won't bother you then. So sorry for the interruption."

"No, not at all, Martha. You're here now, so what did you want?" Palidore asked.

"Actually, nothing important. I just noticed your light on and decided to pop in and say 'hi.' I left my cell phone in my office and was on my way to retrieve it when I noticed your light. So, please, don't let me interrupt you any longer."

"Well, if you have the time, why don't you join us?" Washington asked. Palidore was surprised by his suggestion. "Actually, we're almost done."

"Oh, but I haven't seen the second floor yet," Washington insisted.

Palidore and Martha shot curious looks at each other, not knowing what to say.

"This is the most fun I have had since waking up," Washington continued. "I would really like to see the rest of the building."

"Well, we can go up there, but most of the second floor will be unavailable to us due to privacy concerns. The remains of many of our clients are stored there, and unless we had permission of a relative or family member, we couldn't allow you to enter."

"Well, I suppose, since Stanley is here, *I* could give permission," Martha said having overcome her initial surprise and wanting to stay with Washington a while longer. Palidore didn't seem pleased with the suggestion, but Washington seized upon the opportunity.

"It's settled then. Besides, I am curious about what you actually do here. I looked up the word 'cryogenics' because it is in your business name, but I can't say I truly understand it, so maybe you can explain it as we go."

"Very well, then, but let's finish this floor first," Palidore said, trying to stall their progress just a little. They proceeded out of his office to the procedure rooms.

"When we receive a client, his or her body is processed here for storage," Palidore explained. "Likewise, if we were to attempt to revive a client it would be done in these rooms."

"Was I worked on in here?"

"Yes, you were."

Washington grew silent and looked a little more carefully at the equipment in the room.

"So, what determines when an attempt is made to revive a person?"

"Let me answer your question in another room." He led them out and took them down the hall to the educational room.

"So, in here, we have medical students assigned one or more of our clients. They study what caused the demise of each client and research what progress has been made in curing the problem. When they find any relevant information, they put it in their client's chart. All charts are reviewed on a regular basis. If, and when, we believe we can cure the ailment, we bring the client to the procedure room where we attempt his or her revival."

"So, once a person is processed, can a revival attempt be made at any time?"

"Yes, but that was not true in your case. When *your* body was treated, it had to be kept in that state until the effect of the chemicals used wore off. At that precise moment, we had to act as quickly as possible. That was because of the old way of preserving was set up. However, now, our clients can be revived whenever we decide."

"How did you know it was my time?"

"A small amount of your blood was, obviously treated and put into a jar which we later transferred to a more secure container. When it started to transform from its gelatin state into a more liquid state, we knew it was time to act." Washington grew silent, as if trying to remember something.

"Yes, yes of course, I remember now. Palidore told me that I had to let some blood and treat it. I gave Major Hudson instructions that it had to be delivered to my Palidore along with my body as soon after my passing. It is obvious he succeeded."

"Do you mean to say, you treated *yourself*?"

"That is correct. Dr. Montgomery gave all his patients the choice of taking the . . .the 'compound mixture,' I think he called it, or another mixture for just the pain. He said it was against his oath to make the decision. Except at the time we agreed, I was not ill, so he showed me *how* to do it for when my time came. Then, he said I would know what to do and could also make the decision. He gave me everything to have when the time came . . . but I . . . wait a minute . . . wait a minute. I used them up . . . I used them on Frank! Frank was sick, and I used my mixture on Frank! I had Major Hudson deliver him to Dr. Montgomery. Now I remember. I can't believe I haven't remembered this before now. But where is Frank? Do you have him? Is he okay? Have you revived him? He was treated *before* me, so he *must* have been revived before me. What has happened to Frank?"

Martha stepped in front of Washington who had started pacing around the room. She placed her hands on both his arms to get his attention.

"Please, calm down. Give us a chance to answer your questions. Now, just wait for a moment, and take a deep breath, please." He began to calm down.

"Okay, that's good. Now let's go back into the office for a minute." She took his hand and they re-entered Palidore's office where all three took their seats around the small conference table. While sitting, Martha glanced Palidore, hoping to receive a signal. Who should answer his questions? Seeing no sign, she began slowly talking while hoping Palidore would jump in. But he seemed content to let Martha proceed.

"We do have Frank, and yes, we have successfully revived him."

"That's wonderful! When can I see him?" Washington exclaimed, slamming his hand down hard on the desk causing the container of pencils to tip over. "Let's go now!" He started to rise, but Martha quickly put her hand on his arm.

"Wait, there's more. We can't see him right now. Please let me explain." Washington eased back down in his seat with a concerned look on his face.

"You are correct, it was necessary to attempt to revive Frank before you, but during that process, it was also necessary for him to have an operation to help cure his original ailment. Remember his stomach pain? Well, after the operation, he was placed in a coma.

That's a deep sleep one cannot come out of without medical help. This allowed time for his body to heal.

"He is now out of that coma and awake, but his progress is behind yours. However, he is doing very well. I do not personally work with him. A woman by the name of Susan Trott and another called Lynn Radford are working with him. So, before you can see him, two things must occur. First, you must be ready to see him, and secondly, he must be ready to see you.

"I can see you are ready to see him, but in our opinion, Frank is not quite ready to see *you*. It may be too much for him to understand everything right now. We need a little more time to prepare him. So, for *his* well-being can you agree to be patient a little longer?"

Washington was all smiles. He got up beaming from ear to ear and walking around in a euphoric stupor. "Of course, I'll wait. For Frank, I'll wait . . . after all, I've waited this long, haven't I?" They all laughed as Washington continued. "But this is a cause for *celebration*! I believe we should have a drink!"

Palidore, was all smiles himself now, and went to the credenza behind his desk, slid the door open, and pulled out his decanter of Edradour Scotch whisky along with three glasses. He poured two, but when he started to pour the third, Martha stopped him.

"Please Palidore, not that stuff again. Any chance you have some wine?" Palidore smiled and put her glass down. He slid open an adjoining door of the credenza revealing a small refrigerator containing beer and several single-serving bottles of wine. He picked up a Chardonnay, twisted off the screw top, and poured it into a low-profile wine glass. Then, distributing the drinks, he held his glass in the air.

"Here's to Frank!"

"To Frank!" they agreed.

Chapter 15

The following week was devoted to preparing Washington for the upcoming board meeting. Now, Palidore was sitting with him at a table in the small conference room. He had just handed Washington a background fact sheet on each board member.

In the right-hand corner of each sheet was a photo of the member followed by a list of pertinent facts. Palidore spent the next hour going over all details of each member, adding additional information when it occurred to him. Washington remained silent throughout the process. When finished, Palidore asked if he had any questions.

"I have one request, and one question."

"Okay, what is your request?"

"Can you separate out the ones who were present when I was revived?"

Palidore silently chastised himself for not pointing them out as he had gone through the papers. He quickly separated those who were present during Washington's revival, then handed the smaller stack to Washington.

"And your question?"

"What will they be wearing to the meeting? In their pictures, they each have on a white coat with their name on it. Is that how they will be attired?" Palidore had to think back to previous meetings to produce an answer.

"No, they won't be wearing lab coats to the meeting. They

know that there will be a guest but have not been told it will be you. So, they will likely dress as they normally do."

"And how do they 'normally' dress when they attend these meetings?"

"It varies from member to member, but I would say, for the most part, it will be casual with the ladies wearing pantsuits, or slacks and a blouse or sweater, certainly nothing formal. The men will be wearing slacks and an open collar shirt much like what I am wearing now."

"You mean like you *always* have on?"

Palidore thought about the comment as he glanced down at his attire before responding with a sheepish smile.

"Well . . . I guess that would be right, but a couple of them are what we term 'old school' when it comes to their dress. They have worn a shirt, tie, and sport coat for their entire careers and can't seem to bring themselves to wear anything else. You'll see that, too."

***

On the third consecutive day of his preparation, Washington was growing tired of it. Lynn had told him that before his introduction, the members would be told not to question him. However, as a precaution, she had also instructed him on how best to avoid answering any unwelcomed questions. She assured him that she would jump in, if necessary. She also emphasized that Frank was not to be mentioned.

"I assure you, I will not mention him," Washington promised.

Even though he learned a lot from Lynn, he spent most of the time with Martha. Not because she had more to offer, but simply because he preferred her company. There was something uniquely familiar about her, but he couldn't quite put his finger on it. Preparing for the meeting gave him one more excuse to be near her, and he wanted to spend as much time as he could being close to her. It was just a feeling, but he liked being with her.

TRANSFORMING GEORGE WASHINGTON

For the most part, they didn't even discuss the upcoming meeting, but simply talked on a range of subjects, just getting to know each other. They found many common interests in food, music, and literature. They also laughed together and joked a lot. Even their mutual attraction for each other was discussed. They agreed that if it became too obvious, it could put Martha in an awkward situation regarding her job.

The only suggestion she made regarding the upcoming meeting was for him to relax and be his normal self-assured self. As for Washington, he wasn't concerned at all about the meeting. He felt that Palidore and Lynn were making much to do over nothing. Besides, he had developed his own plans for the meeting and was looking forward to it.

Tomorrow would be the beginning of a new phase of the second half of his life, and he was intent on taking charge of the meeting and making the most of it.

***

The following day, an hour before the meeting, Martha came into Washington's room carrying a suit bag over her shoulder. Washington looked up from his computer station with a smile.

"Is that it?"

"Yes, of course. But what I don't understand is how you knew you wanted these clothes even before you knew you would be attending the meeting."

"I didn't. Like the other clothes you helped me procure, I just wanted them; but then, when I found out about the meeting, I knew this outfit would be perfect to wear, if it arrived in time. And now it has."

"Well, you owe a debt of gratitude to Oliver. He's never altered clothes this fast for anyone, not even Stanley."

Washington removed the clothing from the bag and held them

up for a better look. Pausing, he lowered the clothes over his arm and took a second look at Martha. She was wearing a navy blue pantsuit with a short-waisted coat meant to be left open in front to reveal her white blouse. The simple collar helped feature her ruby red solitaire that adorned her necklace.

"I can't believe it took me so long to notice, but you look stunning," Washington said. "Our outfits will actually match, don't you think?"

"Well, I hadn't thought about it when I picked out my clothes, but I suppose the colors will be similar," she said. "I'll know better after you've dressed."

Washington held up his outfit, once again, and proceeded into the bathroom to change. When he re-emerged moments later, Martha took a long look.

Wow, what a handsome man. How strong, how intelligent he looks, she allowed herself one more thought directed at him in her mind: *I like everything about you, Mr. President. I've grown to admire your white hair which now seems just long enough to give substance to your clean-shaven face. And the scent of your Aramis Cologne is incredible! So, glad you like it. It's not every man I buy cologne for. I still can't believe you are who you are. . . but maybe that's the magic ingredient that has drawn me to you. 'What would I do with you?' Ha! 'What wouldn't I do with you.'*

"Well, what do you think?" Washington asked snapping Martha out of her self-induced trance.

"Oh, I think you couldn't look any better. But I'm not sure about that tie; it may be a little formal for this event.

"That's the point of it," he said. "I don't *want* to dress like the others. I intend to take charge of this event and will start by my standing out a bit."

"Well, I'm not certain what 'taking charge of this event' actually means, but I'm sure you'll do it."

"Right. Now, how will we know when we're supposed to

enter the conference room?"

"When everyone is present and seated, Palidore will send me a signal which I will receive on my watch. He will then open the meeting, and immediately go off the record. Normally, a secretary would be present and would leave the meeting at that point to enter a room where she wouldn't see or hear anything happening in the conference room. But, today, since almost the entire meeting is slated to be off the record, she was told it wouldn't even be necessary for her to attend. So, when Palidore is ready for us, he will send me a second signal. That's when I'm supposed to bring you into the room.

"Let me know when you get the first signal."

"I will. It should be any moment now. Oh, and there it is." she said as she felt the message arrive with a small vibration. "So, in just a few minutes . . . Hey! where are you going? I haven't received the second notice yet." Martha hurried to catch up with him.

"Precisely," Washington said as he strode across the room. "Follow me."

He pushed through the second set of doors leading directly into the conference room. Palidore had just called the meeting to order when Washington entered the room impeccably dressed in white slacks and shirt, complemented by a navy-blue sport coat, and red tie with an American flag embroidered on the bottom of it. Martha was trailing him by three steps, a concerned look on her face.

As he entered, one director after another noticed him, and the room fell silent. Palidore was caught totally by surprise and stopped talking in mid-sentence. Martha was trying to use body language to say 'it's not my fault' as Washington reached the glass podium at the head of the table where Palidore was standing.

"Dr. Montgomery, Miss Radford, so good to see you," he intoned. "And these lovely people must be the members of the Board of Directors. Why don't you introduce me?"

Not knowing what else to do, Paidore followed orders.

"Ladies and Gentlemen, it is my pleasure to introduce

President George Washington." Except for a couple of people catching their breath, the silence continued until Dr. Cotton began to clap.

Then one by one, all the directors rose until everyone was standing and vigorously applauding. The adulation continued until Washington raised his hands in an effort to contain it all. Once he had everyone's attention, he said in an almost comical tone: "Thank you ... I cannot tell you how good it is to be here." He paused, waiting for the expected chuckles. But there were none. Everyone was still in a state of speechless awe. So, he continued.

"I want to thank Dr. Montgomery, Lynn Radford, and Martha Vaughan who have dedicated hundreds of hours working with me and helping to reacquaint me with the modern-day version of our wonderful country. They have been wonderful to work with both professionally, and personally.

"I also want to thank Dr. Cotton and the Alpha team. Obviously, I would not be here now speaking to you if they had not performed their duties so well. Lastly, I want to thank each of *you*. You have dedicated your lives to helping others and offering hope to even those whose lives are about to end. It is truly an honor to finally meet you.

"I find it interesting to note that Palidore's ancestor offered the very first available form of cryogenics which has now been proven successful, so there should be great hope that what you are doing today will be even more successful."

Palidore was sitting motionless. *Where is all this coming from? We never discussed him saying anything, let alone delivering a speech!*

Lynn and Martha were exchanging questioning looks while Washington was speaking.

"So, this is what you meant when you said you were going to take over the meeting," Martha said under her breath. "Aren't you full of surprises?"

TRANSFORMING GEORGE WASHINGTON

"For the past several days," Washington said, "Palidore, Lynn, Martha, and I have been preparing for this meeting. Originally, it was thought this might be a mere meet-and-greet opportunity. Much consideration was given to exactly what should or should not be said; their primary concern was for my well-being. However, after some reflection, I've made an independent decision to expand the scope of the meeting. So, I suppose, I owe them an apology for not sticking strictly to their plan.

"Now, I know that you have all come from work elsewhere, and Palidore, being the considerate person he is, has provided refreshments for you on the side tables over there, so I think I would feel more comfortable if we all just mingle while we munch, and get to know each other a little better. That way, I can have an opportunity to spend a little time with each of you, personally." Washington turned toward Palidore. "Is that all right with you?"

Bewildered, Palidore replied, "Sure, whatever you like."

"It is settled then, please follow me."

With that, Washington headed for the tables which were loaded with a variety of hot hor oeuvres, appetizers, cheeses, veggies, wine, spirits, and more. Everyone got up and made their way to the side tables to join the president. As they crowded around the food, Palidore took the opportunity to single out Martha.

"Did you know he was going to do this?"

"Not at all. But while we were waiting, he said he was 'going to take charge.' I asked what he meant, but he just started toward the door. I am so sorry, but he does seem to be at ease and comfortable."

"And in charge! Look at him over there, he acts like he is everyone's old pal."

"You know, he has memorized each of the info sheets you gave him, and he can associate the faces with their fact sheets It's all very impressive."

"Well, it is impressive, I have to admit," Palidore said.

"You know, he really wants to visit Mount Vernon, and he's mentioned to me that you promised him that he could go, if this meeting went well. So maybe he took that as a challenge."

"Well, he certainly boxed me in on that one," Palidore said. "Quite cleaver, I'd say."

"Perhaps, we need to get closer to him, and see how he's doing," Martha suggested.

"Yes, you're right. Let's see if we can work our way up front."

The two of them drew closer and were relieved to see that Lynn was by his side while he conversed with a couple of the directors. As Palidore and Martha approached, Washington broke his gaze away from his current conversation to acknowledge them.
"Palidore and Martha . . . there you are! I have been getting to know Dr. Miles, I mean 'Sara,' since we are using first names here. Sara was telling me that her son is one of the guides now at Mount Vernon. Quite a coincidence, since we will be visiting there soon, don't you think?" Washington refocused his attention on Dr. Miles. "Maybe we can set it up so . . . 'Jason,' I think you said his name was, can be our guide."

Lynn jumped in. "Well, that *would* be nice but, of course, he would be advised only that a few of your colleagues want to take a tour, so as not to disclose Mr. Washington's true identity. You remember everyone signing the non-disclosure agreement, don't you?" She looked pointedly for agreement from Dr. Miles.

"Oh, yes, certainly," Sara Miles said. "I would not want to violate my confidential agreement. In fact, I could go along, in order to make the request seem more natural."

"That would be perfect! So, all Palidore needs to do is contact you with a couple of possible dates, and you can set it up?" Washington said with enthusiasm.

"I'd be honored," she smiled.

"There's Dr. Beyer, I mean 'Ed'. Please excuse me, I promised him that I would get to him." Washington broke away to greet Ed

TRANSFORMING GEORGE WASHINGTON

Beyer with Lynn trailing behind him.

Martha looked over at Palidore. "Well, he certainly is enjoying this, but somehow you need to regain control of your meeting before something slips between the
cracks."

"I think you are right, but how?"

"Tell them you have one more item of business to discuss before you can adjourn and give them a time."

With that Palidore cleared his throat and announced in a loud voice.

"Ladies and Gentlemen . . . may I have your attention please?" He paused and repeated his request, but no one heard him. Martha held up one finger as if to say, 'wait one minute.' She went to a nearby electrical switch and blinked the lights on and off several times. Everyone stopped talking and Martha pointed to Palidore who once again said loudly: "We do have an item of business before we leave today, so I am going
to give you thirty more minutes to eat and talk, but when the lights blink again, please take you seats at the conference table. Okay?!"

There was a chorus of assorted "okays," "got it," and "yes, sirs," before everyone went back to what they were doing.

"Thank you, Martha, that was helpful but what item of business shall we talk about when we reassemble?"

"Just thank the president for joining us, remind everyone about the non-disclosures, and reinforce that George has not yet made his decision about whether or not he will make his true identity known publicly."

"Excellent! Really, I am so glad we added you to this team."

"That goes for us both," she smiled.

Chapter 16

The lights blinked and the directors started moving toward their seats at the conference table. Lynn still shadowing

"We need to move toward the table," Washington said.

"Should I go too?" Martha asked.

"Yes indeed, please stay with me."

The directors assembled around the table all standing behind their respective seats, but no one sitting, as all eyes were on the former president. He followed Lynn toward the front of the table. Martha followed him but moved close to the wall. A seat originally placed for him between Lynn and Palidore was still waiting for him. Lynn pointed him to it and he moved to stand behind it as the others were doing.

Palidore, clearly in charge again, whispered to Washington: "This won't take long. Please, just do as the others do."

"Certainly," he whispered in response.

"Ladies and gentlemen, please take your seats," Palidore said. Everyone waited for the president to sit before taking their own. When everyone was finally seated, Palidore continued. "I trust this has been as remarkable an experience for you as it has been for me. I want to thank each of you for your dedication to this enterprise, and your time here today.

You may recall our many discussions building up to today's reality. Early on, it was far from certain that this miracle of revival would ever occur. Now, here we are, and as you can see, we have our first president back with us today."

There was instant applause, and everyone stood again, clapping and cheering. Palidore motioned with his arm for Washington to stand and take a bow. Slowly, George stood, showing a bit of emotion in his eyes for the first time.

"Okay, thank you, everyone, please come to order and be seated again. Thank you. Now, to our items of business: "As you know, months ago, we decided that should this day ever come, we would want any revived individual to make his *own* choice concerning the disclosure of his re-emergence. We are at that point now. Each of you has signed a non-disclosure agreement that will prohibit you from talking about anything you have experienced here today. However, I am hopeful that even without such an agreement you would want to do the right thing, and let our guest be the master of his own fate.

"However, I must take this opportunity to remind you once again, as it will truly be hard to resist the urge to share today's experience, that resist, you *must*! What you have experienced here today for the first time, we have been witnessing on a daily basis, for a while now. So, I know *exactly* what you are going through in terms of wanting to announce this extraordinary happening to others. I know just how difficult remaining silent will be. "Does anyone have questions at this point? Any at all?" Palidore surveyed the room and noticed everyone shaking their heads.

"Good. Now I want to also thank President Washington, who we will address simply as 'George' from now on, for his participation here today. Other than Lynn, Martha, and I, *you* are the only people he has met since his revival, and certainly, *this* is the only group meeting he has attended.

"Before today, he has spent countless hours preparing for this meeting, and I think you will all agree, he has done exceptionally well."

Again, everyone was on their feet clapping and cheering. Using both hands now, Palidore motioned for all to sit again, and as the applause faded, he continued. "I was impressed, as I am sure you were, at the degree of preparation and ease with which he has met and greeted you. Truly, an amazing moment.!

"Now I must admit, this meeting almost did not occur. As we were planning for this meeting, the initial intention was to present only a *report,* but our communication director, Martha, suggested that we proceed with a *live* introduction. And so, we did. Now that it is nearly over, I believe she was right." There was applause for Martha as she and George exchanged glances and smiles.

"So, before adjourning, I will ask George if he has anything to say." Without verbally answering, George rose and moved to the glass podium.

"Thank you, Palidore, for giving me this opportunity. First, let me say how much I have enjoyed meeting each of you during our social. It has been truly enjoyable, with one small exception, which Palidore has briefly touched upon. I absolutely would prefer everyone to address me simply as 'George' and not use my former title. It appears that each of you uses just a first name. Well, I would like to do the same. After all, if my true identity is to be kept secret, then we *must* drop the titles.

"I am anxious to expand my social interactions and see more of this country. In fact, when Palidore and I last met, we discussed my desire to visit Mount Vernon. I am sure you can guess why I might like to do that. He suggested we use this meeting as a test to see how well I might do to determine if a visit could be arranged. Well, let's hear it . . . did I pass the test?" Everyone jumped up and cheered.

Washington looked at Palidore and Martha, now seated to his right. He smiled and nodded a 'how about it?' motion to Palidore who gave him a thumb's up sign.

George simply smiled.

Chapter 17

It was seven p.m. when Susan burst into Palidore's office and blurted out "He's gone! Just vanished!"

"Wait a minute," Palidore answered in surprise. "Just calm down, and tell me again, who's missing?"

"Frank . . . Frank is gone!" she said, trying to regain her composure and catch her breath. "I thought he was sleeping when I checked my monitor, so I went to the restroom. But when I came back and looked again, he wasn't in view. I waited, thinking maybe he'd gone to the bathroom, too. But after a while, I became concerned and went into his room to check and he wasn't there!" Her eyes were streaming tears now and she strained to continue. "I looked everywhere, even under the bed. But he's just gone!"

"Did you activate his tracking device?"

"No, you're the only one who can do that! Why do you think I'm here?" she said.

"Oh . . . right."

Palidore went to his desk, bent down, opened the safe, and took out a small box. Opening it, he removed a small device, turned it on, and entered a code. It came to life with a small red dot registering on the lit screen.

"Well, he's clearly still in the building, but unfortunately, I can't be more exact. So, we better start looking. Let's go back to his room; maybe he's returned by now." They headed out the door, bypassed the elevator, and took the stairs, two steps at a time. Bursting into Frank's room, but there was still no sign of him. "Let's think . . . where would he want to go? Did he mention anything he wanted to see?"

"No, he seemed so infatuated with the computer and learning modules. That's all he wanted to do."

"We'd better check on George." They quickly reached his room, knocked, and opened the door.

"What the hell? He's gone, too!" Palidore cried out.

"Did you activate his tracking device?"

"No, just Frank's"

They quickly headed out and down the stairs again, back to Palidore's office where he went through the same process to retrieve and activate Washington's tracking device. They waited for the screen to light up. This time the screen showed a green dot.

"Well, at least we know they're both still in the building. What are the chances they both took off at the same time? Think they found each other and are together?" Palidore asked.

"That seems to make sense," Susan said. "Where should we start looking?"

"You watch the dots while I get Lynn and Martha over here."

Susan was focused on trying to fit both devices in one hand simultaneously, and only heard Palidore's side of the conversation.

". . . well, just get here ASAP!"

She'd never heard such stress in his voice before. Minutes later, both women came in together.

"What do you know?" Lynn asked.

"Show them," Palidore said. Susan held her hand out displaying the devices. Both the red and green dots glowed visibly on the screen. No movement was seen.

"What are these?" Martha asked.

"They're tracking devices for clients Four and Five. Four is the red dot and Five is the green dot."

"Okay, so I still don't understand."

"These tracking devices were implanted in each man's lower leg. But we're not supposed to activate them unless the men are missing."

"Well, from what I see, they don't look to be missing," Martha said.

"Yes, well, now we know they're in the building, we just don't know exactly where. This hasn't happened before, as you can imagine," Palidore interrupted, clearly frustrated. "We've already checked their rooms and neither one is there. So, right now we need to find them. Any ideas or suggestions?"

"You gave George the tour so it seems logical he might be showing Frank something that you showed him," Martha suggested.

"Let's start by ruling out the remainder of this floor," Lynn said.

They headed out of the office and checked each of the procedure rooms. Then they spread to the group study areas and came together again in the reception area.

"We've already checked out most of the first and third floors," Lynn said. "So, I guess we need to go to the second." No one answered as they all headed up the stairs. When they reached the second floor they stopped and looked around.

"Most of this floor is used to house our client cylinders. Beyond that, there is the room with the remaining ancient clients, and the chapel," Palidore said. "The Cylinder room remains locked unless we have a relative visiting, so let's check the room housing the ancient ones." Everyone followed Palidore down the hallway.

Gathering at the door, Lynn quietly opened it and flipped on the light. It was empty. Without discussion, they closed it again and headed toward the chapel. Arriving at the door, Lynn slowly turned the handle and cracked the door open just enough to peek her head in. Immediately, she exhaled, dropped her head, took a step back, and quietly closed the door again.

"They're both in there . . . together, on their knees, at the altar," she said. "They appear to be praying." Everyone visibly relaxed.

"Well, we can't interrupt them while they are praying," Martha said. "It's a holy moment for them . . . finding each other."

"Okay, what should we do, now?" Lynn asked.

"Wait," Palidore said. "Just wait."

"I think we should leave them alone and just go back downstairs," Martha said. "Let them make the next move. They'll have to go back to their rooms eventually. We can't undo their meeting anyway, and they're not in any danger, so let's give them their space.
"Eventually, they'll come to us, and when they do, we shouldn't scold them. They're not children. We should rejoice in their reunion. Sorry to be so blunt, but that's what I think."

"Martha's right," Lynn said "Leave them alone. No one else is in the building right now. When the time is right, we can just warn them about wandering off during hours when the building is occupied."

Palidore thought for a moment. "You're both right. Let's go down to the office and see what happens. Either they'll go back to their rooms or come looking for us."

Everyone turned away from the chapel door and headed back down to Palidore's office on the first floor. As they all filed in, Susan was the last to enter and closed the door. Each one took a seat at the small conference table.

***

George had wanted a more solemn place to pray and decided to find the chapel. When he opened the door, a ray of sunlight streaming through the stained glass window illuminating an image of Jesus praying at Gethsemane greeted him. It was a beautiful site and George made his way to the alter where he knelt on a low prayer bar to give thanks. While deep in thought, he felt another presence enter the room and kneel at the other end of the railing.

When George finished his prayers, he casually looked over to the person kneeling nearby. He caught his breath as he recognized Frank kneeling there. Tears welled in his eyes as he looked at the familiar black hands now folded in prayer. He looked at the curve of the man's head which he had seen so often in the past at Mount Vernon. Thoughts and feelings too numerous to count coursed through him as he realized he was no longer alone on this journey. Finally, Frank looked up and over at him standing nearby.

"Master!" he called out and rose to embrace him.

"Frank," George said hugging him back tightly. They stood for a moment in silent benediction before regaining their composure. "We need to thank God for this moment," George said and they kneeled again to pray, this time in thanksgiving. Finally, George stood and Frank followed his lead.

"I suppose we need to find Palidore," George said. "I imagine he'll be looking for us. I know where his office is; let's go find him."

***

"I just wish I could have seen it . . . their reunion," Palidore asked. "It must have been incredible for both of them. Can you just imagine?" He shook his head. "Anyone need a drink?"

"It's a little early but a glass of wine would be nice," Martha said with a smile.

"Make that two," Lynn added.

"Uh, three, please" Susan held up one finger.

Palidore pulled out three small single-serving bottles of chardonnay from his small refrigerator, fixed their glasses, and poured himself a small scotch. After delivering the drinks, he sat and took a sip of his scotch.

"Okay, give me your thoughts: How are we going to handle this when we see them next?" He saw a variety of questioning expressions around the small conference room, but no one spoke. Before they had a chance to say anything, there was a knock at the door.

Palidore jumped up and for the first time noticed the door was closed which he usually left open. Immediately, he headed over with his drink still in hand and opened it. George and Frank were standing there together. George noticed the drink and smiled.

"Well, that looks good, mind if we join you?"

"Of course, please come in! I think you know everyone," Palidore said, trying to keep his surprise under control.

Frank, however, seemed reticent. "I have not actually met everyone. I know only you, Susan, and Lynn."

"Well, that leaves only Martha," Palidore gestured toward her with his drink hand as she stood and walked forward with her hand outstretched.

"Well, Frank, it is my pleasure to formally meet you. I am Martha Vaughan, the communications director for the company."

Frank shyly shook her hand. Then Lynn broke the awkwardness. "Palidore, I believe you were going to get these gentlemen some drinks."

"Oh yes, of course! Come on over here and join us at the table. There are a couple of side chairs there, let me get you a drink while you're getting situated." The two men each pulled a chair and crowded around the small table.

"I have almost anything you might like, what is your pleasure?"

"A touch of your scotch would be good," George said.

Palidore then gave a questioning look to Frank. "If you have red wine, I would prefer that."

"Actually, I do. Merlot, if that is sufficient?"

"That would be nice, thank you."

Palidore delivered the drinks and joined everyone at the table.

"I see the two of you have had an opportunity to get

reacquainted. We were in the process of planning a reunion for you, but it seems you've beaten us to the punch. I trust you were both pleased to see each other? Can you share with us how that happened?"

"Actually, it was by accident," George said. "When you gave me the brief tour, we never finished the second floor, so I decided to do it on my own. I found the chapel and went in. I thought I had much to thank God for and moved to the altar to pray. While I was praying, Frank joined me at the altar. I thought I was seeing a vision!" All eyes now turned to Frank.

"Well, I became tired of seeing just my room and doing the education modules," Frank said, "so I decided to venture out a bit. I could not see how it would hurt. There was not much on the top floor, so I went down to the second floor where I found the chapel. As I entered, I noticed a man praying at the altar and decided to join him.

"When I finished with my prayers, I saw him standing beside me and realized it was my master, I mean . . . George . . . But he looked so much younger that I almost didn't recognize him.

"As I've told Frank, he no longer needs to address me as 'master,'" George said, "but I know old habits die hard. Instinctively, we knelt back down at the altar to give thanks for this miracle."

"When we finished, Master . . . I mean, *George,* said 'We need to find Palidore.' So, we came to find you here."

"This calls for a toast," Palidore said. Everyone raised their glasses. "Here's to George and Frank and their long-sought-after reunion."

All glasses touched, and everyone took sips of their drinks in an indescribable moment of happiness. While everyone was talking and enjoying drinks, Palidore got up and poured some peanuts into a couple of bowls, placing them on the table. As he sat down, again, he heard George making plans.

"So, I think Frank should be able to join me on our trip to Mount Vernon. What do you think?" Everyone went silent except for Frank.

"Oh, that would be wonderful. I cannot wait to see it. When are we going?"

"A firm date has not been set, but when I was talking to Dr. Miles, I mean Sara, she indicated that her son was one of the tour guides. I think we should find out when he will be available and coordinate to have him as our guide. I believe Sara said she would like to join us. In fact, I thought maybe all of us should go. At least, then, we'll know several people on the tour. We could make a day of it.'

"Well, that sounds like a plan," Susan jumped into the conversation. "Why don't I get in touch with Sara and set it up?"

"All of that sounds fine," Palidore said looking at George. "But remember you are further along in your education than Frank is. And he has not had the advantage of outside social interaction as much. I'm not so sure he is quite as well-positioned to be a participant as you are."

"Nonsense," George said. "He'll do as well as he is doing here, besides, *I* will be with him. We both know our way around Mount Vernon better than any of you. After all, I *built* the place."

Frank looked over at his teacher, Susan, with an almost pleading look. "I am ready. And I *want* to go." All eyes went to Palidore.

"I expect we'll need to be as flexible as possible," he said. "This won't likely be the first time we're going off-script," he paused. "All right, let's do it. Martha, please get with Lynn and Susan to coordinate everything. We'll take the company car. It's an
SUV and big enough to accommodate our group."

Washington slapped Frank on the back and the two of them clinked their glasses together in a victory toast. Their faces were close together and everyone could see the love and friendship between them. Martha brushed away a tear that escaped as she watched the two men enjoying this incredible moment in their lives, together.

Chapter 18

For the next couple of weeks, George and Frank became inseparable. They even had Lynn move their computers side-by-side to work on their education modules at the same time. They chose subjects together and often stopped to discuss them, even question each other. The only difference was that George gravitated to anything related to history, and Frank to technology.

One morning, while beginning one of their joint sessions, Martha came in and asked them to join her, Palidore, Susan, and Lynn in the conference room. Once assembled, Lynn made an unexpected announcement.

"I have a surprise for you. We've decided to take a trip today. Sort of a test run. As you know, we're scheduled to visit Mount Vernon next week. That was supposed to be your *first* venture outside this building.

"However, in anticipation of that trip, we've decided it would be a good idea to go out today on a short trip somewhere." She watched George and Frank exchange joyous expressions. "We feel, perhaps, we'll drive around and let you see things from inside a vehicle today, so everything won't seem totally new to you next week. After all, the world is entirely different from when you were here last."

"That's a wonderful idea," George said enthusiastically, "When do we leave?"

"Very, shortly, but before we depart, you should know that, while we do not anticipate any interaction with people outside of the six of us, we have to be prepared on the off-chance of an unexpected encounter.

"Please remember your situation is special. For now, it needs to remain that way." Lynn handed George and Frank an envelope each. "Go ahead, open your envelopes. Inside, you will find a wallet that contains some paper money, a credit card and a driver's license. The license is not genuine, but looks so good, either one would pass any test. "Hopefully, you will not need to present it to anyone, but today, a driver's license is used as a valid form of identification. So, we are not actually using it to permit you to drive, but just as a form of identification.

"Please note the licenses are from West Virginia. As we have previously told you, we can give you a new identity, so we went ahead and created these new identities for you. Should you later desire to disclose your *true* identities, we will simply discard these, and issue you other ones. The VISA credit cards are valid and can be used as intended. I think you each have covered the monetary education module, so you know that credit cards are used these days to make purchases. Again, we don't anticipate an opportunity to use them. And in the off chance you should be asked for a form of identification, just present your driver's license. You will notice that we have used your actual names."

"So, anyone looking at this will know my true identity?"

"No, not really. Your name is actually a pretty common one now, George. Almost every family with the last name of 'Washington' has at least one relative with the first name of 'George.' So nationwide, there are probably hundreds of people with that name," Lynn said. "Furthermore, no one would ever suspect you are the *original* 'George Washington.' That would only happen if we held a joint news conference and explained how it could possibly have occurred.

"Last of all, we've put one of our business cards in your wallets. If we were to get separated for any reason, you could present it to a taxi or UBER driver and ask to be taken to the MCS building. Again, we do not anticipate any of this ever happening, but you never know, we just like to be prepared. Any questions?"

There was no immediate response as the men busily examined the contents of their new wallets. George took out the paper money and closely examined a one-dollar bill. "I am honored at how many objects the people have named after me," George said. *Still, Gilbert Stuart did me no favors with this portrait,* he thought, looking at his visage on the front. *I didn't like it at the time he did it and certainly don't like it on the money of today. It doesn't really look like me, at least, not anymore.*

Finally, Frank asked a question: "What is our destination, and how long will we be out?"

"Our destination is just to the driveway of Mount Vernon since that's where we'll be going next week. But we're not going to actually *stop* this time. We'll drive close to it and turn around before reaching the public entrance. And since Mount Vernon is quite close, we've decided not to take the fastest way, but another one so you can enjoy a more scenic tour.

"At first, we'll make a couple of small street turns until we reach 14th Street. Then, remain on that street through most of the capital area. You'll get a peak at the Washington Monument and Jefferson Memorial which you've studied. You will also be near Pennsylvania Avenue where the White House is located. We'll then take an expressway to cross over the Potomac River into Alexandria, Virginia. From there, we'll stay on the I-395 expressway, or superhighway, down to The George Washington Memorial Parkway. We'll be on the Parkway about nine miles which will bring us close to Mount Vernon. And we may also take a different route back here.

"How long will all this take?" George asked.

"At this time of day, the normal driving time will be about forty minutes each way, so-o-o-o, I would say we'll be gone about an hour and a half to two hours."

Washington was deep in thought. *A trip of that distance would easily take a day and a half back in my time. Traveling at such speed was unthinkable back then. How different my world would have been with even a small number of these conveniences.* "Will we stop anywhere either going or coming back?" he asked.

"Hopefully not. But I'm glad you asked that question because I need to let you know what to do in the event a stop should become necessary. The most likely reason would be to use a restroom or get a drink. Again, hopefully, that will not be necessary, but in such an event, we should avoid talking to people outside of our group. Stay together at all times; tend to our own business and return to the vehicle as soon as possible. In any event, we believe this will be a delightful adventure and will give us an opportunity to see how everyone does before the real trip," Palidore said. "So, if there are no more questions, why don't we all take a moment to use the restrooms now and meet back here in say . . . fifteen minutes."

Frank and George left the room together talking nonstop as they headed for their rooms. Fifteen minutes later, everyone met again and followed Palidore out the back door where a white Buick Enclave was parked.

"I thought Lynn and I would sit upfront; you and Frank can take the middle seats since Martha and Susan have volunteered to sit in the back third row," Palidore said, giving out seat assignments, George walked around the vehicle, checking it out.

"If Lynn doesn't mind," George said to Palidore, "I'd prefer to sit in the front seat next to you. I will be able to see better from up here."

"Oh, I don't mind at all," Lynn offered. "I'll just jump in next to Frank."   Palidore couldn't help but think: *George is always wanting to change things to suit his desires. I guess he did not consider that I actually had a reason for the seating arrangements such as the middle seats being safer than the front seats. Now, I'll have to answer all his questions while driving instead of Lynn doing it . . . and that is not what I wanted. Oh, well.*

They helped everyone fasten their seat belts as Frank looked around but said nothing. George was pointing to everything on the dashboard asking what each item was for. He was amazed at the air conditioning and kept putting his hand in front of the vent to see if it was still working. He even tried changing the interior temperature before Palidore finally stopped him.

"I think it would be best for you not to touch the instruments, please." George quickly drew his hand back.

"Sorry."

Palidore started the engine, then made his final announcement.

"Okay, we're getting ready to pull out into traffic. Because I'm driving and need to pay attention to what I am doing, please feel free to direct your questions to Lynn, Susan, and Martha."

With that, he pulled out into light traffic. He negotiated the first couple of turns before coming to a full stop at a red light on Riggs Street. While they were stopped, two men ran out and approached the vehicle from each side. They began washing the front window. When they quickly finished, one of the men tapped on Palidore's window with his hand out. Palidore rolled down the window, already knowing the routine, and had a five-dollar bill ready, which he handed the man.

"Bless you," the man said just as the light turned green and Palidore took off. George had watched the activity with great interest.

"Why did those men wash your window? It was not dirty."

"That's how they make money."

"Well, they should have asked you first if you wanted your window washed."

"If they asked permission, then probably no one would allow it."

"You should not have paid them. You did not ask for their help."

"I don't think you understand. It's not really a choice. If they wash the window and I don't pay, they will do harm to my vehicle, so it's just easier to pay and move on."

"Oh, this is very wrong," George said. "If they harm your carriage, you have every right to shoot them. Where is your gun?"

"I don't have a gun with me in the car, besides, you must have a special permit to carry a gun which is almost impossible to get here in Washington. And even if I did, I couldn't just shoot someone for damaging my vehicle."

"Then the sheriff should be called to arrest them. What just happened is a robbery of sorts. Things like that should not occur. How many times a day do you have to pay people to have your window washed?"

"Actually, it doesn't occur that often, George, and almost never twice in the same day. So maybe we should change the subject and just enjoy our ride."

Everyone was silent for a while with Palidore driving and George looking out his window. Then, just when Palidore thought the subject was dead, they were caught by another stoplight, and the unlikely happened. Again, two men approached the vehicle with a bucket and squeegee in hand. Palidore exhaled and started to say something when George unbuckled himself, opened the door, got out, and yelled at the men.

"This window has already been washed! Do not touch this vehicle, or I promise, it will be the last window you wash!" The men quickly backed off and headed to the curb. George jumped back into the Buick and buckled up again.

"*That's* how you handle these thieves, Palidore! People cannot just let those worthless thugs have their way. Up to now, I was feeling pretty good about what has happened in my absence, but now I am starting to have some doubts."

Palidore started to say something, then decided to leave it alone. *Maybe this trip wasn't such a good idea,* he thought. Looking to change the subject again, he was delighted to see the Washington Monument come into view.

"Now, there's a sight! You can see the Washington Monument off to your right. See that tall structure? It's 555 feet tall and was actually the tallest structure in the world until the French finished building the Eiffel Tower in 1889 almost twice as tall.

"This monument, named in your honor, was started in 1848 to commemorate you as the commander-in-chief of the Continental Army during the American Revolutionary War, and because you were the first president of the United States of America. You know, George, you are a very beloved person in this country."

"I am truly honored," George said and was silent a moment. "They honestly built that in *my* memory? It has a very majestic look." Palidore saw he was genuinely touched.

"Yes, they did. Starting in 1848, it took over forty years to build and was finished in 1888. Since then, it was slightly damaged by an earthquake in 2011, but has since been repaired."

"Most amazing!" George said, seeming to have recovered from his agitated state. "I saw a picture of it in one of the educational modules, but it does look more impressive close-up. Can we stop?"

"No, not today. As we've said, this is just a test run, so we won't be making any stops along the way."

They continued to ride in silence another moment until Palidore spoke again. "Just around this next curve, you'll see the Jefferson Memorial. Unlike the Washington Memorial, which was begun within a reasonable time of your presidency, the Jefferson Memorial was not begun until 1939. The stated purpose at that time was to honor Jefferson as the primary author of the Declaration of Independence."

"Well, I am not so sure Thomas was as much the *author* of the document as he was the person responsible for writing down what everyone else said. I will admit, however, that Thomas *did* have a way with words," George said. "He always was a persuasive man, but as you may know, we did not always agree. In fact, we often *disagreed*. Still, I suppose he deserves his own monument. We all worked hard back then making this country come together at its beginning."

Palidore realized he was enjoying the first-person perspective of history from the man sitting beside him. As he approached the expressway he said

"Okay, now, we're going to speed up since we're getting on the expressway known as I-395. We're going over the Potomac River and when we reach the other shore, we will be in Alexandria, Virginia. Soon you will be able to see the Pentagon, the center for our military."

"I remember sketching the shoreline of Alexandria, as you call it, for my older brother Lawrence who wanted a town on the river back then in 1748, when he represented Fairfax County for his father-in-law, William. I was just starting out as a surveyor, and he needed it for a petition he wanted to present to the House of Burgesses." George seemed caught up in memories of the area as he continued. "But it was all open estate land back then. If Lawrence could see it now." George was smiling and taking it all in. However, Frank who had not said much of anything, covered his eyes when the vehicle sped up.

"Are you all right, Frank?" Susan asked. Frank nodded his head but kept his hands over his eyes.

"We are not used to such speed," George offered. "We are used to carriages pulled by horses, you remember."

Funny, Palidore thought, *Should I mention anything about 'horsepower' under the car's hood?* Then thought better of it and said nothing at all.

Shortly after crossing the river, they took an exit which put them on the George Washington Memorial Highway and stayed on it until they reached US-1. They passed through parts of old Alexandria, until it became Richmond Highway and crossed over I-495, continuing until they reached Mount Vernon Highway. A short distance further up the road, there was a sign to Mount Vernon. When they finally reached the entrance, Palidore slowed and turned the SUV around. As they nearly completed the turnaround, Washington spoke.

"Wait! I want to get out for just a moment. Please."

Palidore stopped the car and placed it in park. He started to say something, but in an instant, Washington was out of the car. He didn't go anywhere, but stood and looked around, then took a deep breath of country air. A few minutes later, he slowly got back in the car and buckled up again.

"Thank you, we can go now."

Palidore thought he noticed tears in George's eyes but said nothing. Pulling into the road, again, he headed back the way they had come.

Then it happened. Just as they were proceeding down Richmond Highway, a black car came streaking toward them off Wythe Street Drive at a high rate of speed and slammed into their left front fender, causing their vehicle to spin around once and come to an abrupt stop facing the way they had come, completely blocking the intersection. The GPS now told Palidore to 'make a lawful U-turn'

Meanwhile, everyone's attention was on the occupants of the offending vehicle which was also blocking the intersection. Two men immediately exited and ran. A second vehicle following close behind screeched to a stop. Two other men with guns got out and began shooting at the fleeing figures. With an exchange of gunfire, the men chasing the first two took cover behind the SUV, leaving Palidore and his passengers trapped inside.

Almost without thinking, George unbuckled his seat belt and with a violent thrust, opened his car door causing the man hiding behind it to hit the ground hard. His companion, taken by surprise, stood up and pointed his gun at George. But before he could shoot, was hit by incoming fire from the fleeing men. He lay silent on the ground holding his shoulder.

George immediately recovered the first man's gun and trained it on him. The fleeing men seized this opportunity and made good their escape from the scene.

Now Palidore cautiously looked around. "Is everyone okay?" One by one, they indicated no one was hurt. Slowly, all exited the SUV to find George still pointing the gun at the first man on the ground, now moaning and holding his leg. Palidore wasn't sure what to do next. Finally, he asked.

"Are you all right?"

"He's fine," George answered for him.

"My leg, I think you broke it!"

"You're lucky I didn't kill you. You coward, taking cover behind our carriage and putting us all in danger!"

Now what? Palidore thought, trying to figure out how to protect George and Frank's identities. He gathered the rest of his passengers into a huddle, then approached George and took the gun from him. Frank was now standing at George's side.

"Look, the police will be here soon," Palidore said, "and it will be better if you weren't here. They'll ask too many questions. We need time, and we don't have much. So, you and Frank need to get away from here. Just walk off away. After a while, you can call a Taxi or UBER using your cell phone, or just ask someone to help you get an UBER. When they come, give them my card, and ask them to take you to the address on it, remember? You need to trust me on this. Go now, please, just go. I'll handle things here and we can talk later."

George and Frank headed down the street trying to appear like bystanders.

Chapter 19

Not wanting to follow the fleeing men, George and Frank headed left down Wythe Street until they reached North Fayette Street where they stopped and looked in all directions.

"I think we should go that way," Frank said, pointing down Fayette Street.

"Okay, but what are you thinking?" George asked.

"Just don't think we should be on either of the streets that come together in that intersection."

"You are absolutely right."

As they turned, two police cars sped by with sirens blaring and blue and red lights blazing. Frank looked further down the street.

"Look, there's a restaurant with open-air covered seating down on the next corner. Let's stop there and figure out what to do."

"I agree, let's go."

They reached an establishment called the Bastille Bar and began looking for seats before they were stopped by the hostess.

"Would you gentlemen like a table?" a pleasant voice inquired.

George and Frank both turned to see a well-endowed, attractive blonde woman in a skimpy outfit, showing plenty of cleavage. Both men couldn't help but stare. The sight left them almost breathless. Finally, George was able to say, "Why, yes, that is where we were heading."

"Well, I will be happy to assist you; please follow me," she said, and proceeded to lead them inside the restaurant, placing them in a booth across from the pleasantly dim-lit bar. She left each of them a menu and said someone would be there soon to take their orders. George and Frank were intently focused on the movement of her backside with smiles on their faces as she left. When she was out of sight, they looked at each other and shook their heads before picking up the menus.

"Some of the sights in this modern day are truly amazing," George said.

The clock on the wall indicated one o'clock and the place was alive with noisy customers. Several large-screen televisions displayed different sporting events, all muted, while music played as the primary background sound. Neon lights advertising various brands of beer were everywhere, and the cedar shake walls were adorned with hundreds of individually framed pictures of local patrons.

While waiting for a waitress, the two men were approached by a man who took their picture, then proceeded to show it to them on his camera's small screen.

"Would like to have your picture framed and placed on one of our walls? We call it 'the wall of instant fame!' Only twenty-five bucks. What do you say?" Frank looked across the table at George and answered for both of them.

"We are not interested."

"Sure? All your friends would love to see your picture. Sometimes people just come in and walk around to see who's been here. How 'bout it guys?"

George said nothing, but his look was the only answer the man needed.

"Okay, no problem, enjoy your meal," he said backing away.

No more had the man left then a waitress appeared, dressed in a similar costume as the hostess, only this time she was a petite, but otherwise, well-endowed African American woman. Both men could hardly suppress their smiles.

"My name is Mandy, and I'll take your drink orders while you continue to review the menu. What can I get you?"

"A beer," George said. "I believe I would like a beer."

"Which one? We have an extensive collection." She turned the menu over and pointed. "This is our beer list."

George studied it, trying to understand when his eyes lit up. He recognized a name attached to one of the beers on the list. "I'll have this John Mercer dark ale."

"Very good," Mandy said. "That's a local favorite, brewed nearby in Frederick County. Some say it was one of George Washington's favorite ales. Are you boys from around here?"

"I guess you could say that," George replied.

"And you, sir?" she looked at Frank. "What can I get for you?"

"You may bring me the same."

"Very well, two Mercers coming right up."

The men now silently looked at their menus. Finally, Frank, put his menu down. "I am not sure why Palidore wanted us to leave. We did nothing wrong."

"I was thinking the same thing, Frank. Why shouldn't we have stayed and talked to the police? I just don't know. There seems to be some distrust of authorities and I am not sure all is well with our country."

"Well, do you trust his judgment? Palidore, I mean."

"Yes, I think so, but I am not sure about his decision in this case."

"Do you think we could get into trouble for leaving?"

"Good question, Frank."

At that very moment, most of the television screens simultaneously blinked and changed from their sporting events to signs with the words 'Breaking News!' The scene behind the headline showed Palidore, Lynn, Martha, and Susan standing next to the SUV talking to police. George got up and went close to the nearest television.

It had closed-captioned words displayed along the bottom so he could read what the reporter was saying.

". . . Dr. Palidore Montgomery stated that his SUV was struck by this car over here, before two men got out and began running. Another vehicle came up behind and two other subjects got out and fired weapons in pursuit of the fleeing men. The brief gun battle resulted in one man being killed while the other man returned to his vehicle and drove off. None of the suspects are in custody, and everyone is advised that the men are considered armed and extremely dangerous.

"Should you see or hear anything relating to this incident, please contact the Virginia State Police at the number on this screen. This is Troy Maier reporting for WDCA news."

George returned to the booth and told Frank what he had read.

"But that is not what happened entirely!" Frank said. "Palidore did not tell the truth."

"No, and how did that man get away from Palidore? When we left, Palidore had a gun on him, and his leg was either broken, or pretty badly hurt. What is Palidore up to?"

"What should we do now, George?"

Just then, Mandy, the waitress, returned with both ales. "Have you gentlemen decided on your orders?"

Frank looked across the table at George. "I don't believe I'm hungry right now," he said. George agreed.

"Okay, well, enjoy your beers. I'll be back later to check on you boys."

"So . . . what should we do now?" Frank whispered to George who seemed deep in thought. He wasn't one to answer quickly.

"Clearly, Palidore wants us to go back to his MCS building, but I am not so sure I want to."

"Where else can we go?"

"I am thinking we might go to Mount Vernon."

"Mount Vernon! We just came from there, and besides, aren't

we supposed to go there next week? I think Dr. Miles' son is supposed to be our guide."

"I know, I know, but I am concerned that trip might be called off in light of what has happened today. It may be months before we get another opportunity."

"How could we get there?"

"I thought I might ask our waitress to call that Uber carriage."

Chapter 20

After the police were done questioning everyone, and while the television camera crews were packing up gear, Palidore and the three women got back in the Buick Enclave. Fortunately, after changing the tire, it was still drivable. They started down Wythe Street in the direction they had last seen George and Frank walking. At the corner, they turned down North Fayette Street.

"Palidore," Martha said. "Please stop at that restaurant over there. I think I may be sick. And I need to use the restroom."

"Me, too," Susan said.

"Okay, let me try and find a place to park. Maybe we should all go in and get our heads around this." He spotted an empty parking space. "There's a spot, hold on." As he pulled the SUV into the space, an UBER driver pulled away from the restaurant with George and Frank in the back seat, unnoticed by everyone.

The group of four made their way into the Bastille Bar. The girls headed off to the restroom while Palidore waited for someone to show them to a table. After a short wait, the same blonde hostess who had seated George and Frank, now asked Palidore if he wanted to be seated.

"Yes, thanks, there are four of us."

"Sure, I can show you to a table now, or we can wait for your companions."

"Oh, here they come now."

"Fine, follow me." She took them to a booth. As they were

settling in, she recognized Palidore. "Hey, I think I just saw you on television. You're that doctor who almost got shot!"

"Unfortunately, you are correct, but we need a little time now to collect our wits"

"No problem, baby. Let me get you a pitcher on the house and I'll bring you some peanuts. Just sit down and take it easy. Bless your hearts, you guys have been through a lot today. You need anything, anything at all, just ask your waitress for 'Mary," and I'll be right over. No problem. I sure hope they get those guys."

"So do we."

The hostess left menus and went in search of free beer and peanuts for the table.

Palidore sat with his face in his hands, elbows on the table, Susan's eyes were red from crying, trying to hold back another outburst. Lynn sat motionlessly. Martha pretended to look over the menu. The hostess came back with a pitcher of beer, four cold glasses, and two bowls of peanuts in the shell.

"Hope this helps, but I didn't think to ask what kind of beer you wanted, so I just brought my favorite, Miller's. If you'd rather have another kind or something else, I'll be happy to get it for you."

"This will be fine," Lynn said, just wanting to be left alone. "You're very kind; thank you."

The hostess poured out four glasses and served them before leaving. They each took sips and continued holding their glasses, looking at each other.

"This isn't right. We shouldn't have lied to the police," Lynn said in a remorseful tone.

"Well, technically, we didn't *lie*. We just left out a lot," Palidore said raising his eyebrows.

"You mean, like the fact that George and Frank were with us and left the scene at your direction?" Martha asked.
"Yes, that."

"And the fact that the man didn't just drive off? You had to help him to his car? I hope there are no cameras around," Lynn said. "Why would you do that?"

"I'll admit that in hindsight, I may not have handled it all that well. But had we kept the man there, he would have told the police about George slamming his leg with the door. By letting him go, I'm pretty sure he won't be looking for the police to correct our version of the story. I just don't think George or Frank could have properly answered all their questions. They would have been okay with the facts concerning the accident but would have been lacking in the personal information category. You know the police would have sought out more information, and who knows where *that* would have led. It seems to me that George and Frank would have ultimately been forced to reveal their true identities and it just isn't time yet. We promised them that decision would be *theirs* to make at a later date. I don't know . . . things just happened so fast. I did what I thought was right for them."

Martha's cell phone buzzed, and a picture of George appeared on the screen. "Oh my God, it's George!"

"Put it on speaker," Lynn said. Martha did as requested, then answered.

"Hello, George is that you?"

"Yes, I guess this thing may actually be useful after all."

"Are you okay? Where are you?"

"Frank and I are okay. We are in an UBER on our way back to Mount Vernon."

"George, this is Palidore. Please don't do that. I really want you to head back to the MCS building right now. Please!"

There was silence from George for a moment.

"How can I be talking to you when I called Martha? I am not sure this thing is working right. I don't understand."

"Well, I can hear you because I am sitting next to Martha. Just please ask the driver to turn around and take you back to the MCS building."

"Oh, we will. He has agreed to wait for us while we make our visit. We won't be too long, especially since we are returning next week, but there is something I need to see there *before* next week. Don't worry. I know my way around the place pretty well. We called because we just did not want you to worry. If you like, Frank can give Susan a call when we leave Mount Vernon. That way, he will get a chance to use his phone, too . . . oh, it looks like we are here. Goodbye for now." There was silence on the line.

Palidore, Martha, Susan, and Lynn sat motionless staring at each other until Martha burst out laughing. Lynn and Susan gave her a curious look but then also started laughing. Soon, they were nearly in tears with laughter. Palidore looked on in amazement.

"I don't get it. What's so damn funny?"

Martha tried twice to respond but couldn't stop laughing. Finally, Lynn regained her composure enough to say, "The whole thing. That's what's so funny. My god, George Washington is *back*, has a car wreck, survives a shootout, and then decides he'll just grab himself an UBER and zip on home to ol' Mount Vernon! I mean, who would believe it? It's all so unbelievable, just completely unbelievable!"

Palidore looked around the table at all of their faces before slowly growing his own grin and joining the laughter. Mary, the hostess, came back and looked at all of them. "Well, it looks like everybody is feeling better now; would you like to order something to eat."

They all burst out laughing again.

Chapter 21

George and Frank exited the Uber van and Frank handed the plastic credit card Palidore had given him to the driver.

"I can't take this," the driver said. "You had to sign up on the Uber app for me to even come get you."

George looked at Frank. "Maybe Mandy did that when she asked to see this little plastic thing and then helped us call for this Uber ride."

Frank looked at him blankly.

"Well, then you have been paid already, my good man, yes?" George asked.

"Correct, I'll get my money from the company," the driver said over his shoulder.

"We need you to wait for us, it won't take long," George said as he leaned down to look through the window. They agreed upon a price for the driver to wait for them. "You'll take us back to the MCS building when we return."

"I'll keep the meter running," the driver said as the men headed toward the entrance to Mount Vernon.

As they walked, George looked at Frank. "There is much we have to learn about their customs, but this money thing is something that could have helped Alexander Hamilton. Why it seems no money is needed at all with these little plastic tablets. That could have helped him plan differently when he created the national bank after the war."

TRANSFORMING GEORGE WASHINGTON

They went inside to purchase tour tickets. The gentleman at the counter took Frank's credit card, ran it through a machine, and when it produced a slip, asked him to sign. Frank scribbled his name.

"You're in luck," the man told him. "The next tour will begin shortly. You can join those people waiting outside in the small assembly area."

"Can you tell us who our tour guide will be?" George asked.

"Sure, today your guide will be Janet Rohand." They thanked him, placed the little stickers on their shirts as instructed, and proceeded to the group of gathered patrons. George did a quick headcount and found that including the two of them, there would be thirteen people on the tour unless someone else showed up soon. He pulled Frank aside and talked in a low voice.

"I don't know if our guide will already know how many people she has to guide or if she will do a quick count, but when she comes, I am going to step aside over here so she doesn't count me. Then, I'll join the group as soon as they start walking."

"Why will you do that?"

"I'd rather not be in the beginning count. You'll see why later."

"Okay, as you wish."

A short time later, they saw a young woman walking down the path toward the group. After giving Frank a nudge, George slipped away. When the woman reached the gathering, she did a quick count using her finger to point at each person until she made an announcement.

"Hello, everyone. Okay, we have an even dozen in our group this morning. I thought we were to have thirteen, but twelve is fine. My name is Janet Rohand, and it will be my pleasure to show you the lovely home of our first President George Washington." As she was speaking, George slipped back into the group and gradually worked his way over to Frank.

"I see everyone has on comfortable shoes as recommended," Janet continued. "This tour is listed as a 'moderate activity' event which means that it involves some light walking, and there will be a few steps to negotiate inside the home, so please be careful.

"As you can see, the entire estate is too large to cover in one tour. We also have several optional guided tours you can purchase later, if you wish, to learn more about another area. However, each of your passes includes a 'grounds' pass which will allow you to explore the grounds on your own after our tour of the residence. Today, our tour will be of the main residence, but you will also see a couple of the outbuildings as we approach the home. The entire tour will take about sixty minutes. Now, please follow me and watch your step."

As the group began moving, George took Frank's arm holding him back a bit so they could talk.

"When we enter the residence, you need to be toward the front of the group while I will hang back. They should enter through the main door and hopefully, proceed straight through toward the piazza. When they get past the stairs, I want you to act like you accidentally fell and hurt your leg. It would be good if you could grab someone else with you as you fall. Pretend your leg is hurt."

"Why would I do that?"

"Trust me, Frank, it's because *I* want you to do that. I need for you to draw their attention away from me so I can go somewhere else in the house without them knowing. There is something I want to check on. It won't take long, but you must help me go unnoticed. I won't be away for long. Eventually, I'll find my way back to the group when I am finished. Can you do that for me?"

"It will be as you wish."

"Thank you, Frank, I have always been able to count on you."

The tour guide stopped at the entrance to the mansion and looked at her group.

"You are about to enter the central passage which goes completely through the width of the house almost thirty-one feet. This elegant space is where all visitors would enter the home. Please follow me."

TRANSFORMING GEORGE WASHINGTON

Everyone proceeded into the home. Frank maneuvered himself near the front of the group and George lagged behind as planned. Just past the staircase, while the guide was saying something about the Key to the Bastille, Frank lurched forward and began falling. He took Janet Rohand, the guide, to the floor with him. As everyone gathered around Frank and Janet, George bounded up the stairs thankful for his lightweight comfortable shoes which hardly made a sound. Once on the landing, he went straight through the 'Yellow Room' and into what was once his own bedroom. There, he took the back staircase down, past his study on the first floor, and into the cellar.

As George was making his journey, Frank was brushing himself off and helping Janet regain her footing and apologizing profusely for the mishap while limping around a bit for show.

"Oh, no . . . are *you* okay?" she asked Frank as they both stood up again. Quickly she looked around to see if anything had been damaged in their fall. Seeing nothing amiss, she did another finger count of her group and noted that it matched her original assessment of twelve people. "That's why we must all be careful," she said, smiling again.

Satisfied that all was in order, Janet began telling everyone about the Key to the Bastille again which she said was given to George Washington by the Marquis de Lafayette in 1790. The tour continued.

George had just reached the cellar and was happy to see he was alone. He looked for cameras, having learned of such surveillance devices in one of his learning modules. Seeing none, he was pleased the cellar was not encumbered with such hardware.

Proceeding down the dimly lit hallway, he stopped for a moment at the original cornerstone bearing the initials of his brother, Lawrence. Gently, he touched the deep slits in the stone, thinking of how long ago the marks had been made. *How much has happened since then,* he thought. *No one would believe the journey I am on now. I can hardly believe it myself.*

He stayed only briefly before moving on. He couldn't help but ask himself *I wonder if they found my secret tunnels. If so, nothing in the education modules has mentioned, it. I guess I will soon find out.* He continued east until finding the small room off to the right of the cellar passageway that used to house his favorite whiskey. Now he had to find the correct stones to push that would release the hidden door. He felt along the wall until his fingers touched the old shelving unit. He knew the protruding stone was behind the shelves unless the unit had been moved. It hadn't been. He moved the unit out a bit, feeling around until he found the protruding stone. Then, pushing hard until it moved, he finally heard the latch give.

Now wearing a grin on his face, he pushed the door open and proceeded into the dark hallway. *I know this tunnel goes all the way to the river, but the passageway I want leads off of this one before it reaches the river. It goes to the right and heads toward the stable. I remember the entrance is through a closet or small room, but it is so dark I am not sure I can locate it.* George felt his way along the right side of the tunnel until he found the door. He tried to activate the flashlight on his cellphone but couldn't remember how to turn it on. Then his finger bumped the screen which caused it to come alive, and give him a little light. Finding the stone he needed, he pushed it and the door slowly opened. He stopped inside and began walking again.

Once he reached the stable area, he knew the last passageway he was seeking - the one to the mausoleum - would be a little further down the tunnel and behind one of four ornate doors. It wasn't long before he located the area and remembered exactly which door, he wanted. Simultaneously, he turned the wooden carvings of the snake and bird within the design on the third door and the secret lock released.

Now entering its short dark passageway, he touched the face of his cellphone again to give himself enough light to proceed toward the steps leading up to the mausoleum. He had read that the original mausoleum above this tunnel had been removed, but that did not matter as it was the *steps* he was looking for, and he could see they remained intact just ahead.

Walking over to the steps, he bent down and remembered what his faithful Major Hudson had told him about how to access his secret hiding place. He forced the tread about one inch to the right which then allowed him to slide the step toward him. He was careful not to pull it totally off the base as it was quite heavy. Then, finally, he reached his hand down into the area and touched one of the many leather bags located deep inside the cavern. He pulled the top one out and opened it. His heart was racing as he hit the face of his cellphone again.

To his utter delight, he gazed upon his precious Liberty Eagle gold coins. They were all of the same denomination. Depositing the coins in this hiding place had been one of the last things he had done in his ancient life. The coins had been newly minted in early 1799, and he had acquired as many of them as he could at the time. The currency value of each was only ten dollars when he hid them, but George knew from his education modules that gold was worth much more now.

He began stuffing as many coins as he could carry into each pocket, but not so many that it would make him look bulky or be too obvious. He then put the remainder of the one bag back into its hole with the other bags still inside and moved the step back into place. Then, he proceeded to retrace his journey.

This has taken much longer than I thought it would. I hope I can get back in time.

Arriving back at the door behind the shelves, he reentered the room and moved the book unit back into place. Then, making his way up the rear stairs, he stopped at his study on the first floor rather than proceeding to the second floor from where he had originally come. Now, he entered the study and proceeded into the adjacent parlor where he listened at the door. Footsteps were coming down the stairs. He waited as they passed by and heard the guide open the door to the piazza. He then proceeded to fall in behind the group when he heard her make an announcement.

"We'll end our tour here, near where we started. Outside, you will see the breathtaking view of the Potomac River from the vantage of the piazza." George spotted Frank who was now toward the back of the group. He made his way over. Once everyone was outside, the guide continued talking.

"George and Martha loved the piazza and spent many evenings enjoying this wonderful view. They often entertained here, weather permitting. Well, everyone, that concludes our tour today. Please take as much time as you wish to explore the grounds on your own. On your way back, you can stop and make a reservation for one of our other tours. Thank you for being with us today."

There was a round of polite applause. George was pleased to see a group of individuals surrounding the guide asking her questions. He looked at Frank with a smile.

"Let's go, Frank," he said as they headed back toward their waiting Uber ride. "I found what we came for."

Chapter 22

The Uber driver dropped George and Frank off in front of the MCS building. As they walked up the steps, the door opened and Palidore was standing there.

"Gentlemen! So glad to see you are back," he greeted them. "Please come into my office where we can talk. I'm glad Frank called ahead to let us know you were on your way."

"I'll be right there," George said as he entered the building, "I need to go to my room for just a moment. I'll be right back down."

"I might as well use the bathroom, too," Frank said.

"Well, of course," Palidore said as both men headed upstairs. Inside his room, George quickly emptied his pockets on the bed. He grabbed a shoebox that still held shoes and simply added the coins, wanting to hide them. There were too many for one box, so he put the rest in a second shoebox before returning to the hallway where he met Frank again. They descended the stairs together and went into Palidore's office.

As they entered, the women were standing around with drinks in their hands. Martha quickly approached and put a hand on George's arm.

"I'm so glad you're all right; we've been so worried. Who would think our little excursion would be so frightening? I've never seen anything like it in my whole life and hope I never will again."

"Well, remember I fought in a war," George said. "Gunfire was not the first time for me. Fortunately, it all ended well. But I'm still not sure why we were asked to leave before the police arrived," George said.

"That's what we need to talk about," Palidore said. "Let's all sit down; but first, can I get either of you anything to drink?"

"A whiskey for me."

"Same for me," Frank said. Palidore supplied the beverages, and everyone sat down. Since there wasn't enough room at the small table, everyone pulled back their chairs adjusting the space to make room.

"I don't think you should have asked us to leave," Frank spoke first. "We did nothing wrong. Honestly, I am not sure I can obey such commands in the future."

"Frank, you are correct, of course," Palidore said, "But the decision I was forced to make so quickly was not without reason. However, I think you are certainly entitled to an explanation."

"Which we are anxious to hear," George said.

All eyes diverted to Palidore. Feeling the pressure of the moment, he took another sip of his drink and slowly looked around the table.

"In a *normal* situation, we certainly would have had everyone remain in place for the police to arrive. However, our situation was far from normal in any sense, and I was concerned that both of you would have been subjected to a barrage of intense questioning, which in the end, would have resulted in your true identities being made public.

"As you know, we have previously committed to you that you will be the ones to decide whether to reveal your true identities at the appropriate time. Had you remained, I am afraid, that opportunity would have been lost. In these times, the police are very persistent in finding out what they want to know."

"What questions would have been required of us that would have revealed our true past?" Frank asked.

"For one thing," Lynn said, "the police today are specially trained to obtain extensive background information from any witness, *especially* when there has been a death. Simple questions like your names, addresses, cell phone numbers, dates of birth, education, occupation, and more. They also watch your facial expressions and if they aren't convinced of your innocence, they can take you to police headquarters and possibly interrogate you much further."

"While we have provided you with proper answers to many of their initial questions, there are so many more that you would have trouble answering; like where do you live? Where do you work? Where did you go to school? Where did you grow up? Who were your parents? You get the idea. We just could not let that happen," she said. "If you ultimately choose to proceed with a new identity, which we have yet to provide you, today's incident might have been a real problem.

"I feel that all of this is my fault," Lynn said. "I should have anticipated you might need more information and should have provided it long before now, or at least before ever agreeing to set out on such a journey. I'm truly sorry for putting you in this awkward situation. Please accept my sincere apology. It was my job to prepare you, and I failed." Lynn paused. "You were so excited about seeing Mount Vernon, and we wanted to accommodate you. I'm so sorry for how everything went down today."

"It's not all your fault, Lynn," Martha said. "We all agreed to do this today. Indeed, this walkthrough trip was supposed to help us prepare. Who could have envisioned such a sequence of events would occur. Anyway, the question is not, 'Why has all this happened?' but rather, 'What should we do now, going forward?'"

George, unexpectedly silent until now, stood up and drained his glass. "Well, it is our lives, as you have pointed out, so let the decision about revealing our true identities remain solely with us. Actually, let me get straight to the point. Frank and I have decided, at least for the present, *not* to reveal our true identities to anyone who does not already possess that knowledge. We assume that the people in this room, and the board of directors, are presently the only ones in possession of that knowledge. Therefore, we would very much appreciate it if you would provide us with all the documents and information necessary for us to function under new assumed identities as we very much want to avoid being placed in such an awkward situation again, simply because we cannot describe to others who we really are.

"Please also understand that we will carefully listen to your advice, but ultimately, *we* will decide what we can do, and where we can go. We appreciate everything you have done for us so far, and while we acknowledge that we are still in need of your assistance, we no longer wish to remain captives in this building."

The room went silent for an uncomfortable period of time before Palidore rose from his seat. "I hear what you are saying and understand why you might consider yourselves 'captives' here, but nothing could be further from the truth. Perhaps we should have had this conversation some time ago, but today's events have accentuated the need to resolve these issues. So please hear me out.

"We most certainly honor you, not only for the lives you have previously lived but for the lives you can still live today. We cannot alter the past, but without the great sacrifices each of us in this room have made, to say nothing of the Board of Directors, there would be no future for either of you. Indeed, had we been greedy, we would have simply announced our accomplishments to the world, instantly receiving millions of dollars for book rights alone. We could have filmed every event! But we gave all that up to ensure that your true identities would not be accidentally discovered.

"Furthermore, you should know that there are ongoing expenses associated with your presence which are being paid out of our own pockets. I understand that you were a powerful man in your time, and are accustomed to making all the decisions, but in this moment, it is *not* in your best interest for you to do so. If nothing else, the events of today strongly suggest why I believe you are not ready yet.

"Please understand that we want what you want, but until that can be successfully achieved, the decisions still need to be made by *me*. If you are not willing to abide by that, then there is no reason we should not make public your true identities and receive the compensation to which we are entitled."

The women were shocked at the firmness in Palidore's voice and their faces showed it. Until this moment, he had always led by consensus, but clearly, here he was just taking charge. The room was silent. George looked over toward Frank, then locked eyes with Palidore before speaking in a more conciliatory tone.

"I appreciate your frankness. You are, of course, correct . . . for now. And we shall follow your lead. Should that become too uncomfortable for us, we will let you know. We want to thank you for all you have done, and the personal sacrifices you have made on our behalf. We hope, perhaps, that one day we will be able to repay you for all your kindness." Relief showed on the faces of the women. Frank, as usual, did not reveal his feelings and simply remained silent.

"I believe I could use another touch of your whiskey," George said and held up his glass.

"Let's make it another round," Martha chimed in, glad to have the moment behind them.

"Now, that's something to which we can all agree," Palidore laughed and went to work preparing drinks for everyone.

Chapter 23

As the meeting was breaking up, George asked Palidore if he could catch some fresh air outside. Palidore's eyes glanced over to Martha who was standing next to him.

"I'll stay with him," she said.

"Sure, go ahead and get some fresh air. I'm going home."

George and Martha went out the basement doors and up the steps to the ground street level. When they reached the top, they saw Palidore leaving in his car and waved. Then George took Martha's hand as they stood side by side and stared across the street toward her apartment building. She liked the feeling of his touch and remained quiet.

The activity of the day was setting in and they were both feeling emotionally and physically drained, yet there remained a feeling of contentment as they stood together.

"I have a gift for you," he said.

"A gift? You found time to go shopping while you and Frank were out sightseeing?"

"I didn't have to go shopping to acquire this gift."

"Oh, now I'm intrigued. What could it be?"

"Not here. No one else can know about this, at least for now."

Her curiosity was piqued. *What could he possibly have that he doesn't want anyone else to know?* She looked around. The street was empty. "We can go over to my flat. I live right over there," she said, pointing to her condo.

"You live *there*? I thought you lived in Georgetown."

"I do, but I also have a small flat here; actually, I prefer it, now that I work at MCS. Let's go."

She led him across the street where she entered the garage door code. After gaining entry, they walked toward the private elevator door almost directly in front of her Audi. They entered the cubicle and she hit the 'up' button. Within a minute, they arrived at her flat, and as the door opened, she stopped at another keypad to turn off the alarm system.

"This is it . . . my little kingdom. What do you think?"

"I like it. Looks very comfortable. I can see why you like it here," he said while glancing all around the room.

"Let me give you the nickel tour." Martha showed George both bedrooms and the two baths before positioning herself on a high stool behind the large island in the center of the kitchen area.

"Care for some wine?"

"Sure, what do you have?"

"I'm afraid all I have is chardonnay, and before you get too excited, I should tell you that it's a cheap brand, but it's cold, and I like it as much as the expensive stuff."

"I believe I'll have chardonnay, then. Cold please."

Martha laughed, opened the refrigerator, and fetched the bottle, pouring wine into two decorative stemless wine glasses she and Stanley had bought in Germany. She handed him a glass, then held hers up.

"To an eventful day." They touched the rims, and each took a small sip.

"Not bad," George said. "You know, I prefer my wine cold, too, even red wine."

"Me, too." There was an easy silence between them as they gazed out the window. "Did you say you had a gift for me?" Martha said, breaking the quiet mood.

"Oh . . . yes. I was so impressed with your apartment I almost forgot. Okay, so, hold your hand out." She did what he asked. "Good, now close your eyes."

Martha closed them and felt George put something hard and round into her palm. He closed her fingers around it.

"Okay, open your eyes." Martha opened them along with her fingers, revealing the gold eagle coin. She held it up closer to read the date.

"Oh, it's beautiful. It looks new. But wait . . . it says '1799'. Is that for *real*? Was it minted in 1799?"

"Yes, it was. I was able to secure a significant quantity of the new coins as soon as they were minted in 1799."

"Where did you get it?"

"At my home, Mount Vernon."

"Today?"

"Yes, of course, today. That's why I wanted to go there . . . to find out if they were still where I had left them. They were all there, and I was able to obtain a quantity of them."

"And . . . they just allowed you to go in and take them?"

"Well, I didn't feel it was necessary to ask permission to take what was rightfully mine. So, with Frank's help, I was able to get away from the group just long enough to acquire some of my coins."

Martha wasn't sure how to react. Her thoughts began to race. *What if . . . ?* "You know you took a big chance, don't you? If you had been caught, they would have arrested you. Remember, no one knows that you are back, and wouldn't believe it if you told them. You took quite a risk."

"Perhaps, so, but I did what I had to do. I need the coins."

"So how many coins did you take?"

"Not sure. I haven't had time to count them yet, but maybe a hundred or so."

"Wow! That's a lot of coins. What did you do with them?"

"They're in two shoeboxes in my wardrobe. But I will need a better place to put them. Maybe you could hold them for me. Do you have a safe installed here?"

TRANSFORMING GEORGE WASHINGTON

The question made Martha feel conflicted. She wanted to help George but wondered if she was becoming an accessory to a crime. George was waiting for an answer.

"Well, will you do it?"

"Oh, I'm sorry," she said, lowering her head. "I was just trying to think if there might be a better solution, but for now, I guess that would be all right."

"Thank you, thank you so much," he said, obviously delighted with her support. Then without notice, he took her in his arms and gave her a joyous kiss on the lips. She was completely caught off guard but didn't resist. In fact, the spontaneity of his actions, made her feel a burst of happiness. She felt comfortable being around him but wondered where it was all going. *'What am I getting into here?'* she thought before saying "What am I supposed to do with this coin?"

"Oh, that's *yours,* it's my gift to you. Perhaps, you might take it somewhere to see what it's worth today. Then maybe a jeweler could put a band around it so you could wear it as a necklace."

"Interesting idea, but first, I think we should get an idea of its value. Let's see what we can find out." Martha moved to the couch and picked up her laptop, beginning to type. She patted the seat next to her, enticing George to sit. He took the cue.

"Here we go, let's see. Does that one look like this?"

"Why, that's it! How did you find it so fast?"

"Easy, remember, it's called the Internet. You haven't gotten that far yet. So far you are studying information Lynn has prepared for you to help bring you up to date. But on the Internet, it's like a complete library of everything on your computer. You can look up anything you want almost instantly. But let's see what it says" She began reading out loud: "In the early years, they minted gold coins in three denominations, the quarter eagle, half eagle, and full eagle."

"Mine are all full eagles," George said, "and they look much better than the one on the screen."

"Uh-huh. Let me keep reading. It says: *This coin is one of*

37,449 *that were minted in Philadelphia in 1799. Its weight is 0.9 grams, and the melt value of the gold is $982.23."*

"Let me scroll down and see how much this coin is worth today... holy shit! They say one coin alone is worth $23,436.00 if you wanted to buy it!" She looked at George.

"How many did you say you brought back?"

"Maybe a hundred or so."

"Oh my god, George!" Martha did a quick calculation in her head. "That means the street value of just the coins in your shoebox is $2,343,600.00! Maybe even more." She reached over and gave George a hug, got up and danced around. Then, grabbing both of George's hands, she urged him to stand up. Once on his feet, she swung him around.

"George, aren't you excited? Don't you realize what this means? You've just become a multi-millionaire, which means you're *rich*!"

"I suppose so," he said quietly, "but I was just trying to understand something you said a moment ago." Martha stopped and put her hands on her hips.

"Okay, what did I say that you don't understand?"

"You said: 'holy shit.' What does 'shit' have to do with any of this? Even the shit of a deity. I mean, why did you compare the value of my coins to *shit*?"

Oh, my god, Martha thought, *he's never heard the expression.* She tried being serious while explaining but could hardly contain laughter. "I am *so* sorry, but that's an expression we use today. Apparently, it wasn't used in the late 1700s. But today, it simply means: 'WOW!' People say it, especially when something happens that they didn't expect. Don't ask me how it started because I really don't know."

"Okay, so it is not to be taken seriously," he looked serious.

"Right! It's just an expression related to a surprise."

"I guess, I understand. So, if you give me a gift that I don't expect to receive, I could say, 'Holy shit, thank you?"

Martha burst out laughing. "Well, maybe not *exactly* in that instance, but we should deal with this later. Let's get back to the good news about the value of your coins. The coins you have in those shoeboxes are worth more than two million dollars. That's really exciting, don't you think?"

"I suppose so, but I'm not sure I understand the true value of that number. In any event, that number is probably low because I have many more coins back at the house."

"What do you mean? How many?"

"Well, I brought back about 100 coins, but that's because I could only get a few of them."

"So-o-o-o . . . how many more are there?"

"Well, at the time I acquired them, I put exactly 250 coins in each leather bag." Martha's eyes grew wide, her heart began to pound; she was just inches away from his face. "George . . . how many bags *are* there?"

"Eight . . .there are eight bags full of coins." Martha just stood there not knowing what to say. Finally, she took his hand and pulled him back down on the couch again. She let go of his hand and put her hands on both sides of his face before looking up at him again. George was just staring at her with a questioning look.

"George, this is incredible. We have a lot of things to think through."

"Well, the only thing I think we need to figure out is how to get the remaining coins out of there."

"That's going to be a huge problem, but assuming we get them out, then we have to determine where to store them and how to sell them. I mean, if you put them all on the market at one time, the value of each coin will decrease because you will flood the market. What makes that coin so valuable now is the fact that it is so rare. If there are suddenly 2000 more of them in circulation, then even one won't be so rare. Are you getting this?"

"Yes, of course, I understand. So, we'll sell a few at a time."

"Yes, that's correct, but remember, the buyer may become suspicious if he sees too many coins. He may begin wondering who you are, and how you came to have so many uncirculated ones. It could even become a news story! Today, news travels around the world in minutes, George, even seconds. It really is a different world now. We'll need more than one buyer. We may even need more than one country. We're going to need to be very careful here." She caught herself for a moment. "Oh my God! Will you listen to me? I can't believe I'm saying this. I'm talking about stealing gold worth almost fifty million dollars! We can't do this . . . it's impossible."

"Martha," George said in a serious tone. "The gold *belongs* to me, and one way or the other, I'm going to get my coins."

"But, George, the coins belong to the government now, or at least the government *thinks* it owns everything at Mount Vernon. Without telling them who you are, they will think you're stealing, if you're caught."

"There's the answer, Martha: I won't get caught. They are *my* coins, and I am going to get them, all of them. If I get caught, then I suppose I will have to reveal my true identity. Remember, the government doesn't even know they exist at this point. And I have already shown my ability to acquire them. So, I just need to figure out how to get the rest. In fact, I have a plan, but I will need your help . . . and Frank's. Are you willing to help me?"

Martha looked at him for a long moment, then picked up her wine glass and took a long drink. She looked over the rim of her wine glass at George already knowing what she was going to say. "Hell, yeah. I may live to regret this, but it's just about the most exciting thing I will ever do."

George picked up his wine glass to toast her agreement before noticing Martha's glass was empty. He pulled her hand with the glass closer to his and poured some of his wine into her glass, then held his up for the toast.

Martha's heart was pounding; her eyes were sparkling as she raised her glass to his. Their glasses touched and each took a drink. Then, as their eyes locked onto one another's, George leaned close to her and looked into her eyes. He pulled her closer to him and slowly, gently kissed her lips.

Inside herself, Martha felt something begin to warm. *His strength is overwhelming,* she thought. *Everything about him is exciting.* They embraced and kissed again, but with the second kiss, she felt the passion ignite and suddenly wanted more. Quickly, she controlled her emotions.

'I have to slow down . . . I need more time to think. This is too fast.' She slightly pulled away. "You're an exciting man, George, and that was nice, really nice. I'll help you get your coins back, but I need a little time to understand my feelings for you. My . . . personal feelings. Perhaps, we can talk more about your plans soon."

"Of course, I should get back to my room anyway."

"Let me walk you over, so I can use my card to let you in. It's probably locked now for the evening." They moved toward the elevator, but she noticed that he intentionally avoided taking her hand in an apparent effort to respect her wishes and give her the time she had requested.

There is something about this man that seems so familiar and yet so foreign. She thought about it for a moment, then reached for his hand as they exited the elevator and headed across the street.

Chapter 24

George walked upstairs to his bedroom and found Frank waiting for him. "Frank, I didn't know you were here. I wish I had some whiskey to offer you. It's not like me to be inhospitable. I'd like to offer you a drink like we used to do . . . "

In many ways, it seems like only yesterday, George thought, *and yet I know it has been over two hundred years. It seems impossible!* ". . . From now on, I'll keep a bottle in my room." Frank waited for him to finish talking. "It's good to finally be alone, again," Frank said. He looked silently at his friend, waiting.

"I know you're curious about what happened at Mount Vernon today, but I couldn't talk on the ride back since I didn't want the driver to overhear. Anyway, it might be easier just to show you." He went to the wardrobe and pulled out one of the shoeboxes, taking it over to Frank and handing it to him. "Take a peek inside."

Frank removed the lid, and his eyes grew wide. He looked up at George with a curious look. "Where did you get these?"

"That's why we went back to Mount Vernon. These are my coins from before we fell asleep and woke up here. That's why I asked you to create the diversion. According to Martha, these coins are worth more than two million dollars."

"Two million?" Frank couldn't comprehend the magnitude.

"She looked up the value on the computer, and that's what she found," George said.

"So, Martha knows what we did?"

"She does, but we need her Frank. She's smart and has agreed to help us."

"Help us do what?"

"Go get the rest."

"There's more?"

"Lots more, Frank, hundreds more."

"I don't know. That was pretty scary today. I think we were lucky. It's not likely we'll be that lucky again. I can't keep falling and knocking people down."

"You won't have to, Frank, that was today only. No, there are too many coins to get out that way. This time we'll try something else. Anyway, I want you to know how much I appreciated your help. Without you, Frank, I couldn't have done it."

"Of course, master, you know you can count on me."

"Now, Frank, you know you're a free man. You no longer *have* to do anything I ask. Nor should you call me anything but 'George.' Remember, we're living in the future now."

"I know, but sometimes it's hard to change old habits. I don't mind doing anything you ask. You've been good to me . . . George."

"Well, we've always been friends, Frank, and now we need each other more than ever! With Martha's help, these coins will do more than make us rich men. They will give us our freedom back. Palidore and these people are nice, but we'll soon find a way to support ourselves, and get away from here."

"I hope you are right . . . no, I *know* you are right."

***

The following morning Frank and George teamed up to work on their education modules while Palidore held a meeting in his office with Lynn, Martha, and Susan.

"Last night was not too restful for me," Palidore said, as he opened the meeting. "A lot happened yesterday, and the more I thought about it, the more questions I had. So, maybe today we should think through the events together. I've jotted down some questions as they occurred to me, then went back and put them in the proper time-ordered sequence. Are you guys, okay with that approach?" Everyone nodded, so he threw out the first question

"Why did George get so upset with the window washers? Really, if he had a gun, he all but admitted, he would have shot them."

Lynn responded to the question, first. "We see and judge things by the standards of today. George sees the same things but judges them by standards that prevailed in *his* time. No matter how much we try to educate him, or Frank, we most likely won't be able to alter much of their previously established baseline values.

"Please note that Frank had no adverse reaction to George suggesting the use of a gun as appropriate for someone damaging your car. He seemed to accept George's reaction as correct. Obviously, it wasn't the same for us. Going forward, we will need to anticipate better how someone from his time will react to certain circumstances."

"I suppose you're right," Palidore said. "He definitely did not like the fact that the window washers were forcing their services on us. So, when he saw it happen again, he took matters into his own hands, getting out to confront them."

"Correct. He did that because he knew from your previous conversation with him that you weren't likely to prevent it from happening, which brings us to another point worth noting that George seems compelled to take charge, especially when others don't. Perhaps that's why he was such a great leader in his day. Frank, however, seems to wait for directions before acting out, much like a servant in his day," Susan responded.

"I don't think Frank will ever act without direction unless he is forced to, I'm afraid. It's clear that his relationship with George is special, but behind it all, he still sees himself as subservient to him."

"And I don't think George is likely to take orders well," Lynn added. "He is a true Alpha male, and accustomed to being in charge."

TRANSFORMING GEORGE WASHINGTON

"Well, how are we supposed to control him?" Palidore asked.

"We're not," Lynn said. "The best we can do is try to show him when he's wrong as you did yesterday. You took command, Palidore, and he seemed to respect that."

"Okay, now we have the 'official' trip to Mount Vernon planned for this coming weekend," Palidore continued. "The Board is aware of it, and Sarah's son is going to be our guide. So, in light of what just happened, do you think we should cancel the trip?"

"I don't believe we can," Martha said. "I mean, what would you tell the Board and Dr. Miles? Besides George clearly feels he's earned it."

"Well, if he's 'earned it,' he's more or less already paid himself. He and Frank just took off and went on their own. So maybe he won't feel it's so important to go back again so soon. Martha, he seems comfortable talking to you. Why don't you ask him if it would be all right to postpone the trip for a few weeks?"

"A few weeks?" she asked. "Why so long?"

Palidore and Lynn locked eyes upon hearing the question. Lynn gave Palidore a nod as if to say, 'tell them.' Palidore repositioned himself before answering.

"Okay, this brings me to the big issue that has been troubling me. Lynn and I are supposed to be leaving for Brussels next week to speak at the International Cryogenics Symposium. We have known about this for several months, now, but considering what has been going on here, we weren't sure if we should go. Actually, they've invited me to speak and are paying for me and a guest. Not knowing all this was going to occur I accepted and invited Lynn to go with me. As I've said, at the time, neither of us knew what we would be dealing with here. It's actually quite an honor, but I just don't know about going now."

"That's wonderful news, Palidore," Martha jumped in.

"What'll your topic be?"

"Well, that's the problem. As you know, I did a paper some time ago that none of the publications picked up on concerning our collection of ancient bodies. Seems it caught *someone's* attention and I was invited to speak on the possibility of reviving one of them. So, now, if I go, I cannot tell them: 'Yes, not only is it possible, but we've done it!' I really think I might just have to think of an excuse not to go."

"You should go," Susan said. "You can always talk hypothetically about the possibility, and the efforts you've taken to preserve the inventory of ancient bodies we have on hand without discussing what has actually occurred.

"Later, in the event it becomes necessary, or desirable, to reveal the identities of Frank and George, it may be helpful to have already set the stage," Susan finished. "Those are just my thoughts."

"Well, if we go, that will leave you and Martha here alone. As you know Renee is on maternity leave right now."

"True," Martha spoke, "but we can be in constant contact with you. I mean you won't be *unavailable*, will you?"

"No, of course not," Palidore said. "So, Martha, you agree? This would be a lot on your shoulders."

"I'm sure we can handle it, I mean, what could go wrong?"

There was pregnant pause followed by simultaneous laughter.

"So, you're willing to take charge?"

"Absolutely. And to get back to your original question, I'll talk to George about postponing this weekend's trip."

While Palidore seemed pleased, he did an 'about-face.' "No, I've changed my mind about that. I think we should proceed with the trip as planned. If everything goes okay, I'll feel better about leaving for a couple of weeks. I'd rather have that behind us before we leave."

"What about their authentic identifications?" Susan asked.

"Oh yes, I'm glad you asked," Lynn said. "We've taken care of all that. The documents we've previously given them are now valid, and here are their packets containing everything else they'll need, including a biographical background on each of them which they will need to memorize. You should go over the other documents and information with them so they can begin to assume and feel comfortable about their new identities prior to the trip."

"Very well, then, it's decided," Palidore said. "The trip to Mount Vernon is on, and so is our trip to Brussels. Thank you all. This has been very helpful."

It most certainly has, Martha thought.

Chapter 25

The following day, Martha and Susan met with George and Frank in the conference room. They all sat at one end of the huge conference table. While the table was not lit from beneath, and no lights were on in the room, still the morning sun was providing plenty of light in the room. Frank and George were going over new packets of information containing their altered identities.

"So, here is your birth certificate, Frank," Susan said. "As you can see, it says you were born on the 9th day of April 1981, in New York City. Your parents are listed as 'unknown' as you were left on the steps of St. Eugene's Catholic church.

"Since it was a Thursday, and you were obviously of African American descent, the priest gave you the last name 'Khamisi,' which, as you have told us, means 'born on Thursday.' The document also says you were educated at the church which had a parochial school. Then you set out on your own after finishing high school there. We picked that particular church since it no longer exists.

"Now, this other document is a copy of your high school diploma. Your bio says that you made your way to Greensville County, Virginia, where you found employment doing farm work for Mr. George Washington, who was known at that time as George Walsh. George had a small peanut farming operation there and after a couple of years, he sold his farm, and you and George moved to West Virginia where you worked in a remote part of the state near Franklin. That also happens to be near the George Washington National Forest.

There, you and George began a small timber business known as WTS, LLC, which stands for Washington Timber Services. We created the LLC in Delaware, but had it registered in the records of the West Virginia Corporation Commission. The address of the business is a post office box at a UPS store in Marlington, West Virginia."

"Won't people there say they don't know me?" Frank asked.

"No, because we say that you had little local interaction as you primarily traveled around searching for stands of timber which might have been of interest for other timber companies to buy. So, basically, you are timber brokers with mostly out-of-the-area clients. You can embellish the story as you like but just remember to be consistent," Susan said.

"Also, you were not in the service, have never married, and have no children. In other words, you have pretty much been off the grid," she looked at him. "Anyway, that is an overview. Other details are spelled out here in the summary. Once you've memorized everything, you should dispose of this print copy. We have a social security card in there for you, and our experts have successfully planted a couple of years' worth of tax returns on record. We've also purchased some health insurance so anyone can verify a paper trail. It's a major medical policy which means it only pays the big bills." She looked at him again.

"Are you understanding all of this?"

"Yes," he said. 'But I'll have to think about it some more."

"Of course," she said. "Now, in time, you'll want to get a better policy. We've created a brief medical history for you which is also listed here, and you will find supporting documents also among the papers." She stopped for a moment.

"I know you'll have questions, but for now, I want Martha to update George on his identity."

Martha gave George a brief smile and began explaining his new identity: "George, you've just heard the part about owning a small farm in Greensville County, Virginia, and then selling it. We were able to check the records in the clerk's office there and found that there actually was a small hundred-acre farm on Brink Road, which was once owned by a George Walsh. He only kept it for a couple of years. Then, he sold the farm to a James Ferguson who owns it to this day and has made it a part of his large farming operation. The real George Walsh was not into farming much and was an absentee owner since he inherited the land from his father. The best we could find out about Mr. Walsh was that he went to France as a young man after graduating from college. He returned for a couple of years after his father's death which is when he inherited the farm. His parents were divorced, and his mother continued to live on the farm until her death. That's when George Walsh sold the farm. We've taken his social security number for you as well as his birth date of January 4th, 1980. Sorry it couldn't have been on July 4th, but it is what it is. That's the best we could do.

"We *were* able to successfully create a court record of a name change from 'George Walsh' to 'George 'Washington' which happened to be George Walsh's mother's maiden name. We learned of her maiden name from divorce records on file in the courthouse. As disclosed in the name-change petition, the change was requested by 'your mother,' and made with your consent, to preserve her family's name since there were no other decedents. You were in college when this occurred. We have the name change order being signed by Judge James Luke. The state of Virginia granted your request, as it always does in these situations, to issue you a new birth certificate showing your new name as 'George Washington,'" Martha said and looked at him searching for the paper. "It's in your packet."

"Thank you," George said.

"In any event," Martha continued, "we have now re-scripted Mr. Walsh's life to show that instead of going back to France, as he actually did, we have him leaving Greensville County as 'George Washington' and going to Franklin, West Virginia. Our research indicates the *real* George Walsh died in France last year, therefore, we need not worry about his unexpected return.

"In your packet, you will also find a college degree from East Carolina University. It has the name 'George Walsh' on it, but shows you earned Bachelor of Science degree from the School of Education. So, if asked about this, you can just say you thought it would be easier to finish school with your first name since that's how you began your college education. Sorry, we couldn't change your name on the degree because it's something that really happened, so we just left it alone."

"You've just stolen it for me," George said.

"That's about right," Martha said, looking at him. "In any event, you can pull for the Pirate football team as East Carolina University is your alma mater now. We actually don't know how active George Walsh was at ECU but would suggest you *not* attend reunions or other events on the off chance that an old classmate might want to look you up.

"So that about summarizes it," Martha said. "As Susan mentioned, all other details are in the packet for you to learn and memorize. Any questions?"

George slipped everything back into his packet. "I can't believe you can do this. Are you sure this will work?"

"Absolutely, as long as you learn the details and stick to the script concerning your 'past,' these documents will allow you to have a future."

"One more thing?"

"What is that?"

"Are we going back to Mount Vernon on Saturday?"

"Well, now that you have changed the subject completely, I am pleased to tell you that the trip is still on."

George and Frank stood up which prompted the two women to stand also. Smiles and high-fives made the rounds. As they were leaving George whispered to Martha.

"We need to talk."

Chapter 26

When Martha knocked on George's partially opened door, it swung open. George and Frank were at their monitors but swiveled around when they heard her knock. George motioned her to come over and have a seat. She closed the door behind her and pulled up a chair near the two men.

"You wanted to talk?"

"Yes, indeed. Frank and I need to make plans for our visit to Mount Vernon this coming weekend."

"What kind of plans?" Martha asked. "It's all pretty much scripted. Dr. Miles' son, Jason, will be our guide and several board members will be going along. As you know, they're all aware of your true identity and are looking forward to seeing you back at your home. However, I must caution you to be careful not to offer too much information about the place since the guide, and everyone else, are totally unaware."

"Well, that's not exactly what I am talking about," George said, looking at her. "I'm talking about retrieving the coins."

"Oh, my god, George. You can't be serious about extracting the coins this weekend with all these people joining us?"

"No . . . well, not exactly."

"What do you mean 'not exactly?'"

"There's something that needs to be done in order to prepare for the time we actually retrieve the coins."

"Okay," Martha said, "I'm listening."

"On our last trip, we had a guide who had a small plastic card on a string around her neck. Other guides also had them. One side had a sketch of the main house on it and the reverse just had a bunch of little lines. We didn't actually see her *use* it, but Frank saw a guide with another group hold one up to a door of an outer building to gain access."

"So, what's your point?"

"I think one of those cards could be useful later. There is a tunnel directly under the stables that I will need to visit one day soon. If we could access the tunnel *from* the stables, that would help immensely. When the tunnel system was built, its intended use was as an emergency exit. One passageway would take us to the river where we could escape by boat, and another would take us to the stables where we could escape with our horses over land. In any event, we might need your help with the computer. Frank and I have tried to lookup more about the cards, but we don't understand how to work this 'Internet' thing very well. It seems all we can see is information previously stored on the computer by Lynn. Can you help us?"

"Sure, but I already know a little about those cards. The combination of lines you saw is referred to as a 'bar code.'" Martha looked around the room and saw a box of donuts. She picked it up and turned it over, then held it out for the men to see.

"Here, look at this. Almost every product has a bar code on it. The way it operates is that when the code is passed in front of a bar code *reader* it identifies the product,"

"I was not aware that you could use a bar code for entry access, but I suppose it could be used for that purpose. If the door has a reader, then the bar code would be the password that would allow the door to open. Anyway, I'm surprised to see it used that way as it is not too secure of a system. Do you still need me to research it further?"

"Maybe, but what I'm wondering is whether a picture of a bar code will work as well as the original?"

"Now that I can't tell you, but we could experiment by taking a picture of the bar code for these donuts, then we could go down to the café to see if it can be read."

"Great idea, let's do it!"

"Well . . . we can't go now. People are still in the building, so we'll have to try it later when the building is vacant. But where are you going with all this?"

"I assume that our guide on Saturday will be wearing a badge. At some point, Dr. Miles will want to introduce him to us, and I thought I would hand you my phone and ask you to take our picture. You could gather us together and tend to us for the picture. Meanwhile, you'll make sure the correct side of the card is exposed. Then, when we print the picture later, we can create our own card to use, if you know what I mean."

Martha sat there for a moment thinking: *Is this clever or devious?* She wasn't sure herself.

"Well, at least you are not asking me to try and steal one."

"No, no, of course not."

"I guess this is all part of a greater plan. Do you want to update me on your overall idea?" Martha asked.

George looked at Frank hoping for an expression of agreement. But Frank simply hunched his shoulders.

"Sure. In order to retrieve the quantity of coins remaining, we'll need to make an 'official' trip, and two 'unofficial' ones."

"Will the 'unofficial trips' be in addition to this Saturday's trip with the MCS group?"

"Correct. The only objective on Saturday is to get a picture of the bar code card. On the next 'unofficial trip' we'll use the bar code card at the stable to ensure we have access to the tunnel system."

"You didn't have the card last time, so why now?"

"Because last time, I came from the house into the tunnel. But this time, I need to enter the tunnel from the stable. You see, there are two tunnels underground with one branching off the other. The main tunnel goes from the house directly to the river. The other tunnel branches off the main tunnel and travels to the stable, but also continues on a little further to the mausoleum." George stopped for a moment to see if Martha was comprehending him.

"Okay, I'm following it so far, go on," she said.

"The coins are extremely heavy and it would be very difficult to carry so many bags out undetected. We could never carry them through the house. However, if we use the tunnels, we can get the coins, now hidden under the mausoleum, and take them back out to the main tunnel to the Potomac River. That is exactly how my faithful Major Hudson was able to get my body secretly out of the mausoleum."

"So, if that's going to be your route, why do you need access to the stables now?" she asked.

"I'm getting to that," George said. "You see, the stable has an entrance to the tunnel which I should be able to access unseen. From there, I plan to walk back toward the main branch and out to the river to find the exit hatch. It used to be marked by a tree which is no longer there and the exit is all overgrown. So, I thought, by walking the tunnel and finding the exit to the river, I could poke through to the surface. There, I plan to leave a marker which will help us find it again when we actually attempt to acquire and transport the coins by the river."

"Assuming you and/or Frank can get to the end of the tunnel, I can give you a GPS marker which will allow you to find the spot later with pinpoint accuracy. Then, you won't have to actually 'poke' through the surface."

"You see Frank," George said looking over at him, "I told you she would be invaluable!" Turning back to Martha, he asked, "You can do that?"

"Sure, it's no problem. But I'm still in the dark as to how this all comes together."

"Well, the coins will be retrieved during our last trip through the tunnel from the river. That's when we'll take them across the Potomac at night. Having the opening to the tunnel marked beforehand will make it easier to know where to station a boat. We can tie it off in preparation, and once we know where the tunnel exits, we'll be able to enter, obtain the coins and bring them back out to the boat and make our get-away.."

"Oh, I don't know about that. This is a pretty populated area and there may be other boats out; maybe even security forces of some sort. They're always patrolling."

"That's why we'll need to go during a storm, if possible. A storm will keep people off the river and give us the cover we need."

"I can't believe you've planned all this."

"My dear Martha, during the Revolutionary War I was forced to plan many military operations that were much more complicated than this. "

Martha looked at him in silence. His comment reminded her of just who this man really was . . . a true commander . . . a general. and she was in awe of him once again.

"However, we do have one problem," George said, "but maybe you'll have an answer."

"All right, what's the problem?"

"The access to the tunnel is an old iron door which will probably be almost impossible to open, especially in the rain at night. Any thoughts?"

"Hmm, you could use a motorized winch," she said, glad, once again, that Stanley had educated her on some practical sides of life. "Here, maybe I can show you one." Martha took over George's computer and found a winch system shown on a truck. She played them the video.

"Wow . . . or should I say, 'holy shit!' That would be fantastic if you could get one of those attached to a boat."

"Oh, you can get them," Martha said. "Along with a small electrical motor for a boat." She tapped a few more keys and several items displayed for sale on the Internet.

Frank and George smiled at each other. "Then that's it, except for one thing."

"And what would that be?"

"We'll need to leave on a moment's notice. Especially if our trip is going to be dependent on the weather, and Palidore keeps a pretty close eye on us."

Martha smiled, paused, then said, "Depending on how all this lines up, that may not be as difficult as you may think. I was waiting for Palidore to tell you, but now that you've brought this up, I might as well let you know that Palidore and Lynn will be out of the country at a conference for two weeks starting next week. So, Susan and I will be in charge. I think he wants to present the news to you himself, so please do not let on that you already know."

"No, of course not," George agreed immediately.

"Wonderful," Frank finally said. Until now, he hadn't talked at all. George stood and began walking around the room, talking out loud, not directing his comments to anyone.

"Yes, that should allow us a chance to put our plan into action. Now, we'll need to work out the fine details which may take some time. I need to think this through, but I may need more help."

"Are you talking to me?" Martha asked.

"Just thinking out loud, but 'yes,' I suppose I was thinking of you, and Frank, as I was speaking. Can we meet again, soon?"

"Sure, how about tomorrow? That will be one day before our visit to Mount Vernon."

"Yes, tomorrow will be fine," George said. "My room at nine a.m.?"

"Tomorrow morning," Martha said and rose to leave while giving him a smile. "See you then."

Chapter 27

Palidore sat at his desk and motioned for the girls to come in. Lynn, Martha, and Susan entered the room. He asked if anyone wanted a soda or something to drink but they all declined as they took their seats at the small table. Palidore came around his desk to take the remaining seat.

"Thanks again for joining me. Hopefully, this won't take too long. As you know, day after tomorrow, we will once again venture out to Mount Vernon, and I am hopeful this trip will be a little less eventful than the last. It looks like the weather is going to cooperate, but it will be a bit cold. Anyway, I thought we could just get together and go over a few things to be sure we've thought of everything." There were nods of agreement.

"So, have our gentlemen assumed their new identities, yet?" Palidore continued.

"Yes, most certainly," Lynn said, "and they've also worked on embellishing their stories a bit. George has studied the history of his newly acquired alma mater, ECU, and events that happened during the time he was supposed to be attending. Frank has looked into Saint Eugene's Catholic School and done a background investigation, so he's up to date, too.

"They've memorized their social security numbers, cell phone numbers, etc. We've even set up email accounts for them and hooked them up with some online accounts and apps. I feel comfortable they can handle things now."

TRANSFORMING GEORGE WASHINGTON

"I wish George had been willing to take another name, though," Palidore said. "I mean anytime he's introduced as 'George Washington,' eyebrows are going to be raised and comments made; but I guess if he can handle it, what can I say?

"So, about our trip. It has now become a crowded tour. The entire board is going. Dr. Mile's son, Jason, is going to be our guide but, of course, he knows nothing about the true identities of George and Frank. I have secured a luxury bus and driver for transportation, so we won't have to worry about another issue concerning street window washers, so that little episode won't repeat itself.

"Even so," he continued, "I want it understood that we are to stay together and the four of us need to remain close to George and Frank at all times. I've instructed the board that we'll be out in public, therefore, they must not hover around the two men asking questions that might compromise their true identities. Each of you must act as buffers to help ensure this does not occur.

"Another thing, no pictures, please!" Palidore seemed adamant which made Martha wonder how she was going to pull off the photo George wanted her to take.

"I don't want George's image floating around the Internet. Is that understood?"

"Well, about that," Martha interrupted. "Perhaps we could get *one* group shot, maybe at Mount Vernon, before we all start out, I think the board members might each like a copy."

"I don't know," Palidore said. "Let me think about that. I'll let you know. Now, we'll have a restroom on the bus, so there'll be no need for any bathroom breaks. Sandwiches, drinks, and snacks will also be provided, so no lunch or dinner breaks either. We'll even have beer and wine available for the trip home. Let's just go there, take the tour, and get back. I want this to be as uneventful as possible."

"Where will everyone assemble?" Susan asked.

"Here, at 8:30 a.m. in the conference room," Palidore said. "I've assigned seats on the bus for the four of us, George and Frank. Everyone else will enjoy open seating. We have our own name tags which will be distributed in the conference room. Any other questions?"

None of the women said anything.

"Okay, then let me update you on our trip to Brussels. I've got real mixed emotions about taking the trip at this time, but it appears that it's really going to happen. We were scheduled to leave next Saturday, one week after this week's trip to Mount Vernon. However, a subcommittee has asked me to participate in a pre-conference planning session. Therefore, Lynn and I will actually be leaving *this* Saturday right after the Mount Vernon tour, which means we will now be gone for three weeks instead of two.

"We will, however, be available at all times via cell phone, text messages, or email. But please remember, we'll be seven hours ahead of your time. So, the best time to reach us will be between 11:00 a.m. and 2:00 p.m. your time which will be 6:00 p.m. to 9:00 p.m. Brussels' time. That way, we won't actually be in the conference or meetings at the time you might call. However, let's agree that if there are no phone calls, then I can assume everything is okay. Remember, we're counting on you to keep everything running as smoothly as possible in our absence. Is there anything we need to cover?"

"Yes," Martha said. "Stop worrying! We can handle things here. It's important that you go, but also that you take a breather from all you've been through. Just enjoy yourself. Susan and I appreciate the confidence you've placed in us. We'll be fine. Enjoy your trip."

"Thank you, Martha. We'll try to take your advice, but you'll be in our thoughts every day. I just hope you won't need to be in our prayers, too.

The comment brought laughter from everyone.

"Now, let's focus on getting through this Mount Vernon trip. After that, there won't be any more trips, at least not until we get back. So, if there are no takers for a nightcap, I guess this meeting is adjourned."

***

Martha's next meeting was in George's room where Frank was already waiting.

"Have you secured the winch yet?" George asked her.

"No, but it's been ordered, and should be delivered to my home in Georgetown sometime next week. I can have it affixed to the dingy my late husband and I have on our yacht. We keep the yacht at the Mount Vernon Yacht Club which is, as the name suggests, very close to Mount Vernon," she said, enjoying the approval on the men's faces.

"If you weren't going to do this so late at night, you could have just taken off from the club while it was still open. But we can move it before nightfall and moor it somewhere across the river by Piscataway Park. The dingy is equipped with a small electric motor for navigation. It can also be used to operate the winch," she hesitated.

"But aren't we getting a little ahead of ourselves? We haven't figured out how to get the photo of Jason's badge or settled on a plan for the trip to find the tunnel exit and install the GPS marker."

"True," George said, "but all the equipment needs to be in place. I am so very pleased that you have taken care of so much, and I don't really know why there will be any problem getting the photo of the badge, we've already discussed that."

"Well, Palidore has made it pretty clear there are to be no photos taken. He's concerned about one being uploaded to the Internet. I tried to get him to allow one group shot, but he's only considered it, and just told me no."

"What is his thinking? I mean why would he object?"

"To quote him: 'Remember, George chose to keep his real name, and even though it's a fairly common name I can see the headlines – 'George Washington visits Mount Vernon.' He said it would raise too much attention. With his going away, he just wants to be cautious. I don't blame him."

George was quiet in thought. "Okay, no pictures of me or the group, but why don't you offer to take a picture of Dr. Miles with her son, Jason? Take the picture and tell her you will send it to her. I'll bet she'll jump at the chance."

"Maybe so. We'll just have to see how this all works out and what opportunities I get."

"Well, were you able to conduct the test?"

"What test?"

"You were going to take a picture of the donut box's barcode, then see if the cafeteria could scan your photo."

"Oh, that! Yes, I did, and it worked fine. I even tried different sizes of the bar code and they all worked. So, if we get the barcode photographed, I'm convinced it will work. But I am still amazed they use that technology. I mean that is such an insecure system, surely they wouldn't use it to secure anything very important."

"Yes, well for whatever reason it works in our favor. We know the card works at the stable door. So, if we can make ourselves an access card from the photograph, it will be easier to reach the tunnel from the stables. If that doesn't work, we'll have to try going through the house again which will be much more difficult. Now, how about that GPS device?"

"That part was easy; I have it across the street at my flat. So, any time after Palidore and Lynn leave on their trip, we'll need to get together so I can show you how it works. But there is something else we need to discuss, something that could cause us a real problem."

Frank and George exchanged concerned looks.

"What would that be?" George asked.

"Well, you don't realize it, but a tracking device was placed into the back of your legs. You each have one. They are normally dormant, but Palidore or Lynn can activate them at any time. Once activated, they can monitor you on their cell phones from wherever they are; they'll know *exactly* where you are at any time.

A flash of anger appeared on George's face which Martha

picked up on as she quickly continued.

"They were initially installed for your own protection in the event either of you got lost or became separated from us. But they can also be used to keep track of you while they are on their trip. I thought you should know."

Both men pulled up their pant legs and examined their calves and skin. Frank got down on one knee and ran his finger over George's calf.

"Found it!" he called out, feeling a hard spot. "See if you can find mine."

George returned the favor and nodded when he made his discovery.

Once they knew where the devices were located, they let their pant legs drop and sat back down. George remained silent, deep in thought.

"We'll just cut them out," Frank blurted.

"Exactly! You're exactly right, Frank."

"Wait!" Martha said, "Think about it. I'm not sure who we can get to do that. We can't exactly explain how the chip got in there, or even why we want it out."

"We'll cut them out ourselves, or you can do it."

"Me?! Oh, god, no! I can't do that . . . no way."

"Okay, Frank and I will do it as soon as they leave town."

"I can't believe this!" Martha said. "You're going to just take a knife and start cutting on each other? What about stitches, or infection?"

"Don't worry, we've had some experience with wounds during the war. But you're right. We'll need a few supplies which you can get for us to have on hand. But, first, tell me, how *precise* are these? I mean, if they are turned on, would they know we are in this room?"

"No, more like they would know you are somewhere in this building."

"Oh, that's good. Then once these devices are out, we can leave them in our rooms and Palidore and Lynn will think we are still somewhere in the building," George said. "That will work fine for our purposes."

"But what about Susan?" Martha asked.

"What about her?"

"Well, she doesn't know about any of this. Without her, we'll have to be really careful. But with her in on everything, it could work out smoothly. Do you think we can trust her enough to bring her in?" Martha asked.

"I don't know, but I must confess I have had some misgivings about keeping her in the dark. I believe we can absolutely trust her to do what she says she'll do. The problem is I don't know what she will say. I just don't. I feel like she will want to do what she thinks is best for Frank," George said. "So, Frank, you've spent a lot of time with her. What do you think?"

"I think if she knows this is something I am going to do with, or without her, that she will reluctantly agree to help, but she will try and counsel against doing it, first," he said.

"Is that something you want to handle with her, or do you think we should be there when you talk with her?" Martha asked.

"I think I should handle it on my own, but not until Palidore and Lynn leave on their trip." He looked at George. "I might need one of your coins though."

"Yes, of course." George stood up and retrieved both shoeboxes from his wardrobe. He took one coin out and handed it to Frank. Then, he removed the shoes from one box which allowed enough room for him to consolidate all the coins into it. Then he handed the heavy box to Martha.

"You said you would put these in your safe."

"Yes, I'll take care of it," she said. "But getting back to Susan. I guess she will have to remain in the dark about our plans until *after* our trip to Mount Vernon tomorrow." George and Frank agreed.

"Okay then," Martha said, "We're agreed that Susan will be taken into our confidence, but not until after tomorrow's trip. Then, Frank will talk to her."

He looked at George. "You know George in a way it seems like everything about our country has changed, yet in many other ways it appears that nothing has changed at all."

Chapter 28

"Hello, and welcome to Mount Vernon, home of our first president, George Washington. My name is Jason, and I will be your guide today. I've looked over the list and see someone here who has the name of 'George Washington.' Where is he? Please raise your hand."

George looked at Martha as if to question whether he should show himself. She nodded, and he came forward.

"Well, Mr. Washington, it is indeed my pleasure to meet you. But unfortunately, I must inform you that this magnificent place is not actually *yours*. It belonged to our first president who acquired it in 1761. But don't feel too badly, so far, you are the fifth 'George Washington' I have had the pleasure of showing this beautiful home to and none of them owned it either. However, for today only, we will pretend that this lovely place is all yours."

Only the bus driver laughed. All the board members remained silent and focused on George's facial expression wondering what he was thinking.

"Oh boy, this is going to be one of those deadpan groups," Jason muttered to himself. But outloud, he said, "Well then, please follow me to the home. Right this way."

Once everyone arrived in front of the house, Jason stopped and turned to address the group again. George and Frank had positioned themselves near the front where they were hoping to get a photo of the backside of Jason's badge. He was wearing it around his neck, but, occasionally, it flipped over as he walked.

"Before we go inside, let me give you a brief history of the ownership of this beautiful estate: George Washington's great grandfather, John Washington, was a successful farmer in the area, and in 1674, he and Nicholas Spencer were awarded a land grant of 5000 acres from Lord Culpeper who was the proprietor of this region.

"Upon John's death in 1677, the estate was left to Lawrence Washington, George's grandfather, who upon his death in 1698 devised it to his daughter Mildred Washington. Mildred later sold it to Augustine Washington in 1726, George's father. Augustine then deeded it to his son, Lawrence Washington, George's older half-brother who owned it until he died of tuberculosis in July of 1752. In his will, he left it to his only daughter, Sara, and to her children. If she had no children, then it would go back to Lawrence's wife for life. As luck would have it, Sara died childless two years later, so it went to Lawrence's wife, Anne Washington for her lifetime, and then to George Washington. Therefore, when she died in 1761, it finally belonged to our first president, George Washington."

Jason looked at George with a humorous look on his face and said, "But then you knew all that, didn't you Mr. Washington?"

George seemed a bit agitated and quickly retorted, "Well, actually, after Lawrence's death, and *before* Sara passed away, Lawrence's wife, Anne, remarried and no longer lived here, so she *leased* it to me. Therefore, I was actually in control of the entire estate for many years before she died, and the title finally vested solely with me. And you failed to mention that I already owned other adjacent parcels of land such as the parcel I acquired from John Posey in 1760."

The directors who knew more than they could let on, all laughed. But Palidore, Lynn, Martha, and Susan were all in a state of shock at George's outburst.

For a split second, Jason was also caught off guard. Then he assumed this 'George Washington' was testing him, and quickly responded. "Okay, I see someone else is a student of history. Very good! But, I guess, if you have a name like 'George Washington' you would need to know your stuff. You are, of course, exactly right. I'll try to be a little more thorough going forward. Now let's proceed into the home."

As they entered Mount Vernon, Palidore whispered to Lynn, "I don't know if our leaving is such a good idea. I mean George and Frank keep going off script."

"Well, hopefully, they'll just stay at the MCS building as promised," Lynn said. "Besides, I'm not sure they will ever be a hundred percent ready. Anyway, fortunately, Martha and Susan are spending most of their time with them now and will help keep things under control"

"I guess you're right, but after that little outburst, I'm a little concerned."

Frank was now walking alongside Sarah Miles who was staying next to Jason. He noticed that when Jason turned around to address everyone in the central passageway, the badge around his neck flipped over, displaying the bar code.

Perfect, he thought. He and George had practiced using the camera feature on their cell phones and he was ready. "Sara, jump in there next to Jason and let me get your picture."

"We aren't..."

"No, *you* aren't, but *I* can . . . now, look at me you two." They stood close and smiled at Frank. He quickly snapped the picture.

"I'll send you a copy."

"Okay, thanks," Sarah smiled.

George was taking it all in and smiled. Now for the first time, he was beginning to relax. *Mission one, successfully accomplished,* he thought. *Good for Frank.*

The rest of the tour went smoothly. George had worn a light blue button-down shirt, a pair of nicely creased blue jeans, and white tennis shoes. He had grown fond of these modern-day blue jeans and soft button-up shirts. Frank had on khaki pants and a purple sweatshirt emblazoned with the words, "Howard University" on its front. Martha and Susan wore slacks and sweaters. Everyone seemed to be enjoying the tour and the day. The weather was perfect.

Inside the mansion, George made his way over to Martha and commented, "Look what they've done to the place." She wasn't sure if he was pleased or not.

The walls in the small dining area were colored the beautiful green he remembered from his old days of living there. *My Martha would be so pleased,* he thought, *I wonder what she would think of all that I've been going through now.* He missed having her with him and wondered what it would be like if she could be there next to him. *Wouldn't that be something?*

A couple hours later, after everyone had roamed the grounds at their leisure, Palidore stood by the bus, waiting for his group to assemble as planned. The driver of the transportation bus, provided by Potomac Premiere Bus Service, was waiting with him. They had asked everyone to be at the bus by 2:00 p.m. and it was close to that time now. The board members began arriving and climbing into the bus for the ride home.

On the bus, Frank took a seat next to Sarah Miles for their return trip. She was one of the few people he felt comfortable talking to and he yearned to talk with someone, anyone outside his closely guarded handlers. "Tell me about Jason. How did he get this job?"

"Jason actually had trouble settling down and focusing on a profession. He's attended three separate universities but never obtained a degree. History was always his favorite subject, but you can't make a living just learning history."

"No? Look at him now."

"Well, he's read almost everything possible about George Washington and when he visited Mount Vernon, he loved the history of it. That's what makes him a good guide. Anyway, after his first visit, he looked online and noticed 'Career Opportunities.' Everything more or less fell into place from there."

"Does he like his job?"

"I think so. He talks about all the people he meets and especially enjoys talking to foreigners, most notably, female ones." They laughed at that last comment.

"So how long has he been doing this?"

"I'd say . . . almost three years now."

"So, then he *has* settled down and found a permanent occupation."

"I certainly hope not," Sarah said. "He doesn't make enough money doing this to even pay for rent. He has to share a place with three other guys. If his father and I didn't supplement his wages, he would be a street person."

"If the pay is so little, how do they find people to take these jobs?"

"They're mostly students doing it while they're in school for extra spending money. Jason is the only one who seems to think it's a lasting profession."

Sarah felt comfortable talking to Frank and wanted so much to ask him questions about his past but knew she couldn't. Yet, she found it difficult to imagine that a man of his intellect could ever have been a slave. Clearly, there was a friendship between him and George that she found amazing.

Apparently, all slaves were not equal or even treated equally, she thought. *If only Jason could know who this man was, it might change things,* she reasoned. *But that's impossible.*

Chapter 29

The tour bus pulled into the alleyway alongside the MCS building and discharged all passengers. The three women, Palidore, George, and Frank went to Palidore's office to talk since Palidore and Lynn were leaving shortly for Brussels.

"Well, that trip certainly went better than our last one," Palidore quipped. Everyone laughed knowing it was true.

"Lynn and I will be leaving soon, and I ask everyone to please stay focused and stay *home* until our return. I'm sure our two recent outings to Mount Vernon have whetted your appetites for more adventures, but in an effort to keep you from becoming bored, Lynn has set some educational goals for you to achieve in our absence.

"We've sent them to Martha and Susan via email. Each item will help you prepare for your next outing when we return. Should you achieve these goals ahead of schedule, then your next adventure will include a trip by airplane, boat, or train," Palidore said then paused, expecting to see a display of jubilation, but only Susan seemed mildly surprised. Palidore was disappointed there wasn't more of a reaction but continued talking.

"Well, hopefully, that will be enough motivation for everyone. Again, Lynn and I will be available on our cell phones in the event you need to make contact. Please remember the 'best time window to call' we've discussed, but if there is an emergency, call anytime. Now, let's have a parting toast that our Brussels trip will be successful."

Palidore went to his cadenza to prepare drinks. The gals opted for wine while the guys went for whisky. With drinks in hand, Palidore held his up high to make the toast, but George beat him to it.

"May we *all* achieve our goals during the next couple of weeks!" Everyone touched glasses, but only a few knew the true meaning of his words.

A limo was waiting at the front of the MCI building where the driver had already loaded luggage. Palidore held the door open for Lynn, then entered the other side of the vehicle. Everyone waved as the limo pulled away.

George felt a sense of relief, almost of freedom, and looked toward Frank whose expression seemed to acknowledge a similar feeling. Upon re-entering the building, Susan said she was hungry.

"Sandwiches on the coach didn't quite do it for me; anyone up for ordering a pizza and some wings?" she asked and saw expressions of agreement. "Okay then, I'll place our order. We can meet in Palidore's office again since he has the liquid refreshments. I don't think he'll mind. Let's meet there in thirty minutes." Everyone went to freshen up in their rooms.

When Susan received an email that the delivery was at the door; she went to get it and carried it downstairs. In Palidore's office, they opened beers and made small talk about the day's activities. Looking around, Martha saw everyone draped over their chairs and finally stated the obvious.

"Gee, we all look whipped. What do you think? Shall we call it a day?" Everyone started clearing paper plates and were cleaning up when Frank broke the silence.

"Before we leave, there is something I'd like to do. It's something I've thought I would do alone, but now seems the proper time, with everyone present."

They all took seats, again, while George tried to get Frank's attention. He gave a slight shake of the head as if to say, 'not now,' but either Frank didn't see it, or he ignored it.

"Susan, what I am going to say now is something everybody

else already knows. But just so *you* know, you were *never* intentionally left out of the loop. It's just how things went. First, George told me, then Martha became aware, and quite frankly it was her suggestion that we update you as soon as possible. But then the trip came along and really, this is the first chance we've had to tell you."

"Tell me what?" Susan asked, her eyes fully engaged on Frank's every word. Frank reached into his pocket and produced a gold coin.

"Maybe this is the best place to start."

He handed the double eagle to Susan. "That is a gold double eagle coin minted in 1799. Its face value is just ten dollars, but its *actual* value is near $25,000." Susan who was examining the coin, now almost dropped it, when she heard its value. She tried giving it back to Frank.

"No, that's *yours*. It's a gift," he said.

"Oh no! I couldn't take something so valuable." But Frank refused to take it back.

"Where did you get it? And why on earth would you give it to me?" she asked.

"I am getting to that. We *can* give it to you because we already have a hundred more." Her eyes grew wide, again, as she re-examined the coin.

"And . . . and we are going to acquire about nineteen hundred more of them."

"What?! Whose coins are these?"

"They're mine," George replied.

"So, how much money are we talking about here?"

"We can't be exactly sure, but probably close to fifty million dollars."

"Holy shit!"

"Hey, she said 'holy shit' just like you did," George said.

"Yes, George," Martha said, "This is the correct time to say, 'holy shit.' In fact, I think we should all say it together, now."

"Holy shit!" everyone called out, then had a good laugh. Susan began slowly shaking her head.

"This doesn't feel right to me. Something must be wrong here."

"Nothing is wrong at all," George said. "Back in 1799, I hid 2000 gold eagle coins at my home. No one except me – and now the three of you – knows about their existence. These coins were mine, and still are mine, and I am intent on getting them all back. It is as simple as that. I am not *stealing* anything. I am just retrieving my property."

"Don't you think a hundred coins you've already retrieved that are worth . . . what did you say? Well, anyway, something over two million dollars – isn't that enough? I mean, if you're already rich, why risk everything just to get a little richer?" Susan asked.

"You mean 'a *lot* richer,' George said. "Anyway, it's not just that. I want them because I am entitled to them, and since the government has no idea they exist, they won't miss them." There was silence before Martha spoke again.

"Susan, I must confess, I was just as surprised and concerned as you when I first heard about the coins. But I think the only downside to this would be in getting caught as that would mean George and Frank's true identities would have to be revealed. Once that happens, it would be as George has said, 'there is no crime in going into one's own home and removing one's own coins,' or as the old saying goes 'no crime, no foul.'"

Susan took a moment to consider her words.

"I suppose you're right, but I don't know . . . it just doesn't feel right, and I always avoid things that don't feel right."

"So, you're not going to help us?" Frank asked

"I don't think so, I mean, I don't know. What do Palidore and Lynn say about all this?" Concerned looks shot back and forth.

"They don't know about any of it," Frank said.

"Oh, I see. So, this is sort of a covert operation."

"That would be a good term for it," Martha said.

"Well, I suppose I can't make a final decision unless I know how it's all going to go down."

Everyone looked at George.

"You started this conversation Frank, so you tell her." Frank straightened a little in his seat and noticeably took a breath.

"Well, we know where the coins are. During our first trip to Mount Vernon, George was able to break away from our tour group, with a little help from me, and secure the coins now in our possession. However, there were too many coins remaining in the sacks to get them out that way. He only stuck a few in his pockets then. So, now we have to come up with a different plan to get the rest.

"Today, we accomplished the first part of that plan. During our trip, we took a photo of the back of Jason's badge which has a bar code on it. The guides use that bar code to open some less important areas of Mount Vernon. Martha is going to make us our own badges from that photo which will help us gain access to the stable on the next trip which we are now planning. During *that* trip, George will use the access code on his badge, to go inside the stable area. From that point, he will enter a hidden tunnel system, one which leads to the hidden coins. From there, he's going to walk to another tunnel all the way to the end where a door opens out to the river. He's going to leave a GPS device so we can find the door from the outside at another time. You with me?"

"So far, but somehow, I think you're about to get to the interesting part."

"That would be correct. The final trip will be 'unofficial,' so to speak, and will depend on the weather. We intend to go to Mount Vernon by boat on a very rainy night to avoid detection. When we reach the shore, we'll locate the tunnel door from the GPS signal. After gaining access to the river tunnel entrance, George will proceed through the tunnels and obtain the coins. He will then return the same way. But there are risks involved with the plan. For example, we don't know what, if any, security cameras may be set up at night or how difficult it will be to navigate the river in a storm. The plan is still a work in progress." "Wow, I just don't know what to think," Susan said. "I've never been part of something like this. I almost wish you hadn't told me. Why *did* you anyway?"

"How could we not?" Martha said. "It looks like George and Frank are going to do this with, or without us, and failing to tell you would mean lying to you and sneaking around to get it done. Believe me, I'm not excited about this either, but if it's going to happen, then I feel a responsibility to help because I don't want either of them to get caught or into trouble, especially with Palidore and Lynn gone," she said. "In short, I think helping them is better than letting them flounder out there on their own."

"I see," Susan said. "At least that helps me understand your reasoning." She turned to George and Frank. "But why can't you two see the position you're putting Martha and me in?"

"Susan, we have a limited opportunity here, so waiting is not an option. We don't want to put either of you in harm's way, and if you feel you don't want to participate, then we'll figure it out, and proceed on our own."

"Okay, so, what do you envision my role to be in all this?" Frank smiled at her question sensing she was beginning to relent.

"Your task is the easiest. You need to stay here and be in charge, in case Palidore or Lynn should call. You just need to be our eyes and ears in case the phone rings."

"That's it?"

"That's, it, Susan."

"Oh man, I can't believe this," she was silent as she mulled everything over. "Okay, I guess I can do that much."

Chapter 30

Shortly after lunch on Monday, Martha and Susan entered George's room to set up the new educational goals when they found George and Frank wiping up a considerable amount of blood from the floor.

"What happened! Are you all right?" Susan said deeply concerned. Frank looked up, but George kept cleaning with his towel.

"Oh, we're fine; it's over now," Frank said.

"What's over? What happened here?"

"You didn't know? We needed to cut those tracker things out of our legs. Martha knew about it; we told her we were going to do it."

"Well, yes," Martha said, taken by surprise. "But I had no idea you were going to do it so *soon*. Are you okay?"

"Sure. Just a little sore," George said. "It was bloody, but look at these." In George's hand were two objects still covered in blood. Each was about an inch-long and pill-shaped.

"You didn't mix them up, did you?" Martha asked. "I mean which one is which?"

George pointed to one. "That's mine, the other is Frank's."

"How do you know?" Susan asked.

"They were dated. Frank's date was earlier than mine."

"Let me see your legs," Susan demanded. Both men hiked up one pant leg revealing a bandage wrapped tightly around each one's leg. There was some bleed-through on the white gauze, but not much.

"How did you do this? What did you use?"

Frank held up two razor blades.

"Oh, my god. You didn't use that!"

"Worked just fine," he said, "We sterilized the blades first with a match. Where should we put these, now?" George asked.

"I'll get a plastic bag; you can put them in there. Then, you should rinse off the trackers and get in the habit of keeping them in your pockets so it will look like nothing's changed," Martha said.

"When we leave for Mount Vernon, we'll leave them in our rooms somewhere, right?" George said.

"Right," Martha replied.

"You *knew* they were going to cut themselves?" Susan asked.

"Well, yes, but as I said, I didn't know *when*."

"That was pretty dangerous. You should have had a nurse or doctor do it." Martha shot her a look. "Really?"

It suddenly dawned on Susan that it could never have been done secretly.

"So, I received an email from Palidore and Lynn this morning," Martha said. "They arrived safely in Brussels at about seven a.m. our time and went straight to their hotel. It was two p.m. their time and they were trying to stay awake and acclimate themselves to their new time zone. Right now, it's about seven p.m. there. Most likely they're asleep." She looked at the two men.

"Are you in any condition to see the new educational goals they left you, or are your legs too sore? If you want, I can open the programs for you."

"Yes," Frank said immediately, and walked to his monitor, but George had a different thought.

"You can load the program if you want, but before I sit down at that machine again, I want to see the GPS device and have you explain how to activate it."

"Okay, let me download the files and get them opened first," Martha said. "Then, I'll show it to you." She sat down and began to work. When she finished with Frank's computer, she repeated the task on George's machine, then stood up.

Almost immediately, both monitors came alive with the faces of Lynn and Palidore on the screens. In shock, George and Frank both took a step back. As they did, they heard Palidore say: "Good to see you getting started on your new goals already."

Maybe their greetings are part of the program, George thought for a minute. Then he heard Lynn speak, "Our trip was good, but we were dead tired and about to turn in when our computer beeped, alerting us that you were online."

"You mean, you can *see* us as we work?" George was flabbergasted.

"Yes, we can. It's like doing 'facetime' on your cell phone. Remember how I showed you that application?"

"I remember, but I don't like this," George showed genuine anger. "I am *not a child* to be watched over as he does his homework." He glowered at the images on the screen.

Palidore realized his mood and tried smoothing things over.

"Oh, I'm sorry, George, we just thought it might be helpful for you to see us, but Martha can show you how to turn off the audio and visual if you want."

He could hear George talking to Martha.

"Martha, Palidore said you could turn off this voice and picture, come fix it."

"George, before she does that, please wait for a minute, until we finish talking," Palidore pleaded.

"What else do you want to say?" George's voice was curt. There was silence and Lynn joined Palidore onscreen.

"We just want you to know that we are always thinking about you and available, should you need us for anything," Lynn said.

"We have everything under control," Martha told her. "Please stop worrying. Get some rest and enjoy your conference. We're proud of you, guys."

"Sure thing!" Palidore said. "Okay, thanks, everyone! Have a good day and good luck with your new goals; bye for now." Their images onscreen changed to a page that said, "Special Lesson One."

Martha covered the camera eye on both monitors with a plastic slide and turned off the audio feed. "Okay, they can no longer see or hear us from your computers, but I think we better plan on accomplishing our new goals long before their return."

"We will," Frank said. "In fact, I'm going to start now."

George looked at Martha. "Are you ready to show me the GPS device?"

Martha turned to Susan. "I'm going to take George across the street to my flat and show him the GPS device. Do you mind?"

"Not at all. See you both later."

Chapter 31

Despite the cold temperature outside, Martha's condo was warm and inviting when she and George entered from the elevator. Most of the heat was emanating from the sunlight pouring through the large casement windows.

"Alexa," Martha ordered, "lower the shades." George raised his eyebrows at her invisible "servant" and shook his head in amusement. She headed toward the refrigerator to grab a bottle of chardonnay. He looked around while standing near the kitchen island. Martha held up the bottle. "Care to join me?"

"Sure, but only if it's cold."

"You remembered; I'm impressed," she laughed.

"Don't be. White wine is almost always served cold. I could have been guessing, but then . . . I wasn't. From the last time we were here together, I remember how important it was for your wine to be cold. Actually, I remember *everything* about our last visit here . . . how enjoyable it was."

Martha knew he was referring to their kiss, but rather than respond now, she just poured two healthy glassfuls and waltzed around the island to hand George his glass.

"Cheers."

"Cheers to what?" he asked.

"To us."

"I'll gladly toast to that!" he smiled at her.

They took sips and Martha peeked at him over the edge of her glass. She felt irresistibly drawn to his masculine magnetism. The way he was looking at her with rapt attention made her feel excited inside. She needed an excuse to change her thoughts.

"I think we're here to look at the GPS device."

"Oh, that, yes, the GPS device."

"Let me get it." She said and walked into her bedroom. A few minutes later, she came back with a small box. George noticed it had a smiling arrow on top. She retrieved a knife to open the package and removed the paperwork. George took it from her and looked at the invoice.

"This little thing cost nine *hundred* dollars?"

"The good ones aren't cheap."

"For that kind of money, I could have bought an entire estate," he said, but this time, hesitated to say *when*. "Did you pay for this?"

"Yes, and it's really no problem. Stanley left me plenty of money. Maybe not as much as *you're* about to have . . . but, certainly enough to live out the remainder of my life in comfort."

"So, you don't work for the income?"

"No, I enjoy what I do. It's exciting . . . being with *you* is exciting." She almost wished she hadn't been so honest about her feelings. "I love my job, more than the money."

But he had noticed what she said, and how she had said it. He was looking at her with a penetrating stare.

"I wish I could say the same," he responded. "I mean I very much enjoy being with you but unlike you, I have no job."

Martha didn't know exactly how to respond, so she changed the subject. "We'd better get back to business about the GPS." She took a small item out of the smiley box. It had a magnet on the back and a clear piece of tape coming out the side. She pointed to it. "This prevents the battery from being activated too soon,"

The device had a small screen about two inches long. She read directions out loud, then proceeded to pull the plastic tape out which caused the unit to beep three times. Two lights flashed, one red and one green.

"Why did you pull that out? Did you start it? We're at least a week away from using it."

"Well, the battery is supposed to last five years, and I need to be sure it's working."

"Apparently it is."

"Right, so now, we just need to set a codeword. What word do you want to use? You'll have to use it when you place it at the tunnel entrance."

"A code? I don't know . . . how about GW?"

"Your initials? No, I don't think so. Remember, if something goes wrong, we may never be able to retrieve this, so let's not leave any clues for someone else to find."

"Okay, then let's use 'MM'"

"MM? What does that stand for?"

"My money."

Martha rolled her eyes but proceeded to set the code.

"So, when you place this at the tunnel door, you need to hit this button once to turn it on. After it beeps, then hit this button twice. It will make this little screen light up and show you the alphabet. Keep hitting the button until you see the letter 'M.' When you see it, hit the button twice, and 'MM,' will appear. Whoops, that didn't work. It looks like they need at least a four-letter code. Any other ideas?"

"How about 'A-L-M-M'?"

"What's that supposed to mean?"

"All my money."

Martha smiled and proceeded to enter the new five-letter code while talking aloud as George watched intently over her shoulder. "Okay now that we've programmed in the letters, the code is set. So, when you place the GPS, just push this button and the GPS will be turned on. Then, pull up the alphabet and punch in your code like I showed you and that will activate the device. That's it. Got it?"

"I think so, can we try it?"

"Sure, we can turn it on and off, by using the same button." They successfully went through it twice.

"I think I may need a little more wine if that's okay."

"Oh, sure," Martha said and took both glasses to refresh their drinks. George followed her to the island and watched her pour the wine into a glass.

"Were you going to tell me how you got your job?"

"Oh, didn't I?" She handed him his glass. "Well, let's move to the couch. This may take a while." They sat together and sipped their wine quietly before Martha spoke again.

"Boy, where to start? I've actually wondered when I might be confronted with having to discuss this, but I didn't know it would be *you* who would be asking. What I'm going to tell you is the absolute truth. But I'm hopeful that we can keep this just between us. If it gets out, it could cost me my job. I'm certain about that."

George looked concerned. "Martha, you don't have to tell me anything. It was a harmless question, and I really don't need to know."

"Actually, I need to get this off my mind. It would help to tell you. It's something that has bothered me a great deal, and I want to be truthful with you. I just need your word that it will remain our secret for now."

"Certainly, you have my word."

"As you know, my husband, Stanley, is presently in the care of MCS. Well, Stanley was ill for a long time, and when his options ran out, he turned to MCS hoping that being preserved, and later revived, would occur when there was a cure for him in the future.

"I was very much against it, but he was so insistent that we set up a meeting and met with Palidore who I was not impressed with the first time I met him. I thought him to be an opportunistic salesperson. Then, after showing us around and touting the accomplishments of MCS, he told us about the astronomical price," she looked at George.

"Actually, he could have doubled the price and Stanley would have gladly paid it. Hell, Stanley even paid $50,000 more to hold a space for me in a tube next to him! I was so upset, that I became determined to investigate Dr. Palidore Montgomery, MCS, and all their directors. That's the *real* reason I bought this flat . . . so I could spy on them," she saw George was listening intently.

"Then, when Stanley finally died and was put into one of those tubes, I went to work. I researched everything I could find out about them, but to my amazement, I wasn't able to come up with much of anything negative on any of them." He was listening to every word.

"Now, here's the thing I regret the most: Using my status as a grieving widow wishing to see my departed spouse, I went to visit Stanley. During that visit, I broke into Palidore's office and stole a copy of a thumb drive, you know, one of those little things you store all your lessons and information on, the one that plugs into the computer."

George looked shocked, but amused, at the same time.

"I can tell you later what was on it, but I'm revealing this to you now just to demonstrate how obsessed I had become. Well, as luck would have it, during my research, I noticed an ad for a job at MCS and applied for it. I thought, given my background, I might have a shot. And to my utter amazement, I got the job. I figured that working from the inside, I would finally be able to get my hands on evidence proving that MCS was a fraudulent scam. But I never found any such evidence. On the contrary, everything pointed in the opposite direction. Palidore, MCS, and everyone connected here were truly genuine, on the up-and-up honest people whom I have grown to respect, honor, and love. Looking back, I'm so ashamed of my conduct and how I got this job, but now," she looked at her hands, "Now that I have it, I don't want to lose it." Her eyes were moist by the time she finished. She looked at him, George took her hand and kissed it.

"Notwithstanding your prior motives," George said, "it appears that you were trying to do a good job. That is the sign of a good person. I'm very grateful you have this job, or we never would have met. I certainly don't want you to lose it. So, your secret is safe with me. Actually, *you* are safe with me." He touched her cheek with his fingers and smiled at her. Martha wiped her eyes with one hand and forced a smile.

George cleared his throat, "And your research? What did you do with it?"

"Oh, I destroyed it all, and wiped it off my computer."

"Good, then there should be no problem."

"Well, I haven't destroyed that little thumb drive. I wasn't able to delete the file. When I tried, a message popped up that said: 'You don't have permission to delete this file.' I was afraid to just throw it out, so I still have it. I guess I'll try to crush it or burn it."

"What was on it?"

Martha paused, wishing she had not mentioned it. Then she decided she had to answer. "It's a video clip showing an unsuccessful attempt to revive another ancient person." George showed surprise and paused before asking, "May I see it?"

"Oh, I don't know. I mean I'm not supposed to have it."

"Well, you've obviously viewed it, and now that I know, is there really any harm?"

She looked at him and thought. *Well, it's a little late to hold anything back from this man.* "Okay," she said, "but then we figure out how to destroy it."

"Done," he said.

Martha retrieved her laptop and the thumb drive plugging it in and typing the password her IT guy had set for her. They watched as her screen came to life. Then they sat and watched the drama of client One coming back to life for a brief time before falling back on the table. They sat transfixed, silently starring at the screen until the end.

"Now watch what happens when I hit the 'delete' key." George got closer and put his arm around Martha as she hit the key. A message appeared just as she had said: 'You don't have permission to delete this file.'

Ignoring the message for the moment, George asked, "Do you think they have a video of me?"

"No, I'm sure they don't. Once they successfully revived you and Frank, Palidore became adamant there would be no evidence or record of any more revivals. In fact, I'm sure the original of this clip has been destroyed. He said that if no evidence existed, then nothing could ever be accidentally lost or released. He truly wants you and Frank to be able to decide for yourselves what you want to let the public know about you, where you came from, even whether you want to remain anonymous and start your lives over under new identities. He is an honorable man."

George turned slightly toward her and squeezed her close against him.

"Thank you for confiding in me, Martha. I'm pleased to know that you think enough of me to share the truth with me. I feel I can always trust you."

Martha looked up into his face, aware of his closeness and breathing in his intoxicating presence. "You're a good listener." Then, she leaned in and gave him a short, but meaningful kiss, breaking away before she got carried away.

"Well, I guess I've successfully shown you how to activate the GPS. That was the reason for our coming here, wasn't it?"

"It was one of the reasons, but not my *only* reason. I wanted to spend more time with you. I enjoy being around you." There was a comfortable silence.

"Me, too," she finally said, "but what time is it?" She was startled to realize it was dark outside. "Oh, my goodness, it's nearly nine o'clock! I guess we need to get you back, unless you're hungry, in which case we can fix something to eat here first."

George was all smiles. "In that case, I must confess that I'm very hungry."

Martha was amused at his obvious stalling. Walking to the kitchen, she opened the freezer and got on tiptoes to peep in. "Hmmm, let me see." Then she felt George putting his arms around her from behind and heard his whisper in her ear.

"I didn't say I was necessarily hungry . . . for food."

Martha turned in his arms, looked up and replied playfully, "Why, what else could you possibly be hungry for?" George leaned in and kissed her long and passionately.

"That was just the appetizer."

Martha pulled back a bit and replied, "Our drinks are over there . . . shall we?" They moved to the couch, but never reached for their drinks. Instead, they reached for each other and passionately kissed, over and over again. Entangled in each other's arms, they fell back and stretched out on the sofa. George began to slowly move his hands over her body, feeling each curve, and Martha didn't resist; but then, as his moves became more serious Martha stopped responding. George paused and looked at her.

"You don't have to stop," she said, feeling conflicted.

"But you've stopped."

"I love what you're doing, and I know I've fallen in love with you, but I don't think I'm ready for this. Sometimes, I think of you as just a man, but at other times, you're so much more . . . you're the past, the present, and hopefully, the future. But I'm a little confused right now and wonder which man is making love to me. I'm sorry."

"Don't be," he said tenderly. "We can wait until you figure it out. It will be better then. Any couple can enjoy an intimate encounter, but when such an encounter is coupled with mutual love, respect, and affection, then it is so much more. It is a chance for two souls to meet and become as one, if only for an instant. Some call that 'carnal knowledge,' but I want something that is *shared* between two souls, Martha, I want our souls to meet."

Martha's eyes became moist, again, as she held him close. *He's willing to wait for me . . . he wants our souls to meet . . . oh, my god, how lucky am I?*

TRANSFORMING GEORGE WASHINGTON

"Just hold me, George," she whispered. They lay entwined on the couch and eventually fell asleep.

Chapter 32

Martha opened her eyes slowly and surveyed the room. George was lying behind her with his arm draped over her waist.

Oh, my god, what have we done? she thought. A quick twist of her wrist showed the time on her watch. It was five-thirty a.m. Carefully, she moved George's arm off her side and sat up. *I can't believe we just dozed off like that, and for so long. Maybe too much wine. Okay, Martha, snap out of it; time to stop all this, and get your head on straight. What should I do now? I need a shower. Then, I'll get George going,* she thought.

Martha eased herself off the sofa, checked to see that George was still asleep, and shuffled off to her bedroom in search of a shower and fresh set of clothes. She left the bathroom door slightly ajar, as usual, to prevent steam from fogging up her mirror. But when she stepped out of the shower to towel off, she heard his voice.

"Oh, sorry."

She froze in place. He was standing there looking at her. Strangely enough, instead of feeling embarrassed, she found it erotic, exciting. Quickly she wrapped the towel around her as George started to turn away.

"No . . . please stay."

He stopped, turned, and looked at her again, this time with the towel wrapped around her. His eyes lingered.

"Look, this is a small place, and if you're going to be spending any significant amount of time here, it seems inevitable that we'll eventually see each other naked. That's life . . . it's what happens, and I don't think I should have to change the way I live just because you're becoming part of my life now. So, you don't have to pretend that you didn't see what we both know you saw. We might as well just get used to it."

Unexpectedly, she dropped the towel and raised her arms, turning completely around and giving George a 360-degree view. "So, this is what I look like naked. You like?"

George stood still, taking it all in. "Yes, very much! I can't believe you're so . . . spontaneous." His eyes continued to pour over her.

Then, Martha came toward him, took his hand, and said, "Follow me. While showering I thought a lot about what happened last night and there is something I need to show you."

"What more could you possibly show me?" he said as she led him across the living room to the door of her elevator. She stopped and pointed.

"See that door?"

"Yes, of course."

"Well, *that's* where this 'Commander-in-Chief,' 'Mr. President,' and 'man-of-history' stuff *ends*. Right there. This is *my* flat, *my* place, my little kingdom, and in here; this is where *I* rule! So, if I don't feel like wearing anything to fetch my glass of wine, I won't. I've decided not to be intimidated by your presence, who you are, or who you've been in the past," she said. "For this to work, I need to be me, and you need to be 'just a man.'" She looked at him unflinchingly. "So, I am not changing my lifestyle just because you are here."

She couldn't recall ever doing something so bold in her entire life, nor being so aroused. It was exhilarating. Summoning up her last bit of courage, she turned again to face him.

"So, are we clear?"

"Yes, ma'am," he said, completely enjoying her passion. But as he started to reach for her, she quickly held up her finger.

"Ah, ah, ah . . . no, no, no, you can look all you want, but touching is reserved for the right special time, and now is definitely *not* that time."

Turning away from him, she slowly headed back toward her bedroom feeling triumphant. Halfway there, she stopped and looked back at George who appeared motionless. "

"Well, don't just stand there. Time to get ready. You can use the shower in the other bedroom." Then, she disappeared into her room to dress.

***

As they crossed the street, Martha asked George if he was ready to start on the new goals Lynn had left them to do.

"Let's find Susan and make sure everything is okay," she said. They touched hands briefly and headed inside.

Susan and Frank were just getting ready to work on the computer.

"Well, there you are," Susan greeted them. "Glad to see you two are all right. I was beginning to get worried." Martha shot her a 'we've got to talk' look. After making sure Frank was set, Susan stood so George could sit down at his computer next to Frank. The girls walked out and proceeded down to Susan's office.

"Susan, I need to explain."

"No, you don't need to explain anything, I'm a grown-up and can see with my own two eyes."

"Nothing actually happened," Martha said.

"If you say so."

"Susan, please, just listen to me for a moment."

"Okay, I'm all ears; let's hear it."

Martha explained how quickly the evening had gone, how they had gone over the GPS device, then lost track of time, having a bit too much wine, then dosed off.

"That's it? You're saying there's *nothing* going on between you two?"

"I didn't say that. What I said was: nothing happened last night."

"Okay, so what's going on?" Susan asked, showing more interest.

"Well, clearly George and I have been attracted to each other for some time now. We've tried to put it on hold, but I'm not sure how long that will work. Last night, we kissed in a way that left no doubt about our feelings. We stopped before going too far, but nature has its own way, and I don't think we'll be able to resist much longer."

"So, what kind of plans do you have to control things?"

"That's just it. I don't; I know *he* doesn't, and after this morning, I'm pretty sure this little romance is set to go full steam ahead."

"Martha, you can't!"

"Oh, yes, I can. I'm not going to deny myself what my heart tells me is right."

"You think you can juggle this romance with your job?"

"I don't know, but George is the best part of doing this job, and right now, it looks like George is in my life with or without this job."

"Are you sure that's what's best for him?"

"I'm working on that. Quite frankly, it's my only hang-up right now. But I'm pretty sure I know what his answer to that question will be."

"Well, I must admit, he does seem happy around you. He's really quite a hunk! He sure doesn't look anything like those old pictures of him."

"I know. I have to force myself to remember who he is. That's when it gets weird, and I just don't know how to react."

"So, the good thing is that you're attracted to 'the man' and not the power of the position he once held."

"Good way of putting it. Exactly. I love this man, so I just need to put the history issue out of my mind."

"Can you do that? I mean, if you think about it, this man you're so attracted to once owned slaves, has killed people in war, and as you know, may not have always been faithful to his first Martha."

"I know, I know, I know, but he's different now, it's a different time, and he's adjusting. What he did in his previous life is what commonly happened back then. It's the way people were. It's the way society was back then. And remember, he freed most of his slaves in his last will and testament." Martha looked at Susan's expression.

"And what about Frank?" Susan asked. "You, of all people, should know how much Frank thinks of him."

"Well, I'm just not going to let his past color my view of his future."

"But everyone's past impacts their future," Susan said. "You know that."

"But, this is quite different. He knows that everything has changed, and he's trying hard to understand and adjust," Martha said.

"And yet, he's betting everything on retrieving all those precious coins. He clearly hasn't given up on *everything* from his past."

"I know, his transformation is a work in progress. Maybe helping him face that challenge is part of the attraction. Anyway, I've never been so attracted to anyone in my life. I'm convinced I've fallen head over heels in love with the man I know simply as 'George.' I desperately want to help him face his future while slowly letting go of his past," Martha said.

"Well, good luck with that, but if he makes you so happy then I wish you and George the best and pray everything will work out well."

"Thanks, Susan, it's really nice to have someone know the real truth. "

Chapter 33

Susan brought sub sandwiches back to the office while running errands. Now, Martha, Susan, George, and Frank were sitting at the small table in George's room. Both men had become fond of sodas to the point that each one had a small refrigerator in their individual rooms stocked with a small supply which they kept cold at all times.

While eating, George brought up their next trip to Mount Vernon. "Martha has shown me the GPS device which I need to place at the exit of the river tunnel. It seems simple enough to operate; now all we need do is plan the trip back to Mount Vernon to put it in place. When do you think we should go?"

"Well, I'm not going," Susan reminded him. "Remember, my job is to 'hold down the fort,' so it doesn't matter to me."

"But it *does* matter," George said. "If you recall, Palidore and Lynn indicated the best window of time for them to contact us would be from six to nine p.m. their time or eleven a.m. to two p.m. our time. So, we need to leave after that time window closes , or you'll have to explain our absence if they call. Allowing an hour for travel each way, plus an hour and a half for the tour and planting the GPS, the entire operation should take four hours. So, if we leave here at one p.m., we should be able to make the last tour.?"

"What if they call between one and two p.m.?" Susan asked.

"To make sure that doesn't happen, we'll call them around noon our time," Martha said.

"What day? Frank asked

"I'm thinking Saturday," George said.

Martha started to say something, then stopped. George noticed.

"Martha, what were you going to say?"

"Well, I was just thinking that Saturday would probably be the busiest time. Wouldn't it be better if we went on a less popular day?"

"Actually, we're better off going when the most people are around. That way, I won't be missed when I slip into the stables to access the tunnel."

"Which tour are you planning to take?" Susan asked.

"Well, the tour of the house takes the longest and includes a tour of the grounds. That gives me the most time to complete my task."

"It looks like the last tour is at three p.m.," Martha said as she looked at her I-watch.

"Can you pre-purchase tickets?" Susan asked.

"Yes, there's even a group price. If we buy for a group, I can order online, download, and print them off. But the smallest group is twelve so we would be buying more tickets than we need. But the good thing about a group is that we can use the group name instead of our individual names."

"Since there are only three of you going, where do you get the other nine people?" Susan asked.

"I can handle that," Martha said.

"Okay, what's the name of the group?"

"How about, 'The Ozark Fishing Club,'" Martha suggested. "That's a private club Stanley formed and funded. He used to take his best clients fishing in the Ozarks. Actually, he still has an active account with some funds in it. I can order tickets from there and print them."

"How about transportation?" Susan asked.

"Uber."

"Okay, then it's all set," George said. "Martha will get the tickets and we'll have an Uber pick us up at, say, one p.m. on Saturday afternoon. What about the bar code passes?"

"Done," Martha said. "I've made four badges, but I guess you're the only one who really needs one."

"You're probably right, but I think the three of us should each carry one," George said. "Okay, now that that's settled, there's another matter I need to discuss with you."

Everyone waited for him to spill it.

"On the unofficial trip, I've decided we cannot use Martha's boat."

She looked shocked. "Why not? I thought its proximity and size were perfect."

"Because even if everything goes as planned, we're still going to leave one very obvious clue that we've been there. You see, there's no way to hide or cover up the entrance to the tunnel. The dirt will be disturbed, and everyone will know that someone either went in or came out."

"So?" she asked. "What does that have to do with my boat?

"I think they will quickly conclude that whoever came out of the tunnel escaped in a boat. I mean there is nothing there but the river and, given the bad weather we're hoping for, they'll try and find out whose boat was not at home. One of the first places they'll likely look is at the Mount Vernon Yacht club. Your boat will be the only boat unaccounted for. So, we shouldn't take it."

"Okay, I never thought about that. So, what will we do?"

"We need another boat soon so we can put the winch on it and hide it until our trip."

There was silence as everyone began thinking.

"There are all kinds of little places to rent or buy used boats on the Maryland side of the Potomac," Susan said, "near Piscataway Park. It's also worth noting that the Maryland side of the river is all-natural with lots of trees. So, if you buy a boat, you can probably stash it somewhere over there. I know the area pretty well and that might be a project Frank and I can handle together."

George was surprised at Susan's offer given her reluctance beforehand to participate.

"That would be great. Maybe you could take the winch with you when you buy the boat and have it installed as part of the deal."

"That would work," she said and looked over at Frank who was looking at her. "Frank, want to go shopping with me?"

Chapter 34

It was sunny and cool when the Uber driver arrived to pick them up on Saturday afternoon. The ride to Mount Vernon was uneventful; no one talked much since it was their third trip in as many weeks. When they arrived, Martha arranged for the driver to be available for their return trip a few hours later.

Martha handed George and Frank their tickets, then walked over to a group of people and announced, "Excuse me! I have extra tickets here. Most of our group couldn't make it today," People crowded around her. "I'd hate for them to go to waste." She disbursed the tickets along with quick instructions to follow her. Once gathered, she looked at her watch. "I think we're the next group to go in, so maybe we should head over there. A guide will join us when it's our turn."

As they began walking to the entrance, George fell behind and slowly made his way toward the stables. He stopped when he saw a tour guide coming in his direction with a small group. He stayed at the back of the group as they proceeded to the stables where the guide gave them a small talk about the facility and announced the name of Washington's favorite horse as, "Ol' Nelson." It made George laugh.

Sure, I liked 'ol Nelson, but my favorite was always 'Blueskin,' George thought.

Then the guide used his bar code card to open the door and had the group go in. He waited and timed how long it took before the last person exited outside again.

GIL HUDSON

Only twenty minutes; that won't be long enough, he thought. He waited for the next group to show up and enter the building. This group only stayed fifteen minutes. But the time it took between the first group to enter and exit, and the second group to arrive was an hour and ten minutes.

So, if they are on any schedule, I will have a little over an hour to accomplish my task. That should be enough, he thought. George looked around, took out his bar code card, and moved toward the stable door. He took out his cell phone and pretended to talk on it until no one was in sight. Then, he quickly used the bar code card to gain entry. He next set a timer on his cell phone as Martha had shown him; he was beginning to like this little device. Now, he glanced around and proceeded to the fourth stall. He was amazed to find a horse occupying it.

This will not do. What if he's standing on the trap door when I return?

George moved the horse over to the third stall, then went back in the fourth stall and swept away some of the straw, looking for his old marker which he found carved into the wood. Then he rose and walked three paces to the rear and dug around until he found a hole in a wooden plank. Putting his finger into the small opening, he pulled up hard, but it wouldn't budge. Looking around, he saw a pitchfork and put one of its prongs into the hole and, this time, pushed down hard. Something underneath gave way. Now, he got back down on his hands and knees and removed a small board. With the board out of the way, George lay on his stomach and put his arm into the hole, reaching underneath for a chain attached to a leaver. He pulled and a trap door unlocked. The door opened downward, and George nearly fell in, barely catching the edge of the floor in time to stop his fall.

Now he was dangling above the shallow tunnel, but instead of dropping down, pulled himself back up, retrieved the pitchfork, and tossed it into the hole before jumping into the tunnel himself. Using the pitchfork, he pushed the door back upward and was able to use the chain on the latch to lock it back into place. The remnants of a rope ladder, that had once hung in place, caught his eye.

He glanced at his cell phone. Only sixteen minutes had passed which pleased him, but now he needed to move quickly. By the time he reached the middle of the tunnel, it was dark. Despite knowing his cell phone had a flashlight on it, he didn't trust his ability to quickly locate it, so had brought along a separate flashlight which he now turned on. Its beam of light allowed him to look around.

It didn't take long to orient himself. One way took him toward the mausoleum and the other way toward the house and river tunnel. He headed down the tunnel toward the house and the river tunnel while looking to see if his former tracks were visible as he made his way down the damp path.

Hmm, I'm surprised the government hasn't found this tunnel by now. Clearly they haven't as the wall lanterns still have oil in them. Strange I didn't notice that on my last trip down here when I first came to find the coins. Guess I was in too much of a hurry then..

He found the door that would give him access to the small room toward the river tunnel and quickly moved through it. Now George moved along the dark path but felt it was too dangerous to run. Outside the beam of his flashlight, he could see nothing and the tunnel seemed longer than he remembered. Everything was quiet and damp. Keeping to one side, so his hand could touch the wall, he kept walking until he spotted the old iron exit door in the beam of his flashlight. He stopped briefly and moved the light around to get a better look, then hurried toward the door.

Suddenly, he tripped over something and took a hard hit to the ground, causing the flashlight to fly out of his hand. Now in darkness, he felt around for what had caused his fall and felt something on the tunnel floor. Quickly he recoiled his hand. Now he reached for his cellphone and when he retrieved it, the screen lit up at the touch of his hand. But try as he might, he could not find the symbol for the flashlight on the phone. In frustration, he simply used the light from the home screen to provide some illumination.

Then, he saw what he had fallen over. It was a skeleton. Looking into its face, he recoiled again at the sight. He had seen skeletons before, but this one was unexpected and had caught him by surprise. A few feet away, he saw the flashlight lying not too far up the tunnel. Now, touching the face of his cell phone, he had enough temporary light to keep moving until he retrieved the flashlight. When he finally grabbed it, he slowly stood and backtracked to the pile of bones. The man's flesh was gone, but parts of his uniform were still visible.

Getting down on his knees, he could see this man held the rank of Major. His heart skipped a beat as he slowly realized who was before him. *My faithful soldier, Major Ronald Hudson. He was the only one who knew of or had access to this tunnel. What was he doing here? Why had he died here?'*

Tears came to George's eyes for the first time since his rebirth. Seeing this old friend took his mind back to his former life. For the first time, he felt what he had previously blocked from his mind . . . it was true, all his friends and loved ones . . . were gone. He was alone in this new world, surrounded by strange people. Then, he remembered Frank. He wept until he finally shook his head and glanced at his cell phone - a total of forty-nine minutes had expired. He came back to the present moment. *I need to move; get this device planted.*

Getting up, he proceeded the last several feet to the end of the tunnel where he found three more skeletons. They were not in uniform, and they were not in tack. A sword lay next to them. He picked it up. It had the initials RH on its handle. A gun was also on the floor.

These were intruders, he thought. *Major Hudson slew them with his sword and was mortally wounded in the process. He must have managed to close the hatch and start back before he fell.* Slowly he moved his flashlight over and back across the scene before telling himself to refocus on the mission.

TRANSFORMING GEORGE WASHINGTON

He took out the GPS device and activated it, setting it near the entrance. Then, he made sure the slide bolt to the door was unlocked before starting back. On his way, he stopped once more at the corpse of Major Hudson and saluted the fallen soldier who had served him so well. Quickly, he moved on. When he reached the hatch to the stall in the stable, he checked the time. An hour and thirty minutes had passed. He had missed his deadline and wasn't sure if he should wait, but then knew he had to continue.

Taking the pitchfork, he used it to bring the hatch door down slightly. Hearing nothing, he gradually let the door all the way down allowing himself access to the opening. He jumped upward and grabbed the edge of the upper floor, then pulled himself fully into the stall. The horse in the adjoining stall nickered when he appeared. He struggled to pull the hatch back up and finally brought it flush, inserting the small board again that locked it in place. Covering the structure with straw again, he slowly stood up to look around. Moving to the horse, he brought it back to its original stall, just as he heard voices. A group was approaching and there was no place to hide! Not knowing what to do, he opened the stable door in full view of everyone while the guide was talking and walked out.

"He's a little frisky today," George said, referring to the horse. "You may want to keep your group back a moment. He's got fresh water and hay now."

Without giving it a second thought the guide responded, "Okay, thanks!" Then turned to the group. "You see how well we care for all the animals on the plantation. Now, please follow me." George held the door for everyone to enter, then made his way back to the parking lot.

***

The front door buzzer rang at the MCS building. Susan used her phone to access the intercom. "May I help you?"

"Yes, we'd like to speak with Dr. Palidore Montgomery please."

"I'm sorry, he is not here now, can someone else help you?"

"Wait a minute, umm, yes! We could speak with either Lynn Radford, Martha Vaughan, or Susan Trott. Are any of them available?"

"Lynn Radford and Dr. Montgomery are out of the country right now, and Martha Vaughan is not here at the moment, but I'm Susan Trott. Can you tell me who you are, and the nature of your business? I'll need some identification."

"Yes ma'am, my name is Sargent Earl Sasser of the Virginia State Police and I have Officer Connie Palmer of D.C. Police with me."

"I'm going to buzz you in now," Susan said. "Just push on the door when you hear the buzzer. Please come in and take a seat. The door will lock behind you and I'll be right down."

Susan was concerned and thought: *We're closed on Saturdays, and I'm the only one here right now. I wonder what this is all about. Did George and Frank get caught? No, wait, shit! This is about that damned accident and shooting. What should I do? I really don't want to lie to these people, but I need to warn Martha.* She quickly shot off a text to Martha: *Police are here about shooting last week. Don't return until I text you after they leave.*

After sending the message, she deleted it from her phone, turned the camera on video, put it in her pocket, and proceeded down to the waiting area to meet the officers. As she walked toward them, she held out her hand to greet them.

"Hello, I'm Susan Trott. How can I help you?"

"Thank you for seeing us. I'm Sargent Earl Sasser, and this is officer Connie Palmer." He flashed his badge. "We won't be long, but we need to ask you a few questions about events that occurred last weekend."

"Sure, since you don't anticipate it taking too long, we can just sit here unless you'd prefer to sit at a table."

"No, this will be fine."

They moved to chairs in a corner of the room. He handed her a photo of two men, backs to the camera, walking some distance away.

"Do you recognize either of these two gentlemen?"

She knew instantly that she was looking at George and Frank. Not wanting to directly lie, she answered, "Well, I can't see their faces, so I don't know how you could expect me to recognize them."

"Well, maybe by what they're wearing, or perhaps you saw their faces when you were there."

"No, I'm sorry. Why? Are they suspects?"

"Well, we can't say that just yet, but we find it interesting that they're not looking at the accident scene, and they're not running. Most people run after a shooting. It's unusual for people to pass by an accident without taking a few moments to look at the wreck. Also, they're in the street instead of on the sidewalk. So, they do appear to have left the actual scene. It's reasonable to think one of you would have noticed them."

Susan began to perspire. She wished she hadn't already denied knowing them, but it was too late now to change her story.

"I'm sorry, I just don't recall. Things happened so fast. Who took this photo, anyway? Why don't you contact *them*?"

"It's from a surveillance camera at the stoplight. It not only takes photos of cars going through the light but photos of the area every sixty seconds. This is the only photo it took with these two people in it."

"I see. Is that your only copy? If you want to leave it, I can show it to the others and let you know if anyone recognizes them?"

"Sure, you can have it. We can print as many as we need. As you can see, it's time-stamped on the back. Here, take it along with my card. I'll look forward to hearing from your companions. Sorry to have bothered you."

Both officers rose and moved toward the door. Susan showed them out and when she shut the door, she leaned back against it looked toward the ceiling and exclaimed out loud. "*Shit, shit, shit.*"

She took her cell phone from her pocket to stop the recording and quickly texted Martha: *"They're gone. Safe to come back now. Delete this message."*

Chapter 35

Susan took one look at George's dirty clothes as he walked in the door. "What happened?"

"Let's go to Palidore's Office," he said, "I'll update all of you. I couldn't say much with the Uber driver around, but the task was successfully completed."

They all filed into the office, and Frank headed for the mini-fridge inside the cadenza. "Anyone else need a drink?"

They all took chairs around the small table as Frank brought the beverages. Then George told them about the tunnel and what he had found. He became emotional as he told them about Major Hudson and the essential role the man had played as his security officer which allowed him to transition to his new life. There was silence when he finished his story.

"George, we are so sorry to hear about your friend," Martha finally spoke. "But doesn't that mean *someone* knew about the tunnel even way back then?"

"You know, I've thought about that a lot while riding back here, and now I believe the intruders may have been in the house when they were discovered and chased by Major Hudson. They could have wound up in the tunnel by accident as they were trying to flee.

"When they got to the end of it, Ron slew them with his sword but was mortally wounded in the process, probably by the pistol I found. That must be what happened because the slide lock was still in place. Anyway, I'm just guessing now. It doesn't really matter. What I'm most amazed about is the fact that the tunnel has never been discovered in all these years."

"Well for our purposes, I guess that's a good thing. Right? Nobody will be monitoring the area on the next trip," Martha said.

"Exactly. But I must tell you, that's why I have decided that, in addition to the coins, I will need to get Major Hudson's remains out during the trip."

They were shocked to hear of his change in plans when the phone rang. Susan looked down at the caller ID, then up at the group, looking wide-eyed.

"It's Palidore and Lynn. I'm going to put it on speaker so we can all hear.

"Hello?"

"Hi guys, how are things going?" Lynn asked

"Actually, pretty much as planned."

"Good, glad to hear it. How are George and Frank doing?"

"Very well, actually, they're right here with Martha and me now. We decided to raid the supply of beverages in your office, Palidore. Hey, what time is it there now because it's almost six p.m. here?"

"Yeah, it's late, about half past midnight, but they stay out late here, and we wanted to touch base before we turned in," Palidore said.

"How are things going for the two of you at the conference?"

"Pretty well, I think. We're in the final planning stage for the conference itself. Turns out there's a lot of interest in our ancient inventory of bodies, but not for the reasons we had expected. A doctor in France, Alexandre Arseneau, also has an inventory of ancient cryogenically preserved bodies and is going to speak as well. Seems he has ties that also go back to Egypt from about the same time as my ancestor's father was there. We've enjoyed talking to him. Seems they took a different approach by trying to wake them up with some sort of microwave therapy."

"Really!" Martha said. "Has anyone asked you about your inventory?"

"Well, yes, Alex has. Lynn and I've decided on our way over here tonight that we could talk about our unsuccessful attempts and leave it at that. In that way, we can suggest ways for others not to try revivals. Then, after discussing this with Alex, he asked a curious question: he said, 'If you were successful in reviving one of your subjects, would you tell anyone?'

"I confessed that I did not believe I could do that without the express permission of the person I had revived. To my surprise, he said he had come to the same conclusion. I was curious after that, but he also said: 'So, I suspect that neither of us will ever know if the other one has been successful.'

"I found that amazing, and it left us both wondering if the other had actually already succeeded. Of course, we know we have."

"Wow! That's amazing," Martha said. "I can't wait to hear more."

"How are you guys doing with the special assignments I left for you?" Lynn asked.

"I think it's some kind of puzzle," Frank answered.

"Exactly right," Lynn said. "Good for you! That's a good way to put it. It's a puzzle that forces you to gradually learn how to use the Internet and find answers to your questions. The Education Modules were designed to teach you what I thought you needed to learn.

"But once you've mastered this, you should be able to learn whatever you want in the future, whenever you want. I know it can seem difficult and frustrating at times, so I understand it may not easy but the better you get at accessing the Internet the better off you will be. If you have questions, remember Susan is there to help."

"How about you, George?" Palidore broke in, "Are you getting it?"

"Well, Frank is a little ahead of me right now, but I'm

working on it."

"Okay, Good. Susan. Anything else we need to know before we hang up?"

Susan wanted so much to play the recording she had of her interview with the Virginia State Police but didn't want to discuss it in front of George and Frank, so she just said, "No, not right now."

"Okay then, everyone, have a good evening, bye from Brussels."

***

Al Roker was on the evening news. "Looks like the east coast is about to get slammed by a strong northeaster that's going to bring several inches of rain mixed with snow," he was saying. "The European model brings it in around D.C. sometime late Wednesday where it's predicted to stall for at least a day before making its way up the coast by Thursday, then back out to sea."

He waved his hands before a green screen, pointing to the various area of concern. "The American model isn't much better. It predicts the storm will move in just north of Norfolk, Virginia, before moving further north, but won't stay as long. In either event, we're in for some nasty weather and local flooding."

George looked around the table at his companions before taking the remote and turning off the television. "That's good for us."

"So, this is it, isn't it?" Susan said in a solemn tone.

"It is, and none too soon," George answered her. "It will give us some time before Palidore and Lynn are due back. So, let's go over it again. Frank, what's the situation with the boats?"

"Well, as you know, Susan and I have purchased two identical inflatable watercrafts both powered by electric motors. One boat has been equipped with the winch and is positioned on the Potomac in Piscataway Park along with all necessary supplies. The other one is at the cabin of Martha's friend further downriver. We'll use that one to travel to the hidden boat."

"My friend's name is Dr. Judy Doyle. You might recall she resigned from the MCS board. All the years Stanley and I knew her, we were totally unaware that she was on the board. You can imagine my surprise when I found out." Martha said, "Anyway, she spends this time of year in Florida, so the place is vacant which we knew it would be. They no longer allow homes on that part of the river but her little cabin is grandfathered in - literally - the place goes back to her great-grandfather. I've been there several times."

Susan seemed impressed. "Okay, that's good, but I wasn't sure why you wanted us to buy two boats? Why not just launch the journey from the cabin?"

"Well, several reasons," George said. "First, we wanted a backup boat in the event the primary boat experienced any problems. Secondly, the tools, winch, supplies, coins, and now the remains of Major Hudson may make it too difficult to navigate in the storm. So, as a precaution, we'll take both boats across the river. I'll bring back the coins and Major Hudson. Frank will handle the rest in the other boat. Martha will drive us in her car to the cabin and wait for us to return there. Lastly, after we've returned, we intend to create a small leak in one of the boats, and let it float away."

"What? Why do that?"

"Well, as we have previously discussed, they're going to find out that we were there. The ground around the tunnel will be torn up. They'll immediately start looking for us and eventually find the disabled boat. Hopefully, they'll assume we perished in the storm. With some luck, after a few days of intense searching, they'll ultimately give us up for lost. Since they won't find anything missing from Mount Vernon, and no one was ever aware of the coins or Major Hudson, to begin with, so we should be in the clear."

"Seems you've thought of everything."

"We certainly hope so," George said. "We won't get another chance. So, let's continue. We've timed this out, and the earliest we can safely cast off from the cabin will be eight o'clock p.m. which means we'll need to leave here around seven. So, given the forecast, we need to be ready to go at six-thirty tomorrow night. Martha has purchased us some water-repellant black jumpsuits to wear that will keep us warm. We'll change into them at the cabin."

"How will you find the hidden boat at Piscataway Park at night and in bad weather?"

"You are full of questions today, aren't you, Susan. But that's good. It helps to ensure we *have* thought of everything. So, to answer your question. Martha gave us another one of those GPS things which we left with the boat. We should be able to navigate directly to it. Now, any more questions? Anyone?" They all looked satisfied. George nodded.

"Okay, so let's get something to eat."

"I didn't know when all of this would happen, but I made a big batch of chicken noodle soup. If you want, we can all go across the street to my little place and have a steaming bowl with crackers. But, a word of warning, the only alcohol I have is chardonnay So, if that doesn't suit you, you'll need to grab something from Palidore's stash before coming over."

"We can always count on Palidore," Frank quipped.

Chapter 36

As predicted, the weather turned bad within a day. There was wind and rain all day long as George, Frank, and Martha packed and re-packed her Audi. Finally, it was time. They left the tracker devices which they had removed from their legs in George's room by the computers, said bye to Susan, donned their raincoats, and headed out. It was cold and with cloud cover, it was extremely dark for that time of day.

Arriving at the cabin by six-forty, they made their way inside to change clothes. Then, Frank checked on the boat, tested the winch along with the main battery and the backup one. They used the restroom and ate energy bars before leaving. Martha found the GPS apps on both George and Frank's cell phones and turned them on.

Two red dots showed on their screens, one on each side of the river. Those would be indicating the river door and the second, hidden boat. A third green dot seemed to be located right where they were standing which indicated the cabin they needed to find in the dark upon their return. Everything was working as planned. Frank headed out with George following, but at the last moment, Martha spun George around, threw her arms around him, and gave him a kiss while trying to hold back tears.

"Go, be safe, but come back to me."

George looked at her for a long minute. He seemed to want to say something but was unable, so he squeezed her once, turned, and followed Frank toward the boat. Once they pushed away from shore,

Frank steered the boat as George kept a keen lookout. With the wind, rain, and current, it took longer than expected before they reached the hidden boat. As soon as they came to its spot, they tied off, jumped ashore, and proceeded to inflate the second rubberized boat testing its electric engine. When it was ready, they threw in the backpacks containing the cinch straps, portable lights, and tools. They attached small red lights on the tail of each boat to help them locate each other in the dark and headed out.

The rain made everything more difficult to see and the wind kept blowing them off course. Frank kept adjusting their path as they moved in on the GPS signal across the Potomac until they reached the other side. When they finally arrived at the shore near the entrance to the tunnel, they quickly tied off both boats and started dragging the winch cable from Frank's boat toward the signal.

At last, they were standing on top of the pulsing red light and dropped the cable onto the wet ground. Then they started digging with portable shovels. The wet dirt made digging easier than it might have been on a dry night.

"Hey, I hit something solid," Frank finally said as his shovel hit the metal door. They dug faster now, breaking into a sweat trying to save time. With ninety-five percent of the door exposed, George stopped and dropped to his knees. Frank did the same. George looked around, reached up, and twisted the rim of the small light on his stocking cap causing it to illuminate. Frank did the same. They examined the door searching for a place to fasten the winch cable.

"There's a small handle," George said. "See it near the right edge of the door?" At first, they ran the hook through the handle and pulled hard, but it wouldn't budge. Then Frank noticed the door was hinged on the left. George began working to reposition the cable out and around a tree, otherwise, the winch cable would have been pulling the door shut instead of open.

Now, George signaled to Frank, and headed back toward the boat. Once there, he blinked his headlamp twice and George blinked his back. The winch started up and began to pull. The door creaked opened just enough for George to stick his shovel into the crack before the ancient metal handle broke off and flew past him, just missing his head before hitting the tree. The door slammed almost closed onto the shovel. George, sat back for a second, then signaled Frank with his light and Frank returned.

"I'm going to put this cinch strap through this crack and wrap it around the door a couple of times. Let's attach it to the winch cable again," he said. "Wait for my signal, then start the winch again."

Frank helped him place the cinch strap. Neither of them had seen such a strap before, but following Susan's instructions, they saw how useful it was and were happy to have it now. Then, Frank went back to the boat and waited for George's signal. This time, George stood well away from the door.

He watched as the winch worked its wonder and the door slowly opened. One of the ancient iron hinges broke under the stress of the pulling followed by the second hinge as the door completely slid away after the winch cable. George sent another signal and the winch stopped. Frank returned to see the rusted relic of a metal door lying in the dirt and grass a few feet from the front of the opening.

Now, the rain turned to snow as the men entered the tunnel. George showed Frank the skeletons of the slain robbers as they passed by, then a few feet further on he pointed to the skeletal remains where Major Hudson lay. They both stopped and got down on their knees as George took his backpack off, unzipped it, and retrieved a body bag. Then spread it out alongside the skeleton.

While on their knees, George paused a moment. It was an emotional time for him, and his eyes grew moist. *This may be the only time I will touch anyone from my past,* he thought. *They're gone, all of them, a whole generation of wonderful patriotic Americans.* He looked over at the man waiting for his next move. *Thank God for Frank.*

As George stood, Frank did the same. They slowly moved the remains of Major Hudson into the bag, zipped it up, and left it there before proceeding down the tunnel until they reached the room that gave them access to the tunnel going toward the stable and on to the mausoleum. George hit the correct stones allowing access to that tunnel. Then they proceeded on past the stable entrance to the ornate wooden doors. George said. 'Follow me, it's not much further." Frank followed him down the hall of decorative doors. When they reached the correct door, George put a hand on the head of a carved snake and the other on a bird, turned them at the same time until a latch released. George opened the door, and they went in only a few feet to the steps that had previously led to the mausoleum, but now led to nowhere since the mausoleum had long since been removed.

"Give me a hand with this third step, Frank."

George moved the tread about an inch to the right and Frank helped George slide the heavy step completely off this time, allowing them to finally peer into the hole. There were the eight leather bags of coins . . . all of them. Embracing a moment in celebration, George then laid down on his stomach to reach his arm deep into the hole. One by one he grabbed the bags and passed them to Frank who set them aside.

Once the heavy bags were all retrieved, they put the tread back and slid it to the left locking it into place. Not wanting to rest, they each grabbed four bags and retraced their journey making sure that everything was back in its proper place before reaching the opening of the tunnel.

George stopped for a moment to retrieve the GPS device before they headed out. Carrying the bags of coins to George's boat, they returned for the remains of Major Hudson. His body bag was easy to carry down the embankment where they carefully placed him in the boat with the coins. Then they took out a small vial of blood that Frank had donated to the cause from when they removed the trackers from their legs. He had saved some of his blood knowing it would be impossible to trace anything back to him. Now, they spread the blood near the seat and controls of the second boat.

Then George took out a small handgun and proceeded to

shoot the boat several times from a rear angle, making sure one of the shots started to deflate the boat, and they set it adrift. They clambered aboard the remaining boat and headed out into the fringed weather.

By now, it was snowing heavily made worse by swirling gusts of wind. Visibility was zero. As the currents, wind, and weather thrashed them about, George glanced over at the body bag carrying his friend and faithful officer. *Major, it seems ironic*, he thought, *that I am carrying your remains across the Potomac just as you once carried my remains across this same river so long ago. We have not only crossed this river but also the river of time. It is amazing to realize that both our destinations take us back to a man named Palidore.*

Just then, something caused the boat to spin around. Frank tried to gain control.

"Must have been a rock. I can't see, but we're getting closer to the green dot at the cabin."

"That's fine, Frank. You're doing fine. We're going to make it." Within half an hour, they finally reached the other side but were not able to navigate the small boat up the short creek to the cabin, so with Frank at the helm, George climbed in front and kept grabbing nearby limbs and branches moving them forward. At long last, they saw a light from the cabin and reached the dock.

Martha had been anxiously watching from the window and now ran out to help them tie up the boat. George and Martha briefly embraced but went right back to business. Frank and George deflated the boat and loaded it into the back of the Audi, amazed at how compact the boat had become, and how spacious the trunk seemed void of tools and provisions.

The three of them made several trips to the cabin carrying the bags of coins. Lastly, Frank and George carried the remains of Major Hudson into the house. The men changed out of the black waterproof suits that had served them so well, placing them into a black plastic garbage bag. Then exhaustion hit, and they sank into seats by the fire.

***

"I can't hear you . . . too much static . . . huge storm here. If you can hear me, please call back tomorrow." Susan could hear just fine, but she didn't want to talk to Palidore or Lynn.

She hadn't anticipated their call as the pre-established 'best window of time' was from 11:00 a.m. to 2:00 p.m. EST and this wasn't it. She did the math and concluded right now it must be around 4:00 a.m. in Brussels.

I really hope nothing is wrong, she thought, *but I can't take the chance of talking now because I won't be able to explain why no one else is available.*

"What's that?" she said, again. "Sorry I can't hear you. If you can hear me, please call back tomorrow." She hung up the phone, but almost immediately received a text message:
"Is everyone okay there? We heard about the storm."

"Yes, everyone is hunkered down in their rooms, trying to ride it out." She texted back. "Are you all right? It must be around four a.m. there."

"Were okay, just concerned about the storm."

"It's snowing heavily now, but please don't worry. Everyone is fine. Go back to bed."

"Well, we have redundant generators so you shouldn't lose power at the building, but we understand and will call back tomorrow."

Good, Susan thought. *Don't hurry either.*

***

Martha left a note on the cabin table informing Judy that she had stopped by to check on the cabin for her. It was something she had done periodically in the past anyway. But this time, she left the note just in case someone had noticed her car.

Best to provide an excuse before anybody asks, she thought. Everyone got into the car. Martha and George were in the front and

GIL HUDSON

Frank was in the back along with Major Hudson's body bag and all the coins. Martha started down the drive. They didn't have far to drive, but she had never driven in such a storm before. Windshield wipers were going at top speed as they headed for home.

Chapter 37

The news caught Lynn's attention and she called out to Palidore in the next room. "My god, there's been a break-in at Mount Vernon – of all places! Can you believe it? Listen to this: It appears access was gained through an unknown tunnel near the Potomac River. So far nothing has been identified as missing by authorities, but an inflatable boat was found downstream riddled with bullets and traces of blood. No bodies were found, but the investigation is continuing. Now they're searching the river, but the weather is hampering all efforts."

"That's it?" Palidore asked. "That's all they have to say? News in Europe is so damned concise, *too* concise! Nothing like the news in the U.S. which is anything *but* concise. Shit! I'll bet they're going non-stop about this back home."

"This is going to be upsetting to George. What time is it over there now?" Lynn asked. Palidore looked at his watch and did the math.

"It's nine a.m. here so it's only two a.m. there, too early to call. This likely happened a day ago if they're showing daytime scenes on television. Pretty likely, then, that George and Frank already know. I hope he doesn't go crazy and want to go over there." Palidore said

"It's not likely he or anyone else will get anywhere near the place. I imagine the entire area has been locked down, don't you think? But as soon as we can, we need to call and see if they are all right. What are you doing?"

Palidore was at his computer. "I'm checking a story online. Wait! I can't believe this! It says they found three bodies in an old tunnel, nothing but skeletons left. They were found near the end of some tunnel. Unbelievable! So, that means . . . if this tunnel was previously unknown to anyone in recent times, those skeletons were from a long time ago or they would have been removed by now. Do you remember reading anything about a secret tunnel in your research?"

"No, Palidore, I don't," Lynn said. "I find it interesting that George, who was dying to visit there, never mentioned a tunnel to us. He certainly would have known about it, wouldn't he? Hell, I mean, he *designed* the place."

"You don't think . . . ?"

"I know what you're thinking, but I just don't see how. I certainly *hope* not. Surely not! He was just there *twice* recently, so why would he go back and access a tunnel. Hey, the newscast mentioned blood! Do you think they're all right?"

"Call them right now," Palidore said. "Get them up!"

***

Susan answered the phone by her bed on the fourth ring.

"Hello?" she answered in a sleepy voice.

"Susan, its Lynn. Sorry to call you at this hour, but we've just heard about the break-in at Mount Vernon, and there was mention of blood in the newscast. Are George and Frank all right?"

"Last I checked they were both doing just fine. They're sleeping now."

"Thank God, for that. Well, what did George have to say about it?"

"George told us that the old tunnel was an escape route created for him and Martha should they ever need it. From the house, they had the option to go to the river or to the stable. Clever, don't you think? "

"So, he knew about it, then," Lynn said. 'We figured he had to know."

"Yes," Susan said, more awake now. "He told us he was surprised that no one had found it long before now. Do you want me to wake him, so you can question him about it?"

"No, not at this time of night. We were just concerned for him. You know he has been a bit preoccupied about Mount Vernon lately."

"I know." *Boy do I know,* she thought.

"Does he have any thoughts about who might have done this, or why?"

Susan didn't like avoiding the truth but tried to keep her responses at least tacitly truthful, even if not complete.

"He doesn't seem to be too concerned about who did this," Susan said. *That much is certainly true,* she thought.

"Well, sorry to wake you, but we feel better having talked to you. Please tell George and Frank that we hope this whole matter is not too upsetting to them. I'm sure we'll talk more about it when we return."

"I will tell them, Lynn. Good night."

"Good night, Susan."

***

"What are you going to do with Major Hudson's remains?" Martha asked.

"I don't know except that he needs a proper burial with a proper marker," George answered.

"I don't think that's a problem," Martha said. "The problem will be trying to explain how you came to be in possession of his body. I mean you can't say you stole it from somewhere."

"No, I suppose not, but at least it's safe and sound for now."

"Well, we need to figure this out before Palidore and Lynn return and find him in the inventory room in your old vault."

"Why do you think they'll notice him. Do they frequent the vault room much?"

"Not really, but Palidore has his thumb on everything, and eventually, he will notice. There were five vaults opened before he left, and now there are only four. We need to make a plan. Think . . . Let's figure this out. Where was he from?"

George was silently going over past memories of their conversations. "He mentioned it, once, but I can't remember exactly. He did say he often fished the Meherrin River as a kid."

Martha did a quick search for 'Meherrin River' on her laptop.

"There's a Meherrin River in Emporia, Virginia, which is located in Greensville County."

"Greensville. That's it! I remember now. Funny, but when Lynn was going over my new identity and mentioned that I was supposed to have sold my mother's small farm to a James Ferguson, there was something familiar-sounding about 'Greensville,' and now I remember. Major Hudson was from there."

"Good. So, maybe we should take him back there. Let me see if there are any cemeteries still in business." She tapped the keys. "Wait for it . . . yes! There are two: Emporia Cemetery is the oldest, but there is also a Greensville cemetery. Looks like the Greensville cemetery is now run by a private company that owns a number of cemeteries in Southside Virginia. I'll bet they wouldn't object to selling us a plot, vault, marker, and all."

"Can you contact them?"

"Sure, here's the number. I'll dial it; they should still be open today." Martha listened to the rings. It took three for someone to pick up.

"Greensville Cemetery. This is Amelia speaking how may I help you?"

Martha gave a thumbs-up sign to George and Frank before she replied."Well, I have somewhat of a strange request."

"Honey, there is *nothing* too strange around here," Amelia said.

"Last week we had a woman who left instructions that she wanted her ashes placed in an urn between the legs of her previously deceased lover who is buried here next to his former wife."

Martha's eyes widened. "Oh gosh, what did you do?"

"Still working on that one, just not sure we're going to be able to grant her wish. Now, how can we help you?"

"Well, our problem isn't quite as tricky, but we do want to keep it on the down-low if you know what I mean."

"No problem there," Amelia said. "'Down-low' is what we specialize in, if *you* get my meaning."

"I get it; very funny," Martha laughed. "Well to the point, then, we have recovered some very old remains, more or less by accident, and we probably should not have moved them, but they weren't in a very good place. So anyway, what is done is done, and we want to acquire a decent final resting place for this gentleman. We think he was originally from your area which is why I'm calling you. Do you think you can help us?"

"Maybe," Amelia said, "but you know you're going to need a casket and a vault. You can't just put bones in the ground. I don't care how old they are."

"Perfectly understandable," Martha answered. "and we will probably want a marker as well."

For the first time, Amelia seemed a little more intrigued.

"You understand all this won't be cheap, don't you? You're probably looking at twelve to thirteen thousand depending on the casket and vault you pick out, then there is the opening and closing fees, etc."

"We get it. So do you have any caskets and vaults in stock?"

"Only a couple. Most of the time we have to order them, but we keep a couple of the pricier ones around to show people what else is available."

"How about you just figuring it up for us."

"I've been kinda doing that as we speak, honey. Anyway, I see you have a problem and I want to help you out but looks like the best I can do will top out at sixteen grand, not counting transportation." She didn't wait for an answer. "Where's the body now?"

"Don't worry about the body," Martha said. "We'll bring it to you along with payment."

"All righty," Amelia said. "Let me draw up a contract. When it's signed, I'll need a forty percent deposit. When did you want to bring him here?"

"We're thinking later this week. Probably Thursday, but do you think we could forgo the formalities of having a contract and all, if we bring you say, *twenty* thousand . . . in cash . . . along with the body? I mean you would have to trust us enough to have the hole dug ahead of time, but as I said, we're thankful you'll be keeping this on the 'down-low.'"

"I think I might just be able to help you out there," Amelia said. Martha could almost see her smiling through the phone. "In fact, I own a couple of spots here myself, but my 'ex' is somewhere in Texas last I knew, and I wouldn't want that bastard buried next to me anyway. With no contract, this might be something we could keep between just the two of us if you know what I mean?"

"Sounds like a plan, Amelia. We'll see you on Thursday around noon, if you think you can have the grave dug by then."

"I do the digging around here along with everything else, so no worries, it will be ready. But, say, who am I talking to? How will I know you?"

"Oh, sorry. The deceased gentlemen's name is Major Ronald Hudson and we'll come to your office, I'm looking at your website right now. We'll introduce ourselves when we get there. The important name is Major Ronald Hudson. Our names are actually very unimportant. See you Thursday."

"See you Thursday, darlin'."

Chapter 38

Returning home, George and Martha went straight to his room. Frank was there working on educational models and greeted them as they arrived.

"How did it go?" he asked.

"Well, that was easier than I thought it would be," George said.

"Let's look at the coins," Frank said.

"Yes, I agree; let's take a look, but can we call Susan in here? She may want to see them, too," Martha said.

"I'll buzz her," Frank offered. A few minutes later Susan popped her head in the doorway. "What's up?"

"We're going to get the coins out and wanted you to be here with us. After all, you were a big help."

"Okay, then, 'Show me the money!'" Susan laughed. George went to his wardrobe and removed the eight old leather bags along with both shoeboxes. One by one, he poured the coins out onto his bed. Two thousand shiny gold coins lay in the middle of the covers, now on display.

"H-o-l-y shit!" Martha exclaimed.

"There you go again," George said. "So, is this another time when it's okay to say 'holy shit?'"

"It is, George, it certainly is," Martha said. "Have you counted them?"

"I have, and they're all accounted for. You're looking at 1,994 gold eagles minted in 1799, and never circulated. As you know, we started with 2000. Since then, I gave one to you, and one to Susan. Then we recently sold four of the coins which brought in a little over twenty-five thousand apiece. So, we have in hand, over a hundred thousand dollars plus these coins laying on my bed."

"What did you do with the money you got for the four coins you sold?" Susan asked.

"I put the money into one of my bank accounts for safekeeping," Martha said, "but that's something we need to figure out going forward. We can't just keep putting this much money in one of my accounts. George needs one of his own. I think it's time to bring in JL."

"Who's JL?" Susan asked. She had never heard him mentioned before now.

"His full name is John L. Walston, and it's hard to describe what he does, but I have always heard him referred to as the 'money manipulator.'"

"So, he's like a financial advisor?"

"No, definitely not that. Stanley was a financial advisor, but JL is a money manipulator. There's a difference."

"Okay, so you're going to have to explain to us more about this money manipulator."

Martha seemed surprised to have pricked everyone's curiosity. She took a breath.

"All right then, here's a little background for JL: Years ago, no, actually more like a few *decades* ago, JL got into the debt collection business and became very wealthy in the process. That's when he got to know my deceased husband, Stanley, who became his financial advisor."

"Wait a minute," George said. "I don't understand what a 'debt collector' is. How can you make money collecting debts?"

"Well, when people buy goods or services from someone and fail to pay for what they purchased, people to whom the money is owed can hire debt collectors to try and get the money from these people. If they succeed, then they get to keep a small percentage of the money they've collected from the debtors. That's how they make money."

"But don't they just get put into debtors' prison for failing to pay their just debts?" George asked.

"No, they used to put them in prison, but sometime in the early eighteen hundreds, they did away with debtor prisons," Martha said.

"Well, if you can't put people in jail, how did this JL guy get them to pay when the creditors weren't able to make them pay? What kind of force was he allowed to use?"

"Debt collectors don't use force, they use *persuasion*. There's a difference there, too. They make these debtors understand that unless they pay their debts, no one will sell them goods or services on credit in the future. These debt collectors call them, or write to them, and list all debts on their credit records. It usually does the trick. People are scared not to be able to buy things in the future. Anyway, that's basically how it's done now."

"That is interesting," George said. "It doesn't sound like a very easy way to make a lot of money. How did JL make so much doing that?"

"I have to confess that I don't really know," Martha said. "It doesn't seem possible, does it? I mean most people make money dealing with people who normally pay, but poor old JL had to make all his money dealing with people who *don't* normally pay. I guess he was just very good at what he did, and people who are very good at what they do just seem to make a lot of money."

George looked at Frank who didn't say anything. Both were used to more serious means of dealing with people who didn't do what others wanted.

"Anyway, let me continue my story on how JL became a money manipulator," Martha said. "John made so much money that he wanted to safely invest it so he could earn even *more* money. He contacted Stanley and asked him to be his financial advisor. Stanley was an expert at investing money in stocks, bonds, real estate, trusts, etc. and he helped JL make so much money that JL sold his debt collection firm which gave him even more money to invest with Stanley."

"But I'm still not sure what a money manipulator is," Susan said looking for an explanation.

"I am getting there," Martha replied. "So, when JL's taxes kept going up, he started looking for ways to hide or invest some of his income to lessen that burden. He ultimately became an expert at offshore accounts, creating secret corporate identities, trading in foreign currencies, precious metals, antique jewelry, making private loans, and otherwise secretly moving money around. Stanley and I became really good friends with John and his wife, Phyllis, who we called 'PK'.

"Funny, isn't it? For some reason, we always referred to each of them by only using their initials. Anyway, eventually, JL joined Stanley's firm and ultimately handled the 'special needs' for many of Stanley's 'special' clients who wanted to hide money from the government, their spouses, business partners, or whoever. It didn't matter. If you had money and wanted to keep it without someone else knowing about it, then JL was your man. The money manipulator. Understand now?" Martha sat back and looked around.

"Sounds like this JL and I have something in common," George said. "We both found it necessary to hide money. I shall look forward to meeting him. How difficult will it be to set up a meeting?"

"Not very hard. As I said, he joined Stanley's firm and is still involved with it. So, he is right here in D.C. I can just give him a call and I'm sure he'll be happy to come over to visit with us, either here, or at my flat."

"Well, Martha, you seem to have all the right answers," George smiled. "I wish you could have met Alexander Hamilton. He was very influential in money things, too, you know. But, please set up this meeting as soon as possible."

"I will, but maybe we need to figure out how we're going to get rid of so many of these coins."

"Maybe JL will know some way. Maybe the coins will be a good way for some of his clients to hide some of their money."

"You know," Martha said, 'that just might work, which makes me wonder why you decided to hide so many of these coins in the first place. Did your financial advisor suggest it to you?"

"No, there were no financial advisors back then, just bankers and bookkeepers. My wife, Martha, was wealthy in her own right, so she was not much interested in knowing about my money. She also had her own bookkeeper," George said. "I, of course, also had a bookkeeper and *he* was the only person I needed to hide my money from. He was a bit nosey and wanted to know everything so he could keep track of it all, but I hid a considerable amount from him, including these coins. Good thing I did - don't you think?" Everyone laughed and Martha replied, "I suppose so, George." She leaned in and gave him a joyful kiss on the cheek, then instantly realized as innocent as it seemed, it was her first public display of affection toward George.

***

Later that day, Susan decided it might be a good time to play the recording for Martha of her meeting with the two officers following the car accident.

"I want you to hear this before we talk to Palidore and Lynn again. The police have this picture of George and Frank leaving the scene. Fortunately, the photo was only of their backsides, but they want to know if we saw them, I mean . . . well, you heard it. I played dumb but you must admit they're going to think it's funny if none of us remember seeing them. What should we do?"

"I don't know," Martha said. "I have to think about this. Let me see the photo again." Susan handed her the photo the officers had left with her. Martha took it and studied it before answering.

"Well, for starters, their clothing is nondescript, and you can't even determine their race from that angle. But to be on the safe side, we should get rid of those outfits."

"Okay," Susan said, "so, from that comment, can I deduce that you intend on denying any knowledge of these guys?"

"Correct," Martha said. "Your instinct was right when you answered their questions. I think we need to be consistent, but I think we may want to embellish the story just a bit."

"Embellish it! Like how?"

"I think we should just say: It all happened so fast and there were people who gathered around to help at the scene until gunfire started, then people left. We ducked for cover and can't say for sure if we saw these particular guys or not, but if they were in the area, we probably only got a glimpse of them. We just don't remember seeing their faces."

"Martha! We're lying to the police; that's a crime in and of itself!" Her eyes were wide with concern.

"Susan, you seem to forget that you have already lied to the police, so please spare me the indignation. We are not going to implicate George and Frank. Period.

"Palidore set the stage for this when he ordered them to leave the scene, so I guess he'll have the final say," Martha said. "But you asked what I thought, and that's what I think."

Susan was now trying to hold back tears and attempted to gather herself together. "It's two p.m. our time so we're in the window when we can call them. I think you should make the call."

"I'll call," Martha said. "but since you're the one who met with the officers, just prepare yourself to field their questions. Okay?"

"Okay, just call. We need to get this over with."

Martha dialed, and Palidore answered.

"Martha, is everything okay there?"

"Pretty much, Palidore, but something has come up that we thought you should know about. Is Lynn there with you?" she asked.

"No, she's in her room next door. Let me walk over and get

her." Martha and Susan heard Palidore knock on Lynn's door and her far away voice answer it.

"Palidore, come in. What's up?"

"I have Martha on the phone. She says something has come up and wants to talk to both of us." It took Lynn only a minute to come on the line.

"Hi Martha. What's the matter?"

"Actually, we're all fine, but Susan, who's sitting next to me, had some visitors the other day about the car accident and we want to go over what happened."

"We're listening."

"So, an investigator with the Virginia State Police and a District of Columbia cop stopped to ask Susan some questions about the accident and shooting. Fortunately, Susan had the foresight to secretly record the conversation, so rather than try and repeat what was said, we can play the conversation for you now, if you're ready."

"We're ready; play it," Palidore responded. Susan placed her cell phone next to Martha's and played the conversation. When it finished, she stopped the recording.

"I didn't know what to do, Palidore. Hope I didn't make a mistake."

"Listen to me Susan," he said, "you did fine. There was nothing else you could have done. Even though no one did anything wrong, we can't reveal who George and Frank are. Even if we did, neither of them could possibly help identify the people we had to deal with that day. So, you handled it as I would have."

"But did you notice that they want to hear from Martha and both of you?" she asked. "They want to know if you can remember the faces of George and Frank. I told them I would tell you, and let them know, but that didn't seem to satisfy them much. It's like they want to hear it directly from you. So should I contact them?"

"No, just have Martha call them and let them know she can't recognize them from the photo either. Then tell them when we'll be back. Hopefully, that will satisfy them until we return. We'll put our heads together when we get back and before we call them."

"Martha wants to get rid of the clothes they were wearing. What do you think?"

"I don't want to worry George or Frank about this just yet, so if you think they will miss the clothes or ask too many questions, then just leave everything alone until we return. You've handled everything well so far. Please don't worry about it."

"Okay."

"Anything else we should know about?"

"No. Just enjoy the rest of your conference. We'll be fine."

"Okay and thanks for calling," Palidore said. "Please don't worry about this anymore. Everything will work out. We'll talk again soon."

Susan heard him hang up and was glad the call was over.

Chapter 39

Martha lit a peach-scented candle on the coffee table in front of her couch as George sat looking out the casement windows at the MCS building across the street. There was a bag and a small suitcase at his feet. He had thrown out the old leather bags that once held the gold coins which were now nestled in a small suitcase on wheels.

"JL will be here in about an hour," Martha told him. "I'm going to pour myself a chardonnay. Want a glass?" George reached into the small bag he had brought along and pulled out a small bottle of whiskey. Now, he slowly stood and strolled toward Martha at the kitchen counter where he placed the bottle down.

"If you can provide me with a small glass of ice, I think I'll pour some of this over it." Martha picked up the bottle and read the label. "'Hudson Baby Bourbon Whiskey. Where did you get this?"

"Frank and Susan got it for me. Susan said it was her favorite."

"From the looks of it, seems someone else has grown fond of it, too."

"I have."

"Well then, here you go."

She handed him a glass of ice and George poured a goodly amount of whiskey over the cubes. Without saying a word, they touched glasses and paused for a moment to gaze at each other over the rims of their drinks. Then, each took a sip. Martha moved toward the couch and George followed. They sat silently for a moment, took another sip of their drinks before George finally sat his glass down, and put a finger under Martha's chin to tilt her head upwards. He leaned in and softly kissed her, gently and long.

She never closed her eyes, nor did she resist. When he moved in a bit closer, she held her wine glass between them. "Shouldn't we stick with our drinks? There's really not enough time for what you have in mind."

"How would you know what I have in mind?"

"Oh, I know."

George backed off and picked up his whiskey, swirling the contents. He heard the sound of ice cubes touching. "How long do you think this JL guy will be here?"

"Too long. Sorry but it's business before pleasure." They finished their drinks and moved back to the counter to prepare another round. Just as they finished getting them ready, George turned Martha around, held her in his arms for a moment before saying, "I just want to look at you, if you don't mind. Actually, I believe you recently told me that I could 'look all I want,' and right now, that's all I want."

"Well, I was on display then. I'm not on display right now."

The buzzer rang.

"Saved by the bell," Martha said, as she went to the intercom and pushed the button.

"Come on up, JL." Seconds later, the elevator door opened, and JL Walston entered wearing a blue blazer, open collar light blue button-down shirt, khakis, and brown & black saddle oxford hush puppies that had seen better days. Martha greeted him with a generous hug.

"Hi John, please come in. How is Phyllis?"

"She's good, we're all good."

"John this is George Washington. George, this is my good friend, John Walston who we often refer to as simply JL."

"Pleased to meet you, George," John said. "You certainly have a famous name."

"So, I'm told."

"Let's move to the living area, John. Do you care for a drink?"

"Sure, I'll have a scotch."

"Sorry, we have a very limited menu," Martha said. "Maybe George won't mind sharing some of his whiskey with you though."

"Whiskey is a good second choice. Thank you."

Martha fixed the drink and as they moved toward the couch, John said, "If you don't mind, could we use the table? It may work out better for us."

"Sure, of course," Martha said.

They each took one of six seats at the table. JL took out his computer and set it up as Martha handed out the coasters for their drinks.

"George has a considerable amount of assets and appears to be in need of your services, so I was pleased that you had time to meet with us here on such short notice."

"You know I'm more than happy to help, Martha. It's been a while, I guess we've not had a chance to touch base since Stanley passed."

"I know, it's been a while since we last talked. My new job has been keeping me very busy."

"Okay then, before we begin let me just get down some basic information. What is your permanent address?" George took out his WV driver's license and gave it to JL.

"This is my official address."

"Great, and a good phone number where I can reach you?" George reached into his pocket for his cell phone. But just stood looking at it. Martha grabbed it from him and hit a couple of buttons before reading the number out loud.

"Okay, now about how much money do you need to move around?" JL asked.

Martha jumped in and answered for him. "That hasn't been decided yet. Let me show you why." Martha took out the golden eagle coin George had given her, handed it to JL, and said, "Take a look at that."

"It's beautiful."

"Now, look at this." She handed him a printout from the Internet showing an identical, but slightly worn coin bearing the price of $23,436.00. "As you can see, George's coin is much better, so logically, it could be worth much more. In fact, we have recently sold four of them for a total of more than a hundred thousand dollars."

"So, how many more do you have to sell?"

"Show him, George," she urged. George retrieved the suitcase, set it on the table and opened it, displaying the complete supply of uncirculated gold coins. JL immediately stood up to get a better look

"Wow! they're beautiful."

"Shouldn't you have said, 'holy shit?' Not just 'wow?' That's what Martha says is appropriate when you see something like that. She says you must say, 'holy shit!'"

"Well, okay then," JL said, playing along. "'Holy *shit*, George!' How many are there?"

"We started with two thousand, but I gave that one to Martha and let my friend, Frank, give one to Susan. We've sold four, so what you see there are 1,994 golden eagle coins . . . uncirculated." JL took out his phone, pulled down the menu with the calculator, and did the math.

"So, at twenty-five grand each, you're looking at about fifty million dollars."

"That would be right, but if we sell them all at one time we probably won't get that much because we'll dilute the value," George said. "They're worth it, though, because they are so rare."

"Yes, but the fact that these have never been circulated actually makes them much *more* valuable. In other words, you probably weren't paid enough for the four you've already sold." JL picked up a couple of the coins and looked at them carefully. "May I ask, how did you come to have so many of these?"

Martha didn't let George answer. "Some things we're not prepared to divulge, John. However, as we've said, we've already sold four of them, to four different coin experts and each one confirmed that they were genuine. And I will tell you that George is the lawful owner of all the coins."

"So, why are you involving me in this?"

"We need to convert the coins to money as quietly as we can. We were wondering if they might make a good investment for some of your clients, or if you might have some other ideas." JL thought while he picked up his drink. He peered down at the suitcase full of coins again.

"This is interesting. Very interesting. I definitely think a number of my clients could use these coins to hide some of their money. They're so portable; they could be kept anywhere and sold whenever money was needed. So, yes, I could probably buy half of them now. Most of my clients have given me the authority to invest their funds for them. Others, I would have to contact, but I suspect many of them will jump at the chance to take some of these off your hands. That's assuming you're willing to sell them for 25k each."

"You just said that they're likely worth much more than $25,000 each, and now you want to buy them for that sum," George said.

"They are worth more," JL said. "Of that, I'm sure, but that's why my clients would be willing to buy. If I can't make them money on any deal, then they won't need me. "Besides, I'll charge them a bit more than that to allow for my five percent fee, so you won't have to pay me a commission."

George eyed JL carefully while taking a sip of his drink. "For those clients that you can speak for now, your price is fine. For those that you must seek authorization from, the price is thirty thousand."

"You are a shrewd man, Mr. Washington, and very astute. Time is money, and I think that will be agreeable. So, we are looking at moving twenty-five million dollars now, and more later."

Martha stood abruptly. "Right now? We are going to move *twenty-five million dollars* around right now? I can't believe this. We are really moving fast. I need to refill my wine glass." She moved toward the refrigerator.

"So, let me tell you how we're going to do this."

"Please do," George said.

"In order for all your money to be covered by FDIC you would need 100 separate accounts."

"I don't know about this FDIC thing," George said.

Hard to believe he hasn't heard of the FDIC, JL thought as he glanced over toward Martha with a curious look before explaining. "Well, if a bank should make some bad decisions, and go out of business, then the Federal Deposit Insurance Corporation, known as the FDIC, would underwrite all deposits, you know, insure it, they would then reimburse all depositors up to $250,000 per account. Unless you're married, in which case you are protected up to $500,000," he hesitated. "Oh, I never asked you, are you married?"

"No, I'm a widower."

Martha thought it sounded strange for him to refer to himself as a widower, but that was exactly what he was. She had to hold back a chuckle when another thought occurred to her: *he's probably the only man who could pre-decease his wife and still be considered a widower.*

JL continued, "However, if we are looking to keep some of this money hidden then a good portion of it will be kept offshore or in 'secret accounts,' so-to-speak, therefore, we may only need about ten or twenty domestic banks. How much money do you think you want to have immediately available, George?"

George looked to Martha who quickly responded, "JL, I think around five million will be more than enough, don't you agree, George?"

"Yes, five million would be fine as long as it doesn't take too long to access the other money."

JL began calling something up on his computer as he

talked. "No, the other money can be moved around and be available in five to ten business days. It's not too difficult to move it – it's just that the bank you move it to may want it to sit in their account for a few days. Now just so you know what I'm doing, I have a program that I had created for me that lets me put in data and establish numerous bank accounts all at once. I think we can do a savings account, money market account, and checking account at about seven different banks for a total of twenty-one accounts. I'll transfer the money from my client accounts into these new accounts until we reach a total of five million. There will only be one offshore account, then, and I will move the remaining twenty million into that account.

"Once that's completed, you will give me one thousand coins. I will get back to you later regarding any other clients of mine who might want to acquire some coins."

"You can do that all right now?" Martha asked.

"Yes, I just need his social security number for the domestic accounts, and a password to use with the offshore account."

Martha gave him the social they had given George but looked to George to come up with a password he would remember.

"George, we need a password. We've talked about passwords before, but this would be a very *special* password. Do you have any ideas?"

"WeThePeople1776," George said without hesitation.

"Very well, let's see if that works," JL said and typed it in. It worked. "Okay, we are almost there. Need to know what to do with the money if something should happen to you, George. You can change your mind on this later, but we'll need something to put down now. It's called a 'Pay on Death clause.'"

George got up and walked around with what was left of his drink before turning toward JL with his answer. "I want half of it to go to my friend, Frank, and the other half to Martha."

Martha was shocked. "George! I mean we've only known each other a few months. I couldn't accept so much money. Besides, John can tell you. I already have more money than I will ever need."

JL seemed to take it all in stride.

"Let's stick with that for now," George said, "After all, he said I could change it later. Right now, it covers the two people most important to me." John was staring at his computer screen.

"I know Martha's last name, but what is Frank's?"

"Frank Khamisi is his full name," Martha replied as JL keyed in the name finishing with a hard last key entry leaving his hand dramatically in the air. "Okay, wait for it, wait for it and . . . boom! I just love it when that happens! Look George, there are all your new domestic accounts with the five million evenly distributed among them, and there is the offshore account with another twenty mill. Done! So, let's start counting out a thousand of those beautiful coins."

"Let's first refresh our drinks so we can properly toast this accomplishment," Martha said. Everyone made their way into the kitchen.

"Is this an appropriate time to say: 'holy shit' again?" George asked.

Chapter 40

Martha opened the package and took out the uniform she had found at a costume shop. George gazed at the elaborate coat and pants. "It's not exactly right, but I guess it will have to do," he said. "Did you get the 'major' epaulets?"

"Yes, George, right here, but this is going to look very strange on a skeleton."

"I know, but Major Hudson deserves a proper burial in exchange for all his courageous sacrifices in service to me. How about the marker?"

"I've ordered one from the cemetery, but it will have to be put in place once it is completed. Amelia said it would be placed on the gravesite in a couple of weeks."

"I'm not sure I trust her. How can we be sure it will be done?"

"Final payment won't be given until it done," Martha said. "Five thousand to be exact. I will give her a small lockbox, and we've agreed that I will send her the combination when she sends me a photo of the marker properly in place."

"Good! I like that. When do we leave?"

"I wanted to talk to you about that. It will take us about four hours to drive there, or we can fly. Actually, there is a nice airport facility there in Emporia. Stanley and I have used a private air service for years. If we do that, then we can be there and back in less time than it takes to drive just one way, but I wasn't sure how you would feel about flying. It's up to you."

"How would we get Major Hudson from the airport to the cemetery?"

"Amelia said she would take care of that. She has a friend at Echols Funeral Home, I think she said her name was Dale, who is willing to pick us up and handle everything we need. So, what do you say? 'One if by land, or two if by air?'"

George smiled. "Two. I pick two by air."

"You sure? You've never flown before and some people . . . "

"I'm sure. When do we leave?"

"Tomorrow morning."

***

The following morning, Martha's air service picked them up and took them to the airport along with a black body bag containing Major Hudson's remains. George was excited. He had read about the Air Force and warplanes. Now he stood at the entrance to the private hanger watching aircraft come and go.

I know it's safe, he thought, *I'm just not exactly sure how I feel. These are incredible machines! This future was unimaginable in my old time. How far this country has come . . .* his thoughts were interrupted as Martha touched his arm.

They walked over to a waiting Lear jet and were greeted by an attractive woman who approached and welcomed them. Martha recognized her.

"Sandy! Good to see you, again. Are you going to be our pilot today?"

"No, I have first mate duties today. Gene, I mean Caption Wills will be at the throttle this time, but welcome aboard, it's been a while. How is Stanley?"

"I'm sorry to say that Stanley passed away a few months ago. It wasn't unexpected as he'd been ill for some time. Most people didn't realize just how ill. He kept it well hidden. Today, I'm here with my traveling companion, George Washington."

"I'm so sorry to hear about Stanley, Martha, I always enjoyed his company," she said, then turned to George. "Mr. Washington, it is a pleasure to meet you."

"Madam," George nodded and shook her outstretched hand, grateful she didn't comment on his famous name. *Women today are very confident*, he thought.

"Please follow me and we will get you all set." They went up the steps settled into the plane's comfortable seats. There were six: four in the rear that faced each other, but they chose the two forward-facing seats near the cockpit.

"You'll see better out the windows from here," Martha said.

"Once we're in the air we can provide refreshments," Sandy said. "Just go ahead and buckle up now. Martha, you've flown so much with us, I'll spare you the boring recital of our normal safety instructions. They're here on the card in the pocket if you want to review them at your leisure."

George took one out and studied it. A few minutes later they heard the pilot announce overhead: "Okay, folks, we have a green light to proceed to the runway. The flight should take only about forty-five minutes, and we anticipate a touchdown in Emporia around 10:45 a.m. Looks like we have a beautiful day to fly. I've called ahead to Emporia, and they are awaiting our arrival. Enjoy your flight."

George sat back and took a deep breath. Martha reached over and took hold of his hand. He felt the power as the engines revved up, then the plane moved out of the hanger and taxied onto the runway. Sandy took a seat in the back and buckled up.

Finally, the Lear jet started rolling faster and picked up speed rapidly. Martha noticed George had not changed his grip on her hand and showed no signs of apprehension. He was looking out the window with a steady gaze, totally fixated as the plane launched upward into the air and the ground fell away beneath them.

No one in their wildest dreams could imagine this, he thought.

My god, I could have seen all the troop movements from up here. We could have won the war so easily. What a world this is. I am without words.

Once the plane cut through the light cloud cover, he looked over toward Martha.

"This is amazing, totally incredible! I could never have imagined this. I did, however, once take a balloon ride, but this is much better."

Sandy was up and asked, "Can I get you anything to drink or a snack? Maybe a Mimosa or Bloody Mary?"

"Let's do the Mimosas without the orange juice," Martha said. 'In other words, just the champagne."

"Coming right up." Sandy returned shortly with two fluted glasses bubbling with champagne. They took the drinks and as Sandy left. Martha raised her glass causing George to do the same.

"To us!" she said.

"To us, indeed!" They clinked the glasses, then sipped their drinks contentedly.

As George looked out at the land below, he couldn't help but think of how much his world had changed. How the land below them was developed with houses and roads and buildings. It wasn't long before Sandy was back to inform them, they would be landing soon and collected their empty glasses. Martha and George buckled up and sat back as they felt the plane beginning to descend. Again, George looked outside and watched everything below grow larger as it all came up to meet the plane. Then they smoothly landed and taxied toward a small terminal building.

When the engines finally powered off, Captain Wells came out to greet them before opening the exit door.

"A pleasure to have you onboard, today," he said, touching his cap.

"And you, sir, drive a mean pair of horses," George said

as they laughed.

A portable staircase had already been put in place for them, and they descended to the tarmac, making their way to the terminal where they were met by an attractive lady.

"Hi, I'm Dale Echols with Echols Funeral Home. Amelia said you were bringing remains with you, so I brought a hearse in addition to my vehicle."

"Nice to meet you Dale, I'm Martha, and this is George. The remains are still on the plane, but you should know that other than transportation I do not believe we will need any of your services as the major's remains consist of only his skeleton. We have, however, purchased a new uniform we would like to have put on him."

"While my assistant is getting the remains moved to the coach," Dale said, "why don't we sit over there for a second." They moved to a corner and took three of the four available seats. "We can put the uniform on the skeleton if you like, but you know how that will look. On the other hand, we could improve his appearance if you like, at no additional cost to you."

"What are you suggesting?" George asked.

"Well, we have a Styrofoam container that comes in four sections, an upper and lower section for both the top portion of the body and the lower portion. It's really a container shaped like a body. You place the skeleton inside the lower sections, closing the top over it, then you put the clothes or, in this case, the uniform on the top portion, and presto, the body has a realistic shape. You don't have to touch the head, but if you choose, we have a container for that also. So, the entire body is encased in the Styrofoam container which will then be placed inside the casket. We even have several applique masks that can be applied as a face. Does any of that interest you?"

"Well, I have never heard the word 'Styrofoam' before, and I am curious as to what it is, but yes, what you suggest does interest me." Dale gave him a look of surprise as George continued. "But why would you not want to charge us for such a service?"

"My father started this business decades ago," Dale said, "and he was prone to buying everything that came along associated with the funeral profession. He bought five of these things when they first came out to have on hand, and we've not used even the first one. I mean how many skeletons is a funeral home going to be asked to handle?" she said, pausing before answering her own question.

"The answer is none, until now. So please allow me to help out if I can. Besides, it would be an honor to help a veteran."

Martha looked over to George before asking, "That's very nice of you, but if you don't mind me asking, how long would this take as we are on a fairly tight schedule."

"No time at all. Echols Funeral Home is on the way. We can stop just long enough to put the skeleton inside the Styrofoam container and dress him."

"Well then, let's do it," George said.

As they were leaving the terminal Dale said, "By the way, Amelia could not get hold of her source for a gravestone marker. She reached out to me about getting one so I'm handling that for you now. She will pay me from the funds you have given her. However, I couldn't help but notice that according to the inscription for Major Hudson's remains, he's more than two centuries old! How did you come into possession of such extremely old remains?"

Martha smiled, "Some things we are not at liberty to divulge but you can rest assured there's nothing nefarious afoot, and Amelia has assured me that this will all remain confidential."

"Oh, yes, of course, no problem there," Dale said.

The process at the funeral home did not take long except for the part of picking out an appropriate facial applique' which was then applied to the Styrofoam head via shrink wrapping it and using a hairdryer.

"From a distance, Major Hudson actually looks pretty good," George said.

"It's the least we could do," Martha agreed.

They met Amelia at the cemetery where funds were paid. The actual burial took only moments. Amelia, Dale, Martha, and George were the only ones at the gravesite and George was the only one to speak, reciting a short prayer.

"Heavenly Father, you have already received the soul of this brave soldier into Your care and custody. He is now a part of Your kingdom, part of the whole; but today, we pause to remember the time he spent here, among us, what he did and who he served. He has never been, nor ever shall be, forgotten, Amen."

Chapter 41

As the jet slipped effortlessly through the air, Martha turned to George. "I thought your prayer at the gravesite was beautiful, very appropriate, but I wondered what you meant when you said he was 'part of the whole.'" George, about to take another sip from his glass, put it down and looked at her.

"I'm not sure I can properly explain it to you. I believe that when your soul departs from your body, it becomes part of the whole."

"What is 'the whole?'"

"The universe. Everything. It's, actually, quite wonderful. You see, you feel everything. In the presence of God, you are finally at peace with yourself and the universe."

Martha was quiet before asking, "Well, what is it like . . . there?"

"You feel so at home, and part of all that is good. You doubt nothing, because you fear nothing, and in an instant, you finally see the purpose of life, the vision God has for you. Finally, you realize that somehow you have always *been* part of the universe, even before you were born, or your tenure here on earth. Everything has real meaning, real purpose. I can't explain it any better because until you see it, it's impossible to put it in words," George looked at her as she was clearly waiting for him to say more, so he continued.

"I mean, how would you explain to an infant, prior to his birth, what he is about to see or experience? He just spent nine months in the comfort of his mother's womb, wanting for nothing; then he is suddenly placed in this world full of mountains, oceans, trees, birds, animals, and everything else. Even if he could hear and understand you, he would not know what you were trying to describe. Put another way, it would be like trying to explain the colors of the rainbow to a person who has been blind since birth. It's really impossible."

"Well, what do people do? I mean, you were there for a couple of hundred years. What did you *do*? What went on?"

George smiled and reflected on how to answer her question while peering out the window at the sun. "You always have a purpose. You always have meaning, and you are always part of the whole. But . . . there is no such thing as 'time.' It's just always 'now.' You live in an ever-present 'now.' You don't age. You don't tire. You don't hunger. You are in the presence of Almighty God and that is more than enough. It's wonderful. It's all you could ever want."

"So, now that you have experienced the Afterlife, are you afraid of anything?"

"Yes," George said. "I experience fear. I am human and my body experiences fear. You see, the primary purpose of your body is to protect your soul, so it can achieve its mission. That's why your survival instincts are so strong. You can't help it."

"But you came back," Martha said, wanting to know more but not sure how far she could push this conversation. Finally, she shifted in her seat and turned more toward George. "So, who are you now? What does all this mean for me, for *us*?"

George smiled. "Right now, I am once more, a mortal man. My soul is once more encased in this old body of mine that Palidore restarted. But I would not be here if it were not God's will. For now, I am human. And I feel and behave like a human being, again." He looked at her before he said the next words. "And my feelings for you are as real as they can be. You and I are part of the universe, and the feelings and love we share is good, very good. You just need to be 'you' and I will be 'me,' and together, we will be 'us.' What we have is good, Martha. If it were not so, I would not have told you anything."

Martha was nearly overcome with emotion as she heard his words. She took out a handkerchief and dabbed at her eyes. Inside, she was trying to sort her feelings along with memories of her late husband. Stanley had never spoken to her about such things. It made her feelings for George even stronger.

Then Sandy appeared in the aisle. "Touching down soon. You may want to finish your champagne, or shall I take your glasses now?" Martha and George noticed that they had been so engrossed in conversation they had not consumed much of their drinks. Picking up their flutes, they toasted with a small sip before, handing the remainder of their drinks to Sandy.

*** .

Arriving back at the MCS building by three o'clock, they were met by Frank and Susan. George told Frank about the flight and the funeral. Frank remembered Major Hudson and was pleased everything had gone so well. Martha showed Susan photos she took on the trip with her cell phone.

"So, what's next?" Susan asked.

"I think we need to plan for Palidore and Lynn's return," Martha said. "A lot has happened, and I suspect we need to decide what we're going to share with them."

"That's not difficult," George said. "We need to tell them everything. I don't want to lie or mislead them. They're good people and have been good to me. So, it's time to confess."

"You don't think they will be upset?" Frank asked.

"They probably will be, but had they known what we were going to do, they never would have left on their trip. But they did, and we did what we did, and so here we are. I'm quite satisfied with what we have done and where we are. Hopefully, in the end, they will come to realize everything has worked out for the best."

George's cell phone rang. With a surprised and perplexed look on his face he said, "Someone from Charlottesville, Virginia, is calling me? Who could that be?"

"Maybe it's Palidore or Lynn," Frank said. "Who else would have your number?"

"Well, when it rings, just answer it and find out who it is," Susan said. George touched the green button and held it to his ear.

"H-e-l-l-o?" he said very slowly. Everyone listened carefully to his side of the conversation.

"I am not sure." Silence.

"Actually, I just don't know." Silence.

"What does it cost?" Silence.

"Actually, I don't own the car, but I can check and see if the owner thinks we should have this warranty."

Susan laughed. "George, just hang up."

George put the phone to his chest. "That would be rude. This woman seems to be genuinely concerned about this."

"They will never stop talking. You just have to hang up on them. They are used to it," Susan said.

George put the phone back to his ear. "I'm so sorry, but I have to hang up now. Thank you for calling." He pushed the red button. Martha and Susan were nearly overcome with laughter, but Frank wasn't sure what had just happened. Martha and Susan took several minutes to explain how robocalls worked. George listened but didn't seem sure it was a scam.

"Well, how did she get my number?"

"George, those are just random calls, they dial all possible numbers. Anyway, we should get back to our subject. We were discussing what to tell Palidore and Lynn," Martha said.

"I thought we had settled it. We are going to be truthful and tell them everything that has happened."

"Okay, I understand that is what you *said*, but sometimes when you have significant news, you need to plan where and when to make such a disclosure," Susan said.

"I agree with that. What do you suggest?"

No one said anything for a few moments. Then Martha started to say something but stopped mid-sentence as if she suddenly had second thoughts. Frank saw it.

"Martha, you were going to say something?"

"Well, I did have an idea, but decided that maybe it would seem a little too informal." She now had everyone's full attention.

"Why don't you give us your idea and we can all decide whether or not it's workable," Susan said.

Martha stood up and walked around a bit before responding. "I was going to say that maybe I could hold a dinner at my flat and that's where we could explain everything that has happened."

"Well, that's a great way to handle it." Frank said. "Everything is better with food."

"We could tell them that we just want to celebrate their return," Martha said. "So, let's see, its Thursday today and they're due back next Wednesday. That should give us plenty of time to make arrangements." Susan said.

"They're coming in late on Wednesday, so I think next Thursday is out. They'll need time to rest. So, how about next week on Friday?" Martha asked. Everyone nodded in agreement.

"It happens that my calendar is clear on that day," Frank said. Everyone laughed

His sense of humor is really coming out, Martha thought

"Then it is settled. I think I will have it catered," Martha said. "That way, I can remain focused on the meeting. I know just the right person for the job. I'll give her a call. However, there is something else I could use some help with."

"What's that?" Susan asked.

"Follow me."

They all followed Martha down to Palidore's office. Martha went to his liquor credenza and started taking out liquor bottles. They all watched and waited for an explanation.

"You see, apparently Palidore likes all of these, and I do not keep anything but chardonnay at my flat. Well, now I do have half a bottle of Hudson Baby Bourbon whiskey . . . and that's it. Maybe you and Frank can write down the names of all these liquors and get them for me along with whatever mixers are used with them. I guess it's time for me to expand my bar selections."

"Sure, we can do that, but it looks like he prefers this Edradour single malt scotch whisky since he has, let's see . . . six and a half bottles of it," Frank said. "You might just need to borrow the opened bottle of that and buy the rest."

"I agree," George said. "Palidore once told me that Edradour is not available here. He has to order it special, which is probably why he has such a supply."

"Well, anyway, Frank and I will take care of shopping. Is there anything else?" Susan asked.

"No, I can handle the rest of it, but George and I have not eaten, so we are starved. Want to join us for an early dinner?" Susan looked at Frank.

"Actually, Frank and I ventured out for a late lunch not long ago, so I'm going to pass, but Frank, you can join them if you want."

"No, I might just spend another hour or so on the modules. I'm learning a lot."

George was pleased at how the evening was developing since he wanted to have time alone with Martha.

255

Chapter 42

Martha and George made their way across the street to her flat. Once inside, Martha suggested ordering Chinese. George agreed, and while Martha called to place the order, George went to the cupboard to store Palidore's bottle and reach for the opened bottle of Hudson Baby Bourbon. Then he poured himself a drink. Opening the refrigerator, he took out a cold bottle of chardonnay, held it up to Martha, and pointed at it. She gave him a thumbs up and he poured her a healthy glass. When she was off the phone, she took her glass from George, and they moved toward the couch.

The late afternoon sun was pouring in, so Martha ordered Alexa to lower the blinds halfway. Then asked for some Roger Williams music to play. With the pleasant music on, and the sun no longer a distraction, she held up her glass to George and they touched the rims.

"That's three," he said.

"Three what?" Martha asked.

"Three toasts we've had today. But I like it . . . I'm not complaining."

"Well, it seems we have a lot to celebrate, don't we?"

"Indeed, we do."

"You've accomplished a lot since your return, George Washington."

"I'm pleased with what we have been able to do."

"Let's see, you've mastered many of your educational modules;

met and impressed the MCS board; visited Mount Vernon not just once, but four times; survived a car accident and shootout; retrieved all your precious gold coins; converted half of them into a fortune and available cash; found and buried the remains of your faithful Major Hudson, and last, but not least, you have won my heart."

"You saved the best for last," he said. "If I've indeed won your heart, then truly that is the most amazing feat I have accomplished since my return." George leaned in and gave her a light kiss on the lips. He looked into her eyes and returned for a longer, more passionate kiss. When they paused, Martha smiled

"I expect the food will be arriving soon," she said.

"So practical," he sighed.

Not long afterward, the doorbell sounded, and the food arrived. While they were eating at the table, Martha brought up another subject.

"George, can we revisit a portion of the conversation we had on the plane? I still have a question or two."

"You may ask all the questions you want, but be forewarned, I'm not certain I will be able to properly answer everything you may want to know."

"That's all right. But you mentioned that our lives all have a purpose and meaning and that in the Afterlife, you finally understand what that is. Does that mean we will never know what our purpose or meaning is until *then*?"

"Not necessarily," he answered. "But you need to understand that during our lives here on earth, many of us spend too much time trying to figure it out instead of just living our lives in a way that will allow us to find and complete our mission. Some of us may even think we *know* what our purpose is, but only in the Afterlife will everything truly fall into place. Then, you'll be able to see how important your purpose was here on earth, what it means to the universe, the whole, and how significant you really are. Once there, you will revisit the multitude of small things you ever said or did, the kindnesses you showed to others, and you'll quickly come to realize that the sympathy and feelings you showed outside yourself to others is the glue that holds everything together. You'll come to understand that all your accomplishments are not nearly as important as your *willingness to make the effort*," he looked at her."We all have meaning, and we all have a purpose, and we are all equal in God's eyes," he said. "Does that answer your question?"

"I'm trying to understand . . . I want to understand. What you say makes so much sense but, to be truthful, I should confess that I'm still struggling with it."

"Okay, let me give you an example. Maybe this will help: Suppose you are a clock. During your lifetime, as a clock, you are not sure why, but you work very hard to keep your three hands circling in front of your face with exact precision. You observe people stopping to look at you. Some look and hurry away. Others look and just sit down. You don't understand their actions, but you keep doing the only thing you know how to do – show the time - until one day your spring breaks, and you stop working altogether. Your soul escapes from the clock and looks back. That's when you realize you had a real purpose in life. You helped people keep their appointments, enabled them to make decisions, and plan events in their lives. You remember all their faces and suddenly it all makes perfect sense to you. Your life, as a clock, had real purpose," he said and paused. "Does that help?"

"Yes, it does. It really does. Thank you so much. But that leaves me with one more question."

"Go ahead, I'm listening."

"Well, now that you're back, do *you* already know what your new purpose will be?"

George smiled. "Actually, I suppose I *do* know, and I believe you probably know your purpose as well. Somewhere deep inside all of us, we secretly know, or at least have a sense of what our purpose in life is; unfortunately, sometimes we just don't *consciously* realize that we know it. So, we keep on searching. However, I believe that when events occur, you will respond appropriately. As long as my faith in

God does not waiver, I will make the right choices and, accordingly, will fulfill my purpose. I need not worry now about what I must do. I only need to keep my faith, love my God, and all will be revealed to me in due time."

"Well, that's a lot to think about."

"No, it's not. You don't need to wrestle with it, Martha. Just live the life that God has given you and you will accomplish your purpose. True understanding will come later."

They were silent, just letting the conversation settle around them. Then Martha arose, blew out the candle in the center of the small table, and cleared it off before asking, "Would you care for another drink? I'll make this round."

"Sure," George replied, as he made his way to the kitchen counter. Martha handed him his glass refilled and took her glass of chardonnay. Roger Williams was playing "The Impossible Dream" on his piano. The moment was pregnant with emotion. George put his glass down, removed Martha's glass from her hand, and took her in his arms. They began to dance to the music, slowly, romantically.

For Martha, it was a magical moment. *I truly am living the impossible dream*, she thought. When the song ended, they didn't part but chose to stand there holding each other. When the next selection began to play, Martha took George's hand and headed toward her bedroom. Once inside, she kissed him lightly on the lips.

"I think it's time for our souls to meet."

Chapter 43

The next morning George was the first to wake as a bit of sunlight caught his eye. He noticed that during the night, he had gathered all the covers onto himself, leaving Martha, still asleep on her stomach, with nothing to cover her unclad body. The sun, coming in through the partially closed plantation shutters, had the effect of casting shadow stripes across her body. George was mesmerized at the sight.

This is the most beautiful woman I have ever known, he thought. *Both in body and spirit.* Unable to resist an impulse, he began lightly running his hand over her soft skin, causing her to stir. With her face less than a foot away from his, she opened her eyes.

"I need some covers."

"But I much prefer you as you are."

"Well, then you need to figure out how to keep me warm."

George needed no further encouragement and threw back his covers enough to draw her in toward his warm body. She stirred against him, and he became excited again. When they had exhausted their lovemaking, they lay together looking up at the ceiling fan as it moved slowly above them hanging from the ornate ceiling.

Finally, Martha kissed George on the nose.

"I'm going to shower and get ready. You should do the same, but you'd better go to the other room. We don't have enough time to enjoy each other again right now."

They both showered, dressed, and eventually found themselves at the kitchen counter. Martha popped two frozen sausage biscuits into the microwave for a quick snack before they headed back across the street to the MCS building. Susan saw them come in.

"Well, hello," she said in a coy tone of voice. "Did you two just happen to accidentally doze off again?"

"Something like that," Martha said, in no mood to explain.

George went to find Frank and Martha stopped by her office where she started planning for the dinner celebrating Palidore and Lynn's return. She called her long-time friend, Patsy, who answered on the first ring.

"Martha, how good to hear from you again. I was wondering how you were doing now. It's been a while since Stanley passed. Is everything okay?"

"Actually, things are going so well that at times I actually feel guilty for feeling so good," Martha said.

"That's wonderful to hear. You sound happy."

"That's why I'm calling. I'm having a small party next Friday and was wondering if you could cater it for me."

"Next Friday? Let's see . . . yep, I'm clear on that date, and even if I wasn't, I would still make it happen for you somehow."

"You're too sweet, Patsy."

"So, what were you thinking?"

"Well, this has to be something that you can prepare ahead of time and leave here. I'll have to serve it at an appropriate time. It's for my boss and colleagues. There will be just six of us."

"What time?"

"Oh, early evening; we probably plan on eating around six, but I can text you the exact details."

"Let me think about a menu for you. Some things don't keep well if they are not served right away. I'll come up with a couple of suggestions and you can decide then."

"That's why I love working with you, Patsy, you're perfect at planning these last-minute dinners. I'll never forget all those wonderful impromptu Saturday night get-togethers you invited Stanley and me to. I can't thank you enough for always being there for me. I'll let you think, and we'll talk again later." When she hung up, she knew the dinner would be perfect.

***

George peeked into Frank's room and caught him at his desk. Frank heard him enter and spun around, getting up to greet him. Meeting in the middle of the room, they threw arms around each other and embraced in friendship.

"Always happy to be together with you, my friend," George said. "I can't imagine how I would manage this new life without you. How's it going with the modules? By now, I would imagine you are way past me."

"You know, George, this thing is addictive. The more I learn, the more I want to learn. But as much as I like it, I need to find something else to do. I can't just keep doing this and nothing else."

"That's what I want to talk to you about. I know there is still much we have not mastered, but I'm not sure we ever will. I think it's time we set out on our own. We certainly have enough money, and we have our new identities. So, what do you say?"

"When are you thinking about doing this?"

"I'm not exactly sure, but probably sooner rather than later," George said. "I have to run this by Martha. You know we are quite attracted to one another."

"George, that's been obvious for some time now. Susan and I have discussed it," Frank said. "So, where should we go?"

"Well, we are supposed to own a business in West Virginia, so I was thinking we should head there."

"And how are we supposed to get there?"

"We'll need to buy a car or truck, but I guess we should learn how to drive first."

"Let me surprise you, then. Since you have been spending so

much time with Martha, Susan and I have been doing a few things ourselves. In fact, she has already been teaching me how to drive."

"Frank, you are full of surprises," George said, smiling broadly.

"Actually, I think I have it down pretty well. I've also covered the module and passed the practice driving test," Frank moved his hands in the air as if he were turning a wheel. "I know we already have valid West Virginia drivers' licenses, but I thought I should learn this stuff anyway."

"That's wonderful," George said. "Funny how things just seem to fall into place at the right time. So, us getting a truck shouldn't be too difficult. I'll ask Martha where she gets her vehicles."

"So, George, what will we do in West Virginia?"

"Well, as you may recall, we are supposed to own a timber business. We find tracts of timber for lumber companies. You remember our business name, don't you, the WTS, LLC? Now that we have millions of dollars, we can buy the timber ourselves and resell it at a profit instead of finding it for others. What do you think?"

"I am in, George, but I'm not sure either of us knows enough about the value of timber today to make intelligent investments."

"We'll learn, Frank, we'll learn."

Chapter 44

On Friday, Martha left work early to prepare for the dinner party. She had just finished dressing and setting the table when her buzzer rang. She went to the elevator door and hit the intercom button.

"Patsy, is that you?"

"It's me."

"I'll be right down to help you bring things up. The elevator to my flat is in front of my car. I'm putting the garage door up now. See you in a minute."

With boxes on a service cart, Martha and Patsy were able to manage the transfer of all items in one trip. Once everything was in the flat, the two women bustled around the kitchen unpacking and storing things everywhere.

"Gosh, that smells s-o-o-o good," Martha commented.

"I hope you like it," Patsy said. "I chose to leave the meat a little undercooked so we could finish it off in the oven on low heat here. Let's warm your oven now to 300°. Then one hour prior to eating, just put both dishes in, and that's it. I've already put the fresh salad in the refrigerator to cool. I just wish you had let me bring dessert."

"Oh, I know your desserts are amazing. But Susan, one of my colleagues, wanted to bring something. You know how that goes. So, I wanted to let her do her part. She's a big part of this evening's dinner/meeting. Now, how about a drink. Have the time?"

"Well, maybe one, for old times' sake," Patsy said.

"If I remember, you like vodka tonics with two limes. Right?"

"That's it; you've got a great memory."

Martha got out the new bottle of Tito's Vodka and Fever-Tree tonic and made the drink, adding a tiny bit of sugar to top it off.

"Here you go," she said, handing the glass to her friend. "You're in luck, too, because until yesterday the only alcohol I had in my flat was chardonnay. Now, I'm newly stocked up, just for tonight."

Patsy held up her glass and Martha did the same. "To friendship," Patsy said, taking a sip. "Hmm, this is perfect; maybe the best I've ever had."

"If you remember, Stanley liked vodka tonics in the summer, and he showed me how to make them. He said it was the special tonic water that made all the difference." Martha and Patsy spent the next hour catching up before Patsy packed up her empty containers and left.

Martha checked the time and put the dishes in the oven at 5:30 p.m. Then, she lit candles, put on soft Roger Williams music, poured herself another chardonnay, and waited for her guests.

George was the first to arrive. He had previously mastered the code to her garage door and elevator, so he came in unannounced and surprised her by putting his arms around her from behind and nuzzling the back of her neck.

"Well, welcome to you, too." She said and turned to hug him.

"It's always good to be here with you."

"Now that I have a fully functional bar, please feel free to fix yourself a drink."

"Don't mind if I do."

He was fixing his drink when the buzzer rang. Martha opened the garage door and elevator for the remainder of her guests. She warmly greeted Palidore and Lynn who brought a gift from Brussels for her condo. They had arrived back in town late Wednesday, and she hadn't seen them on Thursday or even earlier Friday before she had left the office early to prepare for this evening. Frank and Susan arrived soon afterward with a glorious dessert in hand.

Soon, everyone had gathered around with a drink, enjoying the aroma of the Chateaubriand and the homemade scallop potatoes wafting in from the oven.

At 6:30 p.m., Martha asked for everyone's attention. "If you'll all take seats at the table, George is going to say grace for us; then we can eat."

"It smells so good," Lynn said. 'Better than anything we had in Brussels. I can hardly wait."

George said grace, after which Martha served salad followed by the two main dishes on the table, uncovering them both at the same time. Everyone raved, but Martha gave all the credit to her friend, Patsy.

Halfway through the meal, Palidore put his fork down.

"This is great, Martha. Thank you so much for hosting this evening. Now, tell me how everything really went in our absence. We've been asking, but everyone has been telling us to wait until Friday, so our curiosity is completely peaked." Martha shot a glace to George who had previously volunteered to narrate the entire adventure.

"Well before we start, let me simply say that from *my* perspective, everything could not have gone better. However, I understand that it's possible *you* might take a slightly different view."

Palidore and Lynn looked at each other. Then George began to explain what he had done during his first trip to Mount Vernon and in the subsequent trips to retrieve his coins. He also told them about finding the remains of his friend, Major Hudson, and the airplane ride to re-bury him. Lastly, he explained how Martha had introduced him to JL Walston who set up his bank accounts. When he finished, he presented a small, wrapped gift to both Palidore and Lynn. Neither of whom had interrupted him throughout his presentation. They did, however, look as if they were in a state of disbelief as they accepted the small packages.

"Go ahead, open them."

Lynn and Palidore exchanged glances and slowly began opening the packages. Lynn finished opening hers first; then Palidore waited until she finished. Inside was one of the Golden Eagle coins made into a necklace.

"This is gorgeous!" she exclaimed. "Is it one of your coins?"

"It is," George smiled. "Martha helped me find a jeweler who could put the gold band around the edge so it would fit on the chain, but not harm the coin."

"Thank you, George," she said gratefully, "This is *very* thoughtful."

"Palidore, please go ahead and open yours."

Inside, he found one of the coins converted into the face of a watch.

"Why, this is *beautiful*, how on earth did you do it?"

"I didn't. Again, Martha gets the credit for knowing who to contact. I just provided the coin hoping it would get done in time."

"How much did you say one of these coins is worth?" Palidore asked again.

"About twenty-five thousand dollars," Martha said.

"I don't know . . . I just don't know what to say," Palidore stammered. "All of this is almost too much to comprehend. I have very mixed emotions going on right now. I guess my first impression is to be thankful that everyone is okay, and no one is in any trouble. On the other hand, it's like a father watching his children growing up too fast." Everyone laughed.

"But wait! I heard on the news that after the break-in at Mount

Vernon, they found a boat downriver with blood on it," Palidore said.

"That was Frank's blood. None of our blood is on file anywhere, obviously, so we took some and spread it around to make the authorities think that whoever had entered the tunnel system had perished. Since they never knew about the coins in the first place, no one would know they were gone. Hopefully, they won't need to spend too much time investigating the whereabouts of any persons they think are responsible," George said.

"Well, you seem to have thought about it all. I'm not sure where we go from here. Is there anything else you need to tell us?

"Yes, something more, and it's the most important thing."

Lynn and Palidore's faces seemed to turn pale. What more could possibly be revealed?

"I have fallen madly in love with Martha," George said. Martha's face showed shock as she had no idea, he was going to divulge their secret. When he told her that he was going to tell them everything, she never dreamed it was about their relationship.

I guess when he says 'everything' he means "everything, she thought.

Lynn appeared shocked and looked at Martha.

"Is this true?"

Martha looked around the table at all faces now fixated on her.

"Yes, Lynn. It's true. What's more, I'm in love with George, too. I know that allowing this to happen is professionally irresponsible, but for me, it's the most wonderful thing I have ever allowed myself to do. So, to you and Palidore, I apologize, and will hand in my resignation tomorrow."

Then turning toward George, tears now streaming down her face, she took his hands in hers. "And to you, George, I offer *no* apologizes, only my undying love."

***

The following morning, Martha's letter of resignation was on Palidore's desk which he would not accept. Instead, he convinced her to let a couple of weeks pass, hoping in that time, somehow, the turmoil of emotions would settle down.

In the meantime, Frank and George resumed their educational modules. Lynn spent time working with Susan and Frank but somehow avoided Martha. They filed reports with police concerning the car accident traffic-cam photo but heard nothing back.

***

It was early on a Monday morning when Lynn rushed into Palidore's office holding a letter in her hand.

"They're gone!"

"I know," Palidore said as he held up another letter.

"What are you going to do?"

"I don't know, Lynn, probably nothing. What does your letter say?"

"Well, it just thanks me for all I've done for them and says they'll be back in touch at a later time. It also says that I shouldn't try to contact them for now. Oh, and it also contains a check made out to me for one million dollars! Can you believe it? What does yours say?"

"Pretty much the same thing; but mine has two one-million-dollar checks. One is made out to me, and the other to MCS. Oh, and they left me something else."

"What?"

"These." Palidore held out two tracking devices in his hand. "They're going to West Virginia. I think Martha is going with them. She left a second resignation letter."

"What about Susan?" Lynn asked.

Palidore held up another envelope and waved it at her. Nothing more needed to be said.

GIL HUDSON

Sneak Peak
into Book 3 of the POTUS 1 Series

The Rise of George Washington

GIL HUDSON

Chapter 1

George awoke in the dark at the sound and glanced over to Martha who was fast asleep. He listened carefully and heard the sound again. The night clock displayed 5:00 a.m. He grabbed his cell phone off the nightstand and rose slowly. When Martha stirred, she could hear him talking in a whisper to the 911 operator.

"I can tell you there is someone in our flat and you need to hurry because someone is going to get hurt really bad and it's not going to be me." With that, he hung up as the operator's voice beseeched him not to confront the intruder. Martha tried to process what she had just heard as she watched her naked lover peer around the cracked open bedroom door.

"George, what are you *doing*?" She said in a whispered voice.

"Martha, listen to me. You need to get in the bathroom and lock the door. Do not open it for anyone except me. Do you understand?"

"George, please listen to me . . . "

"No! you listen to *me*... wait, wait . . . be quiet! There it is *again!* The guy must be drunk because he keeps bumping into things. Frank is out there on the couch and in *danger*. Now, do as I say and get in the bathroom!" His command was in as firm a voice as his whispered tone would allow. "I am going out there and I know this is your little kingdom, but I am going to *defend* it."

Martha's eyes grew large as she realized what was making the noise, but there was no time to explain it to George as he crept out the bedroom door. She grabbed her cell phone and went into the bathroom as fast as possible to dial 911 and cancel the police arrival she knew was on the way

Susan heard George yelp and peeked out the door of the second bedroom where she had been sleeping. Seeing the naked first president jumping around on one foot made her quickly retreat. Frank, who had been asleep on the couch, quickly sat up just as George yelled.

"I've got you! What the *hell* kind of creature are you?" he called out, rushing toward the casement window with the small, dark object in his hands. Cranking open the casement window with one hand, he tossed the object outside with the other and watched it smash onto the ground below. Martha came running from the bedroom in her robe and handed a very distraught George Washington his own robe to cover up.

"You're bleeding, George! Are you okay?"

"I think so. That thing bit my foot! I kicked it away, but it started coming right back at me! It had a hard black shell and funny feet. I've never seen *anything* like it. How the hell did it get in here?"

Martha knew George was upset and actually being quite brave. She didn't want to make fun while he was so distraught, but was having a hard time holding back her laughter.

Standing by, Frank realized what had just happened and what his friend was going through, so he tried to explain. "George, it wasn't a creature. It was a machine."

"A machine? What kind of machine! And why on earth would anyone want such a thing in their home?"

"It's a self-propelled vacuum cleaner that roams around and cleans up dust and dirt," Frank said.

"You have to be kidding me!"

"No, he's not, George," Martha said. "I am so sorry, but I forgot to turn it off, so it started to roam at five this morning because that's when I've programmed it to clean. I know that's early, but normally, I am here alone and want it to finish before I leave for work," she said.

"How come I've never seen it before?"

"Well, it's base is out of view under that little table so it's not easily seen. Also it's not programed to clean every day and I normally have it turned off when I have guests. I forgot this time; I'm so sorry. Let me see your foot. Gosh, the cut is kind of deep."

"Is it? I thought it was *alive* and had bitten me so I kicked it really hard. I suppose that's how I actually got cut."

Martha went around the counter to the kitchen sink, grabbed a paper towel, moistened it with water and returned to George, now seated, and dabbed at the wound then wrapped the paper around it.

"How much did you pay for that worthless piece of junk?" George asked.

"About eight hundred dollars."

"Eight hundred dollars! For *that*? I can't believe it! Well, it's gone now." George said triumphantly, but with a sheepish grin on his face. "Hey, how come the police never came?"

"After you ordered me into the bathroom, it occurred to me what was happening, and knowing no one was *really* in danger, my first priority was to call off the 911 report. It turns out that it is not a very easy thing to do. I had to prove I was the owner here, and not the alleged criminal. However, I *was* successful in calling off the police who were already en route."

Everyone sat in silence until one by one they began to laugh, even George. And so began their first day of independent living.

***

GIL HUDSON

If you've enjoyed this Sneak Peak into Book 3 of the POTUS 1 Series

The Rise of ***George Washington***

You can pre-order it soon on Amazon.com.

Five- Star Reviews for the POTUS 1 Series

5.0 out of 5 stars **Could not put it down**
Reviewed in the United States on January 17, 2022
Verified Purchase

I usually do not read books. Loved this one.

Amazon Review – J.L.W.

5.0 out of 5 stars **Top Rating for this Story**
Reviewed in the United States on January 17, 2022
Verified Purchase

I am an avid reader of Stuart Wood, John Grisham, James Patterson, and believe me, Gil Hudson has done an excellent job with this book. Definitely a top rating for this story.

Amazon Review – J.H.

5.0 out of 5 stars **Interesting Story Well Done**
Reviewed in the United States on January 11, 2022

In general, I am not an avid reader. However, I really enjoyed reading Reviving (George Washington) and look forward to reading subsequent books in this series. The story is interesting, well-written, and an easy read. I found myself not wanting to put the book down until I was done---pretty rare for me. The author, Gil Hudson, is to be congratulated for a good storyline and a job well done. Stu

Amazon Review – B.O.

If you missed reading Book 1
of the POTUS 1 Series

Reviving
George Washington

Here is a Sneak Peak
into Chapter 1

You can find it on Amazon.com
and TheWritersMall.com

GIL HUDSON

Chapter 1

The Accident

April 2, 1798

The door to the clinic banged open and five disheveled men rushed in carrying a stretcher on which a bloody young boy was crying in agony, blood pouring from a wound in his left leg.

"We need help! Get the doctor . . . he's been shot!" One of the men yelled as they placed the stretcher in the middle of the clinic floor. The other patients in the waiting area jumped back to make room as nurse Althea White ran over to the boy. Dr. Palidore Montgomery came running from an examination room at the sound of the commotion.

"Sam, run back to room Two and tell Kevin to get out, so we can get this boy in there. You men, help me move him." Four of the men grabbed the stretcher again and passed a shaken Kevin in the hallway as they rushed into the exam room placing the stretcher and the boy on a high table.

"Thank you, now please leave, so nurse White and I can work." As the men began leaving the room, one man remained.

"I am not leaving!"

"Who are you?" the doctor asked.

"I am his father, and the one who shot him."

"Then stay out of my way, and don't talk," Dr. Montgomery

said. "Whoever put the tourniquet on, saved his life so far, but he is bleeding badly." He nodded to his nurse, "Aletha, cut his pant leg off, and let's clean this up."

Aletha moved swiftly as instructed and continued working rapidly on the wound without need for further instruction. The doctor noticed the boy about to nod off and yelled, "Hey! Not yet! Stay awake, Son . . . you need to stay awake!"

Aletha put a cold washcloth on the boy's sweat and tear-stained face as his eyes opened again. Palidore pressed down on a specific spot below the tourniquet with his thumb. "Still bleeding too much. Aletha, run to my office, and get me the brown satchel near my desk, quickly please."

Nurse White did as requested; when she returned, she placed the bag on a small table next to the high one Palidore was working on. The boy's head was lying still; the father was standing anxiously to the side with pain in his eyes.

"Now, listen carefully to me. Take out the jar labeled 'A' and unscrew the top. Be careful not to spill any contents." Aletha carefully followed instructions. Palidore looked at the man. "Sir, come over here and keep your son awake, slap him, if necessary, but do not let him doze off." The man stepped next to his son on the opposite side of the table and began talking to him and touching him to keep him awake.

"Althea, give me a scalpel; I need to open this wound up more to see where the bleeding is coming from. I am afraid the bullet may have hit his femoral artery, so this may be difficult to control." He inserted a retractor and enlarged the wound opening to see inside the leg as blood continued to seep out in with a slight pumping movement. Nurse White pressed against the edges of the wound with gauze attempting to keep the area free of new blood so the doctor could look.

"Now, listen to me, Aletha. Take a spoonful of that powder from Jar A and gently spread it out on the tray next to me." She did as instructed. Palidore took his finger and pressed against the powder, then placed his finger into the wound, repeating this several times.

TRANSFORMING GEORGE WASHINGTON

Each time his finger hit the wound, the blood would immediately congeal and appeared almost to freeze. Slowly, the bleeding stopped except for a small amount still leaking from the artery. Palidore examined it closely to see if his powder had taken effect, but when he touched it, blood spirted out hitting Aletha in the face. Quickly, Palidore applied the tiniest touch of the powder directly onto the artery. Almost instantly, the blood congealed and froze. He looked carefully. All bleeding had stopped.

"Quickly, now, sit him up!" Palidore commanded. Nurse White and the boy's father helped the boy into a sitting position on the table. "You have him? Hold him up. I've got to prepare something." Palidore took another small jar from the bag labeled "B" and put a small amount in a glass of water, mixed it, and handed it to his nurse.

"Make him drink all of this." She put the glass to the boy's lips and after multiple sips, he had drunk the entire contents. "Ease him back down on the table," Palidore said. "He can rest and sleep now if he likes." They laid him back down and Althea washed his face with a wet cloth.

"You're okay now," Althea said in a soft, calm voice. "You're going to be fine. Just relax and rest." When she looked up, she saw the father's tears streaming down his cheeks and watched as he began sobbing almost uncontrollably. She went to him and guided him to a chair along the wall.

"You will have to leave us for now, sir, we are not done here, yet, however, we must not disturb him with your upset. You can sit right outside the door." The father nodded and quietly left the room. Althea resumed her position next to the doctor who instructed her,

"Please take some of that peroxide in the blue bottle and clean the wound. It's something new that should help prevent infection."

"I know what it is, Palidore, you told me all about it when you were able to acquire it."

"Right. Well, just pat some around the wound and wipe gently with some gauze." She followed his instructions while Palidore manipulated the wound opening again. He could now see the artery clearly and spoke in a whisper.

"The bullet, indeed, nicked his femoral artery. I have put some of my special compound on it and sealed it, but I am uncertain about what might happen when we release the tourniquet. I am going to try and strengthen the artery, so please, open the jar that is labeled 'C' and take a small amount and place it in a small dish. Next, add a small amount of water, maybe only a teaspoon." Aletha stirred the mixture, creating a thick solution.

"Now take a small amount of gauze and soak it with the solution." Aletha followed his direction, but Palidore interrupted her. "A much smaller piece, please." When she had the new piece ready, Palidore held out his hand to receive it, and gently wrapped it around the artery. As they watched, the gauze began to slowly shrink and formed what appeared to be a perfect bandage around the artery. "Okay, let's hope this holds," he said while reaching to untie the tourniquet and holding his breath. A few seconds passed before Palidore was able to breathe normally again. He looked over at his faithful nurse and smiled.

"Good job, Aletha, I think, with God's help, we have saved this boy's life. Now, let us clean this up, sew up the wound, and apply a bandage around his leg."

"I can do that," Althea smiled. "Why don't you go inform the boy's father." Palidore, nodded and walked out into the hallway where the father was leaning against the wall. "It is a bit of a miracle, but I believe your son will recover. He has lost a lot of blood, so he will need rest and nourishment for the next several days. His artery was, indeed, nicked and had you not tied a tourniquet and brought him here so quickly, it would have been a different story. But we have stopped the bleeding and he will heal. However, he also needs to avoid any activity with that leg for at least a week."

"I don't know how to thank you enough," the father said emotionally.

"None is necessary, but I am curious how it happened."

"It was entirely my fault. Steven found my handgun and was looking at it. Being afraid, I grabbed it out of his hand, not realizing he had already cocked the hammer back. It just went off like that, discharging a bullet right through his leg."

"I see, well, as I've said, you also helped to save him with your quick action. But if you don't mind, can you share with me how it is you wound up bringing him here?"

"My assistant, Jeffrey, a patient of yours who is in your waiting room, suggested we bring him here and you were closer than my own doctor." Palidore seemed to accept the explanation.

"Well, again, I am sorry, but in all the excitement I failed to get your name, I am Dr. Palidore Montgomery." He held out his hand to the man.

"Of course, and I am William Grayson."

"*Senator* William Grayson?"

"Yes, the same."

"Well, Senator, why not tell your friends in the waiting room that your son is going to recover thanks to their help." They proceeded into the small waiting area where Senator Grayson made the announcement. Aletha, who was finishing, could not help but smile as she heard the loud applause erupt from the waiting room. Arrangements were made for where the boy would stay to rest before being taken home, again.

Later when the last patient had gone, Aletha cornered Palidore. "Are you going to tell me about the ABC jars?" Palidore paused and looked at her, knowing he owed her some explanation, but not just yet.

"Althea, the truth is, I had no right to use those medicines on that boy. They are not approved and never will be."

"But they worked so well, why not?"

"I want to tell you, but cannot, at least not now. All I can say is that they won't be approved because there is a finite quantity, and they can't make anymore, so they will never be approved. Please never mention this to anyone or they may take my license away."

"You know you have nothing to worry about. I'll never tell another soul, but will you ever be able to tell me more? I mean, what did we give that boy to drink?"

"Aletha I just can't talk about it, but the solution he drank helped insure he would not get a blood clot caused by the other medicine I used on the wound. Now as much as I would like to, I just can't go into this in any more detail. I shouldn't have used them, but I was at my wits end, and I knew I had to try something. It worked this time, but without you, nothing would have worked. So that boy has you, and God, to thank."

"Palidore, what if Senator Grayson tells someone."

"He won't – he has no idea what we were doing. Besides, I think he will want to put the whole incident behind him as soon as possible."

"I suppose so, but I won't ever forget what we did here today, even if I am sworn to secrecy. "

***

Enjoyed this Sneak Peak from Book 1 of the POTUS 1 Series?

Reviving George Washington

You can find all books of the POTUS 1 Series on Amazon.com and TheWritersMall.com

GIL HUDSON

About the Author

GIL HUDSON

Gil Hudson is a retired attorney from Virginia who now resides in The Villages, Florida. For many years, he was actively involved in politics having served as a local party chairman and as a delegate to the 1980 Republican Party National Convention during which Ronald Reagan was nominated to run for President of the United States. He stepped back from politics to accept a substitute judgeship but his interest in politics and history never waned.

He often wondered how our forefathers might view the state of our country today. This curiosity was the impetus for his writing the historical fiction POTUS 1 series. Artfully written, the reader has an option of reading all the novels either sequentially or independently.

Made in United States
Orlando, FL
12 May 2022

17815297R00165